ALFRED BESTER

THE
COMPUTER CONNECTION

Alfred Bester was born in New York in 1913. After attending the University of Pennsylvania, he sold several stories to *Thrilling Wonder Stories* in the early 1940s. He then embarked on a career as a scripter for comics, radio, and television, where he worked on such classic characters as Superman, Batman, Nick Carter, Charlie Chan, Tom Corbett, and the Shadow. In the 1950s, he returned to prose, publishing several short stories and two brilliant, seminal works, *The Demolished Man* (which was the first winner of the Hugo Award for Best Novel) and *The Stars My Destination*. In the late 1950s, he wrote travel articles for *Holiday* magazine, and eventually became their Senior Literary Editor, keeping the position until the magazine folded in the 1970s. In 1974, he once again came back to writing science fiction with the novels *The Computer Connection*, *Golem100*, and *The Deceivers*, and numerous short stories. A collection of his short stories, *Virtual Unrealities*, was published in 1997, and his final novel, *Psychoshop*—completed after his death by celebrated author Roger Zelazny—was published in 1998. After being a New Yorker all his life, he died in Pennsylvania in 1987, but not before he was honored by the Science Fiction & Fantasy Writers of America with a Grandmaster Award.

AVAILABLE NOW

THE COMPUTER CONNECTION

ALFRED BESTER

ibooks
new york
www.ibooksinc.com

DISTRIBUTED BY SIMON & SCHUSTER, INC

An Original Publication of ibooks, inc.

Pocket Books, a division of Simon & Schuster, Inc.
1230 Avenue of the Americas, New York, NY 10020

An ibooks, inc. Book

ibooks, inc.
24 West 25th Street
New York, NY 10010

The ibooks World Wide Web Site Address is:
http://www.ibooksinc.com

ISBN 0-671-03901-6
First Pocket Books printing February 2000
10 9 8 7 6 5 4 3 2 1
POCKET and colophon are registered trademarks of Simon & Schuster, Inc.

Cover design by Jason Vita
Cover photograph copyright © 1999 by Jesse Cooday
Interior design by Michael Mendelsohn at MM Design 2000, Inc.

Printed in the U.S.A.

FASTER THAN THE
SPEED OF BESTER:

*A Few Words of Introduction to One of the Most Fecund
Writers the World has Ever Spawned*

by Harlan Ellison

Once upon a time, when the world had less rust on its pinions, when it sang the *Missa Solemnis* less off-key in the shower, when a good idea could beat both the tortoise *and* the hare to the tape, there lived in this enchanted land a creator of ornate and filigreed dreams whose talent was a Catherine Wheel showering wonders in every direction.

His name was Alfred Bester, and he died in 1987, and even if some of you parvenus are scratching your heads—on which that little squishy place, the fontanelle, has not yet congealed with puberty—asking yourselves, "Well, if this Bester dude was so awesome, like why haven't I heard of him?"—you had better believe the world is a less sumptuous banquet because of his absence. You are worse off than you might have been, even if you don't know it.

You had to love Alfred Bester.

Or, wait a minute, writing it in Besterese, y'hadda *luv* Alfie!

Some people think and speak and sometimes write in a left brain way; and some people think and speak and once in a while write in a right brain way; but Alfie was the only writer who ever existed and spoke and sure as hell thought and wrote in a WonkBrain way. It wasn't left or right or centrist or doublethink or pig Latin, it was so Bizarre City, so dearly skip-logic, so all-encompassing of concepts and extrapolations and surmises and impossible mountain goat leaps from what-is to what-might-be, that it seemed he was almost as one with his character in this novel, the 13-year-old seductress Fee-5: he heard it all, on neurasthenic telepathic cross-lines (you could look up the term on page 20-something).

Alfie's great aptitude was a mutant chameleon's talent for learning other writers' tricks—perhaps only partially unearthed or explicated—maybe just a cornice edge protruding from the muck or loam of style, perhaps just the whisper or nuance of that ecstatic note trembling midst the cacophony of hack verbiage—and yanking it out, dusting it off, hosing it clean; reifying those tricks; distilling them; turning them on their axes; standing them on their heads, and wildly reconstituting them in a dementedly brilliant newAlfie way. The caprices and conundra that Alfie got from writers he admired, like Charles Harness and Henry Kuttner and A. E. van Vogt and Robert Heinlein, were aided and abetted by the even stormier knavery he had picked up from Dumas and James Joyce and Laurence Sterne.

And, of course, for all of his daring and singularity and purely American literary cozenage ... he was never included in an annual O. Henry best-of-the-year, or *Best American Short Stories* volume. When the Burkes and Hares of modern belles-lettres stitch up the final borders of the last patch in their quidnunc quilt, nowhere will you find mention of *The Demolished Man* or *The Stars My Destination* or the hundred great short stories. And *that*. Is. Why. You. Ain't. Heard. Of Alfred Bester. You dummy.

So I am here, today, right now, to tell you that Bester was an 8-lane turnpike interstate freeway running full-tilt-boogie North *and* South, at the same time.

Never his like before; never his equal since.

But hark: I pause in mid-essay, during the raw copy retype (yes, Virginia, I still work on a manual typewriter, my raven having moulted and ceased producing broad-nib quills), to share a few pages of juicy prose with that estimable editorial icon Howie Z., and he vouchsafes as follows: "Aren't you being a bit unfair to the potential reader? Aren't you presupposing a lack of familiarity with Bester's work on the part of an audience not dumb, but merely untutored?"

Curse you, GrandSavant Z. You tweak me in my weakest place: my theantropic obsession for evenhandedness, that fastidiousness of regimen that simultaneously I despise and to which I pay obeisance. ("An artist trying to create a powerful atmosphere can't be expected to embrace the banal method of tv documentaries, which always illustrate both sides of a situation—and leave you nowhere." *David Denby*, 1979.)

So, okay, I'll jam back into the closet of memory that incident two summers ago, when I was teaching a writers' workshop in imaginative literature, and idly mentioned Bester as d'bomb, and this teen-aged student, nice kid, came all over cloudy and said, "Who?" and I was shocked that he didn't know Alfie's name and *oeuvre*, and I began to have this creeping (and creepy) epiphany, and I asked the class of twenty-five or so men and women of varying ages, "How many of you have never read Bester . . . and how many don't even know the name?" So okay, I'll jam that creepy memory, that recalled moment of so many hands in the air. I'll pretend Howie Z. inveighs against rank prejudice *a priori* in a world that slathers homage on *Pokémon, Chicken Soup for the Soul*, and Britney Spears while *Little Nemo*, Stanley Ellin, and Jane Green recede at light-speed into the Terra Incognita of cultural amnesia where the only citizenship is that of the non-person.

So okay, you all know Bester intimately; you've all read and delighted in *The Demolished Man* and *The Stars My Destination*; and you know that the Science Fiction Writers of America, that noble and humane organization, finally got around to awarding Alfie their much-vaunted Grand Master Nebula award—the winning of which was conveyed to Alfie as he lay in a coma on his deathbed in a nursing home in Pennsylvania; and you know the short stories by heart, particularly "Fondly Fahrenheit," which is one of the best short stories produced in this last half-century, though you won't find it in any *Best American Short Stories* anthology . . . aw, but there I go again, being cynical and unfair, sorry Howie. I'll straighten up, and give y'all the benefit of the barest, that you *do* know Bester, and that is why you're here, wasting your time with my blather, rather than getting on with it and reading *The Computer Connection*.

Which may not be the absolute best thing Alfie ever set down on paper—at least that's the general consensus, having been reiterated chitteringly since it was first published in 1974–75. (Come with me, if you will, to page 114 of *The Encyclopedia of Science Fiction*, a 1993–95 variorum reference work, where we find the following: ". . . while full of incidental felicities, did not quite recapture the old drive in its ornate story of a group of immortals and an omniscient computer; perhaps it lacked a natural 'Besterman' as focus. The pace and complexity were still there, but somehow looking like self-parody.")

But that's like saying we ought to level and sub-divide Mt. Kilimanjaro because it ain't as high as Everest.

Alfie wrote *Tiger! Tiger!* (which was the other title of *Stars*) in 1956. *The Demolished Man* in 1953. They were novas in comparison to every other bright star in the genre. They blew everyone away. But Alfie wrote to amuse himself; he used to say it was for therapy. And when he felt right with the world, he packed it in, the writing, and he went off and did other things, such as working as a Senior Editor for the then-enormously popular *Holiday* magazine, or writing for television, or working on *Green Lantern* for DC Comics.

When he came back to the novel length—he'd kept on writing the occasional brilliant short story without any protracted lapse of endeavor—it was twenty years later. The story was serialized in *Analog* as "The Indian Giver" in '74, in England as *Extro*, and in hardcover in the U.S. by Berkley Putnam as *The Computer Connection*, 1975. And, no, it wasn't Everest, it was merely Annapurna, a measly 26,493 feet.

As I write this essay, we're about a month and a half shy of that arbitrary chronological goose-egg called The Millennium (and even *that's* commercial self-delusional bullshit, as we all know damned well that the 21st century doesn't truly begin till January 1st, 2001) and every moron media venue is inundating us with "Best of the Century" lists. Best athletes, best movies, best rectal suppositories; most significant men and women of the last hundred years, the hundred top entertainers of the 20th century, the top ten toys, the top fifty inventions, the best this and the best that.

Playing this "best" game is rankest hokey-pokey, a scam, a *mot injuste*, a waste of time, a debasement and demeanment of anything and everything good and worthwhile that has slipped out of fashion or is simply white noise to a generation that actually lays out money to watch Adam Sandler. Memory is as capricious as the fad frenzies of the Great Wad. Al Jolson, Glen Miller, Lightnin' Hopkins, Carl Perkins and Stevie Ray Vaughn could carve Garth Brooks, Ricky Martin, and the Backstreet Boys a collective set of new assholes if talent were the criterion, but the former are no-price with institutionally ignorant audiences who have been dynamited into believing that the latter rock and rule. So, no, *The Computer Connection* isn't *The Demolished Man*. It is only a terrific book, filled with ideas and "incidental felicities" that will make your mouth gape.

It is a wild ride, as deranged as a fruit-bat, a demented science fictional transmogrification of the chaotic and hilarious household of the Kaufman & Hart Broadway hit *You Can't Take It With You* (later a famous Capra-directed film). This novel is pure Screwball Comedy!

Bester wrote a locked room traditional mystery with *The Demolished Man*, and a straight action-adventure revenge rewrite of *The Count of Monte* Cristo with *The Stars My Destination*, but *this* goofy, deliriously tasty book you hold, this was Alfie's Hollywood sitcom *manqué* tribute to all the hijinks he'd seen and dealt with and chuckled over and suffered while working in the TV and film business. Not the straight mainstream view he presented in his novel *Who He?* but a revivified, gussied-up lampoon of the Ultimate Dysfunctional Family, with all the sibs and aunts and uncles writ huge as Immortals, not the least of whom are Jesus, H. G. Wells, Samuel Pepys and . . .

Oh, hell, why go on like this!?!

The Computer Connection is an unsung treasure of Alfie's later years. It is a great book to read, a couple of evenings of delight, best imbibed while some elegant rinkytink music is playing in the background. So throw on a little Scott Joplin—I suggest the *Red Back Book* collection—or some of Ernesto Lecuona's piano music—try Thomas Tirino playing the *Rumba Rhapsody* and the 19th century Cuban Dances—and settle back. Kick off your shoes, kick off your mundane workaday cares, kick off your inhibitions, and let one of the most fecund writers of the century massage your risibilities.

I assume you know Bester, because Howie Z. implores me to assume so; but if you don't, and if you miss this chance, I will seek you out, I will take you down, and I will—as the great philosopher Savanarola said—open a can of whup-ass on you. And did I, by the way, tell you that I knew Alfred Bester as a friend, that his Grand Master Nebula resides here in my home because there isn't an appropriate museum or archive setting for it, and that you are far worse off than you know because Alfie is gone? Oh . . . I told you that, did I?

So go on and read the book, dummy, and stop gawping at me. I'm just the road-sign pointing into the town.

Bester is the road. And Bester is the destination.

1

I tore down the Continental Shelf off the Bogue Bank while the pogo made periscope hops trying to track me. Endless plains of salt flats like the steppes of Central Russia (music by Borodin here); mounds of salts where the new breed of prospector was sieving for rare earths; towers of venomous vapors on the eastern horizon where the pumping stations were sucking up more of the Atlantic and extracting deuterium for energy transfer. Most of the fossil fuels were gone; the sea level had been lowered by two feet; progress.

I was headed for Herb Wells' hideout. He's perfected a technique for reclaiming gold (which nobody wants these plastic days) and is schlepping ingots back into the past with a demented time-dingbat which is why the Group has nicknamed him H. G. Wells. Herb is making gifts of gold to characters like Van Gogh and Mozart, trying to keep them healthy, wealthy, and wise so they'll create more goodies for posterity. So far it's never worked. *No Son of Don Giovanni. Not even The Don Meets Dracula.*

Following the Thieves & Vagabonds road signs that Herb puts out for the Group, I went under a mound and tunneled through the salts, absorbing $NaCl$, $MgCl_2$, $MgSO_4$, calcium, potassium, bromides, and probably traces of Herb's gold which he'd grudge me. I came out at the bunker hatch.

Locked, of course. I hammered on it while the pogo bounced and thrummed overhead and it was six, two, and even they'd get me before Herb heard me, but he did; he heard me.

"Quien dat? Quien dat?" he called in Black Spanglish.

"It's Guig," I hollered in XXth Century English.

That's the secret cant the Group uses. "I'm in a jam. Let me in."

The hatch swung down and I fell in. "Freeze it, Herb. The fuzz may have spotted me."

He slammed the hatch and froze the grommets. "What the hell have you been up to, Guig?"

"The usual. I killed another guy."

"The fuzz making a fuss about murder? Don't put me on."

"He was the governor of the Corridor."

"Oh. You shouldn't kill the importants, Guig. People don't understand."

"I know, but they're the only candidates worth killing."

"How many failures have you had so far?"

"I've lost count."

"And no success." Herb meditated. "Maybe we ought to sit down and discuss it. The first question should be, is it a problem of perplexity or complexity? I think—"

A pounding made the hatch vibrate.

"There's goody two-shoes," I said without joy. "Can you shoot me timesome in your dingbat, Herb?"

"But you always refused to shoot a trip." He gave me a mournful look. "You hurt my feelings."

"I've got to disappear for a few hours. If they don't find me here they won't bother you. I apologize about the ding-bat, Herb, but I was always scared of that thing. The whole Group is."

"So am I. Come on."

I followed him into the Chamber of Horrors and sat

2

down in the insane machine which looks like a praying mantis. Herb handed me an ingot. "I was just going to give this to Thomas Chatterton. You deliver it for me."

"Chatterton? The kid poet?"

"In the flesh. Commited suicide in 1770, greatly regretted. Arsenic. He was out of bread and out of hope. You're going back to London. He's holed up in an attic in Brook Street. Got it?"

"Neither rain nor snow nor gloom of—"

"I'll put it on a three-hour snatch. That ought to give you enough time. I'll shoot you to a prominent place so you can get your bearings. Don't wander too far or the thing won't be able to grab you."

The pounding got louder and more peevish. Herb did things with calibrations and switches and there was a crackle of french-fried power (which I'll bet he never pays for) and I was sitting in a mudpuddle in the rain and a George Washington type on a chestnut horse nearly rode me down and bawled hell out of me for obstructing a public road.

I got up, backed off the road, and someone kicked me in the brain. I jumped and turned around and it was a pop-eyed corpse hanging from a gibbet. Herb had shot me to a prominent place, all right—Tyburn. I hadn't been in London in years (rotten with fallout residues) and certainly never in 1770, but that gave me my bearings. Tyburn had been turned into Marble Arch. I was on the outskirts of eighteenth-century London. No Bayswater Road, yet; no Hyde Park; just fields, trees, meadows, and the little Tyburn creek meandering. The city was on my left.

I walked down a path that would someday be Park Lane and turned left into the fringe of houses. They became thick and crowded when I reached a cow pasture that would become Grosvenor Square. A Saturday-night market was in progress. Hundreds of barrows and stalls illuminated by flaring torches, grease lamps with flags of flame, humble tallow candles. Roars of hucksters: "Eight a penny! Stunning pears!" "Chestnuts all 'ot! Penny a score!" "Beautiful whelks, penny a lot!" "Fine walnuts, sixteen a penny!" I was hungry but I didn't have any current coin; just two pounds of refined gold.

I remembered that Brook Street led off the north side of Grosvenor so I took that route asking for a writer named Chatterton. Nobody ever heard of him until I came across a Flying Stationer hung with broadsheets offering "The Life of the Hangman," "Secret Doings in Soho," "The Treacherous Servant," that sort of thing. He said he knew Chatterton. The kid wrote long-song poems for him at shilling ea., and he pointed out the house which had no business to be standing.

I ran up the crumbling stairs, convinced I'd fall through at every step, and burst into the attic with a merry, "Gold! Gold! Gold! Bright and yellow, hard and cold!" (Thomas Hood, 1799–1845) The kid was writhing on a pallet in the last agonies of arsenic poisoning. "Ah-ha!" I thought.

"He's dying. He knows he's dead. If I can save him maybe we've got another Moleman for the Group."

I did my best. The first thing to do is make them vomit. I pee'd into a tumbler and forced it down Chatterton's throat. No nausea. Too far gone. I ran down the stairs and banged on a door. It was opened by Betsy Ross' grandmother, complaining. I shoved past her, saw a jug of milk, took it and a clutch of charcoal from the cold fireplace. She had now graduated to screaming. I returned to my house call. Charcoal and milk. Nothing. He was gone, greatly regretted, and what the hell was I going to do with 24 oz.

(troy) of gold which was dragging the butt pocket of my coveralls?

Well, I had to stall anyway until the Mantis put the snatch on me so I went for a walk in the rain. At Fleet Street I turned off and went into the Cheshire Cheese to see if I could parlay the ingot into a drink and maybe dry off in front of the fire, which was eclipsed by a snorting whale and a simpering dogfish. The Grand Cham and Boswell.

"What would you do, sir, if you were locked up in a tower with a newborn babe?" dogfish was asking. The whale heaved and growled but before he could answer that monumental question I was yanked back to the dingbat, dripping all over the circuits to the anguish of Herb.

"OutOutOut!" he hollered. "They've left."

I out.

"Why didn't you give Thos, the gold?"

"Too late, man. He gone when I get."

"Oh, drat."

"Try again, a little earlier."

"I can't. The damn thing won't shoot the same decade twice. To tell the truth, Guig, I think it's a lemon."

Maybe that's why his Health, Education, and Welfare program never works. I thanked Herb, still using the Group XX English and returned to Spangland, the Gem of the Ocean. I know all this sounds kind of lunatic but I'm up against a tough proposition keeping these notes. I have to translate from Black Spanglish—Benny Diaz, gemmum, ah gone esplain any pagunta you ax—which is now the official language of the country, and then go on from there. It runs: Spanglish XX English Machine Language. It's one hell of a job, especially when it's compounded by sorting out centuries of memories. So I ax you to dispensar when I jumble. My damn diary won't. How many times when I compile data for it has the print-out snapped, "090-N. READ." which is machine language for, "I can't understand a goddamn thing you're saying."

We all have this trouble. Not remembering—our memories stick like graffiti—but placing events in their proper sequence. I have to compile notes and diaries because I worry about this. I'm the baby of the Group and I'm still trying to train myself to develop an organic filing system. I've often wondered how Sam Pepys manages. He's the Group historian and diarist and he tries to explain his system to me. It's perfectly simple for Sam. Like: A $1/4 + (1/2B)^2$ = The breakfast I ate on Sept. 16, 1936, and Good Luck to Sam.

I've only been around since Klakatoa blew up in 1883. All the others have been on the scene much longer. Beau Brummel survived the Calcutta earthquake of 1737 in which 300,000 were killed. Beau says nobody back then would ever believe the mortality figures, and he's still sore because the honkies didn't give a damn about how many quote niggers unquote died. I'm with him on that. He—Oh, I'd better esplain about our names.

The famous names I mention aren't the realsies. We have to move on and change our names so often—the Shorties begin to wonder about us—that nobody can keep track. So we stay with our nicknames in the Group, and we pinch them from real people. They reflect our crotchets and main interests. I've mentioned H. G. Wells and his time-dingbat. There's Tosca, an actress type; Beau, the epitome of the beautiful people; Sam Pepys, the historian; the Greek Syndicate, our financier; Bathsheba, the *femme fatale; und so weiter.* I'm nicknamed *Grand Guignol*, Guig for short, and I don't like it. I don't think of myself as a Theater of Horrors. I'm sincerely trying to do good, through horror, yes, but it's a small price to pay for what I'm offering. Wouldn't you pay an hour of agony for eternal life?

But about our ages: Oliver Cromwell was buried alive in a mass grave during the Black Death and still doesn't want to talk about it. He says dying by suffocation is something to forget forever. Scented Song escaped the sack of Tientsin by the Mongols when they piled 100,000 severed heads into pyramids. Her description makes Dachau sound like a picnic. The Wandering Jew is Christ, of course. You can pick up the clue in Luke 24:3. A writer—D. H. Lawrence, I think—smelled the truth when he met Jacy in 1900 and turned it into a fantastic story about how Jacy might have lived a normal life if he'd only balled a bod. He didn't know Jace. We call Christ Jacy because if you use his real name it sounds like you're swearing.

There are many others whom you'll meet later on. The oldest, by far, is Hic-Haec-Hoc. He got that nickname because that's what his grunts sound like; he's never learned to speak any language although he can unnerstan simple signs. We think Hic may be from the late Pleistocene or early Holocene and got his charge in some cataclysm that was dramatic enough to make a Neanderthal aware. Who knows? Maybe he got clobbered by a meteor or trampled by a Hairy Mastodon.

We don't see much of Hic these days; people scare him and he's always pulling back from the edge of civilization. We used to wonder how he was going to adapt to the population explosion but the space explosion solved that. He's probably homesteading in a crater on Mars, Mother of Men; a Moleman can live on anything except nothing. Pepys, who keeps track of all of us, like Celebrity Service, claims that

Hic was spotted once, mousing around the snows of the Himalayas, and he swears that Hic started the legend of the Abominable Snowman.

I use the word "charge" advisedly when I try to esplain our immortality. They call it "nerve-firing" nowadays. As near as I've researched, we all underwent identical traumas which destroyed or discharged the lethal secretions that are the crux of old age and death. If your cells accumulate lethal secretions you're not forever for this world, and all creatures have been endowed with this metabolic suicide. Maybe that's nature's way of wiping the slate clean and trying again. I'm intensely anthropomorphic and I can see nature getting disgusted and closing the show on the road.

But our Group has proven that death doesn't have to be inevitable. Of course we did it the hard way. Each of us knew we were going to die and received a psychogalvanic shock that wiped out our lethal cell products and turned us into Molecular Men; Molemen for short. I'll explain that later. It's a sort of updating of Cuvier's "Catastrophism" theory of evolution. In case you've forgotten, he argued that periodic catastrophes destroyed all life and God started it all over again on a higher level. He was wrong about the God bit, of course, but catastrophes do alter creatures.

As described in each case (with the exception of Hic-Haec-Hoc, who can't describe anything) the circumstances were almost identical. We were trapped in some natural or man-made catastrophe that gave us no chance of survival; we were aware of it; a psychogalvanic charge ripped through us as we toppled into extinction; then some miracle aborted the death and so here the Group is forever. The odds against this sort of freak are fantastic, but the Greek Syndicate says that even the longest odds are bound to come in sooner or later. The Greek ought to know. He's been a professional gambler ever since Aristotle kicked him out of the Peripatetic School in Athens.

Jacy often describes the wild surprise of death that shocked through him on the cross when he finally realized that he was not going to be rescued by the U.S. Marines. He wonders why the same thing didn't happen to the two thieves who were busted along with him on Golgotha. I keep telling him, "Because they weren't epileptics, Jacy," and he keeps answering, "Oh, hush. You're obsessed with that epileptic delusion, Guig. I wish you'd take a lifetime off and learn to respect the mysteries of God."

He may be right. I *am* obsessed with the belief that our Group is epileptic-prone and that there's an historic linkage between epilepsy and the unique. I suffer from it myself, and when that aura hits me I can encompass the universe. That's why we scream and spasm; it's too magnificent for the microcosm to endure. I've trained myself to recognize the epileptic type and every time I spot one I try to recruit him (or her) for the Group by killing them horribly, which is why they call me Grand Guignol. Bathsheba always sends me a Christmas card with a picture of an Iron Maiden.

That's not fair. I torture and kill from the best of motives, and if I describe my own experience with death you may understand. Back in 1883 I was an export factor, it says here, on Krakatoa, a volcanic island in the Sunda Straight. Krakatoa was listed officially as uninhabited and that was the swindle. I'd been established there secretly by a San Francisco firm in an attempt to muscle in on the Dutch trading monopoly. Did they say "muscle" back then? Wait a minute; I'll ask my goddamn diary.

TERMINAL. READY?
READY. ENTER PROGRAM NUMBER.

001
SLANG PROGRAM HAS BEEN LOADED.
LOC. + NAME. START COUNT 2000 N.P
SLANG HAS FINISHED RUN.
MCS, PRINT. W.H. END.
NO.

So all right, they didn't say "muscle" back then, and happy birthday to IBM.

Now only an idiot would have taken the job, but I was a twenty-year-old kid intoxicated by the Discovery Mystique and mad to make a name for myself. Headline: NED CURZON DISCOVERS NORTH POLE!!! Like it was missing. Or, NED CURZON, THE AFRICAN EXPLORER. "Dr. Livingstone, I presume?" Only M'bantu says Stanley never said that, and I take M'bantu's word; he was there with a bindle on his head. Bindle? Bundle? McBee was there with a crate of four-buckle arctics on his head.

I was alone on the island in a bamboo warehouse with nothing but a terrier for company, but the locals sailed over to trade. They asked for the damndest things and offered me the damndest things, including their women, who would bounce into bed for a gill of trade whiskey. Ah! Those fabulous tropical beauties immortalized by Stanley! Not Sir Henry Morton Stanley of Africa; Darryl F. Stanley of Hollywood. Their skins were crocodiled with ceremonial scars and they cackled when you balled them, displaying teeth blackened by betel nut. Bring back Dorothy Lamour.

The natives knew that Krakatoa's Mt. Rakata was an active volcano, but it was so small, compared to the boss jobs on Java and Sumatra, that it never prevented them from visiting. Rakata would complain and steam up pumice occasionally but you got used to it. There were earthquake grumbles now and then, so slight that I could hardly distinguish them from the pounding of the surf. Even my idiot dog didn't have the sense to be alarmed. You know, the dumb friend barking to give warning of the unseen menace.

The big blowup came on August 26 and I did receive a rather odd warning. The day before, old Markoloua sailed over with his young men and women and a boatload of bêche-de-mer, which I loathe, but the Inscrutables love. They cook with 'em. The locals were all chattering excitedly about fish. When I asked Markoloua what the fuss was, he told me that there were devils in the deep blue sea; when they landed on Krakatoa they were chased by great shoals of fish. I laughed at this but he led me to the beach and pointed. By God, he was telling the truth. The shore was littered with fish, gasping and flopping, and every comber brought in hundreds more, all of them bursting out of the water as though they were pursued by the devil.

Many years later I discussed this phenomenon with a vulcanologist at the Mt. Etna station. He explained that the heat building up at the base of Rakata must have spread across the ocean floor and raised the temperature so high that the fish were driven onto the land in their attempts to escape. That was much later. At the time I thought it was some sort of pollution.

Markoloua left, having traded the bêche-de-mer for ten (10) tin mirrors. Next morning the first blowups came, four of them in succession, and it was the ending of the world. I didn't hear the noise, it was too loud to hear, I felt it, an accoustical battering that made me scream. The entire north end of the island went up in a mushroom of lava. The main cone of Rakata was split down the middle, exposing the central shaft. The sea poured into the molten interior, was instantly transformed into live steam, and blew up in another series of explosions that crumbled the rest of the cone.

I was hammered by the noise, blinded by the smoke, suffocated by the livid vapors, slammed out of my senses, and there came that tidal wave of lava creeping toward me like a swarm of red-hot caterpillars. I could feel nothing but the wild incredulity of death shocking through my body. I *knew*. I knew what nobody believes until the extreme moment. I knew I was dead. And so I died.

Actually it was the vibrations of the explosions that produced the miracle. They burst the withes that bound the bamboo walls of my warehouse and twisted the stems into a birdcage, a logjam with myself inside incorporated with wooden debris; and then the quakes must have blasted me out into the ocean. I was not aware of it at the time; I only realized it later when I was reborn, floating in a caul of bamboo on the surface of the sea.

Krakatoa was gone. Everything was gone. There were new reefs thrusting up, black and stinking of sea bottom. There were black clouds of volcanic smoke and dust rumbling with thunder and lightning. I was in shock for five days, which might have been five eternities, until I was picked up by a Dutch freighter. They were sore as hell about the disaster, which had delayed them by three days and acted as though it were all my fault, like I'd been playing with matches. That's the history of my death and the miracle that saved me. That's what turned me into a Molecular Man.

Now the hell of it is that it's pretty tough to arrange a volcano or a Black Death or a Hairy Mastodon when you want to recruit a man into immortality, and it's even tougher staging a miraculous save from the catastrophe. I'm pretty good at cruel killing but when it comes to the rescue

I keep failing no matter how carefully I prepare. I did succeed with Sequoya, but I have to be honest and admit that the miracle was an accident.

Jacy is always pained when I call it a miracle. He spent a few months with me in Mexifornia and when I repeated my theory about what happened to the Group (the hell of longevity is that you get garrulous and repetitious) he said, "No. Miracles are the constituent elements in the divine revelation, deeds which display the divine character and purpose."

"Yes, yes, I know, Jace, and what could be the divine purpose in keeping the likes of me alive forever? All right, I'm the product of nineteenth-century rationalism. Would you buy a rare coincidence of improbability and biochemistry?"

"You sound like Spinoza, Guig."

"Now that's a compliment. You ever meet him, Jace?"

"I bought a pair of spectacles from him in Amsterdam."

"What kind of a guy was he?"

"Splendid. He was the first to refuse to worship gods fashioned by men in their own image, to be servants of their human interests. That took courage in the 1600s."

At this point my own servant came in with refreshments; cognac for me, Romanée-Conti for Jacy, who's been a wino ever since the Jerusalem days. The urchin was wearing a classic French Maid's costume, something out of a movie from the archives. God knows where she dug it up. And then she had the impudence to wink at Jacy and say, "Hello. I'm your Bunny."

She flounced out. Jacy stared at me.

"She's always springing surprises on me," I said. "She tries to crunch my cool."

"She speaks XX."

"I taught her."

"Does she know about the Group?"

"Not yet."

"What is a Bunny?"

"An antique waitress."

"But who is that child?"

"She adopted me and I can't get rid of her."

"Now Guig. . . ."

"Would you like the whole story?"

"Of course."

"Well, I was editing *Dek Magazine*, freebie cassettes full of comics and commercials, and, believe it or not, I got a letter. A *letter* in this day and age. I was absolutely flabbergasted, so I answered it. Wait a minute, I'll pull the entire correspondence out of my diary."

TERMINAL. READY?
READY. ENTER PROGRAM NUMBER.
147
FEE FILE HAS BEEN LOADED.
LOC. + NAME. START COUNT.
FEE FILE HAS FINISHED RUN.
MCS, PRINT. W.H. END.

The printout rattled like a machine gun for a few seconds. I handed Jacy the length of tape, printed in XX, of course; I don't want outsiders reading my personal private diary. We'd both written in Spang but I'd translated.

2 the edt. of Dekkk. I wish to rite a article on hisory of minor groups in cuntry like Indians & sib-

erians who discover America in 1492 comeing over from Rusia on boats. Coloumbus was a liar. Truley yrs.

> Fee-5 Graumans Chinese
> Mexiforn, USA

DEAR MR. CHINESE:

Thank you so much for your interesting proposal. Unfortunately we feel that the subject is not suited to the editorial policy of *Dek* which is entirely dedicated to comics, commercials, sex and sadism.

> Most sincerely,
> The editors

Two edtrs. Dec. Your ansr irellevant. Indians and eskimos minor groups been put down in U.S. of A. since 1492. You robing them of man hood 320 yrs. Make them 2rd class cityséns. Gen. Custer got what was comeing to him.

> Fee-5 Chinese
> Mexiforn

DEAR MR. CHINESE:

Subtracting 1492 from 2080 gives *us* 588 years. What happened to your other 268 years, or will that be part of your proposed article?

> Most sincerely,
> The editors

Edtrs of Dk. Nomber is irelivant. You don't do something too wipe out injustice to grt indians who made U. Spangland of A. grt proves you not relateing 2 valus for meanful dialg and our MSs will confront you.

Fee-5 Chinese

DEAR MR. CHINESE:
What is MSs? Is it the abreviation for "Manu-scripts"? We must warn you that *dek* will only con-sider one submission at a time.

Most sincerely,
The editors

Rottn establish mint edtrs. Not MSS. MMS. Stands for militantes for more militante socity. We take over yr office. We throw you out. We sit in foreverr. Bring p-nut butter & jelli sandwich & sleep on floor.

Fee-5 (mad)

DEAR MR. FEE:
Could you give us some idea of when your mil-itant organization will take over our offices? We'd like the chance to clear out in advance. You see, we're on the twentieth floor, so we can't go through the windows like deans and faculty members.

Most sincerely,
The editors

You think MMS gone give you warneing in ad-vance so cort orders & police pigs can comit fashist brutality? We confront you when MMS decide & if no meanful dialog you go out windows we don't care if even 268 floors hi.

Fee-5 (Pres. MMS)

Dear President Fee:
Is that what happened to your missing 268?
            Most sincerely,
            The editors

O Kay. You reject democratic prosiss. You force
MmS to take militante actions for militante soceyety
& indians & eskimos & 100% minor groups will
arise.

            Beware

That was the end. Jacy looked at me in such perplexity
that I had to laugh. "She showed up all right," I said. "Ten
years old, militant as hell, and we fed her so many peanut
butter and jelly sandwiches that she got sick and I had to
take her home. Now I can't dump her. She's adopted me."

"How long has she been here?"

"Three years."

"But has she no family?"

"They were happy to get rid of her. They're just average
goons and this kid jumbled them. She's a *lusus naturac*, a
freak, a sport. She actually taught herself to read and write.
There's no end to her potential."

"What does she do here?"

"Makes herself useful."

"Guig!"

"No, no. She's ripe but she's only thirteen. Too young
for me. It's not what you think, Jacy. For shame."

"I do not apologize. I know your reputation. You live
entirely for mechanical pleasure."

Mind you, this to me, who'd cleared every woman out
of the house for Visitation. That's the trouble with these
dedicated reformers; they're wonderful guys but they have

no sense of humor. Scented Song says that Confucius was exactly like Jacy, always serious. Sheba says the same thing about Mohammed; you could stand all that earnest wisdom for just about an hour and then you had to sneak out for a few laughs. None of us ever dated Moses but I'll bet he was the same.

This is what got Jacy into trouble, but I'm not complaining because that's how I met my first successful recruitment. The bods at Union Carbide, our local university, were mounting their ritual protest. It was the traditional daily rioting, with screamings, burnings, and killings. The only thing that changed was the cause, and the pressure groups had to sign up months in advance for representation. Jacy said he was going down to the campus to see if he could stop it. He was all for the kids' goals but he didn't like their methods.

"You don't understand," I told him. "They love their tradition of death and destruction. They don't even ask what it's for. They're issued posters and scripts and then they have themselves an orgasm. The ones that dig the death wish are obliged."

"Destruction of any of God's work is an attempt to destroy God," he said earnestly.

"Maybe. Let's find out what they're destroying for today. Hey, Fee!"

Fee-5 came in, playing the vampire bit now. "Kiss me, my fool;" she said and smote me across the chops with an artificial rose.

"Tune in. What's the riot about today?"

She cocked her head and listened hard.

"What is she doing?" Jacy asked.

"Jacy, you live in the homes of our Group and you don't know what's going on in the crazy culture outside. It's a bugged and drugged world. Ninety percent of the bods have bugs implanted in their skulls in hospital when they're born. They're monitored constantly. The air is crisscrossed with thousands of broadcasts. Fee is unique. She can pick them up and sort them out without a receiver. Don't ask me how. The kid's a genius. Let it go at that."

"Honk Lib," Fee-5 said.

"There you are," I said. "Would anybody in his right mind burn down a library for the sake of Honkies? There aren't a million pure whites left in the world, and most of them are Jukes and Kallikaks from inbreeding."

"Come here, my child," Jacy said.

Fee sank into his lap and kissed him seductively. He put his arms under the vampire to make her comfortable and instantly the scene was transformed into Michelangelo's "Pieta" That's Jacy's magic.

"Do you use drugs, my love?"

"No." She glared at me. "*He* won't let me."

"Do you want to?"

"No. They're ditt. Everybody else does."

"Then why are you angry with Guig?"

"Because he makes me do what he wants. I have no identity."

"Then why don't you leave him?"

"Because—" She was hung up. She fell back and re-grouped. "Because I'm waiting for the day when I make *him* do what I want."

"Are you bugged, love?"

"No," I answered. "She was born in the gutter and she's never been in a hospital. She's clean."

"I was born in the fifth row from the front in Grauman's Chinese," Fee said with enormous dignity.

"Good heavens! Why?"

"That's where my family lives," Fee said reasonably. Jacy looked at me in bewilderment.

"She's stuck-up because her family made it down to the orchestra from the balcony," I esplained.

He gave up, kissed Fee, and disengaged himself. She actually clung to him for a moment before letting go. Charisma. He asked Fee if the riot had started and she said yes, half the fuzz were picking up the bug broadcasts and sounded irritated with it. They were getting bored with the repetitions. One of them was suggesting sending in an *agent provocateur* to incite a more entertaining sort of riot.

So off Jacy went, the dearest Knish-head I've ever known. He still wore the longish hair and the beard and still looked his Mole age, thirtyish, so I thought that would make him safe but I followed all the same, just in case. I didn't think the bods would hurt him but the fuzz might try to incite him to a more entertaining riot. He was capable of it. Nobody's ever forgotten the brouhaha he started in that temple in Jerusalem.

The campus was the traditional mess: missiles, lasers, firebombs, and burnings, so everybody was happy. They were chanting and shouting jingles, "One, two, three, four," and something that rhymed with four. "Five, six, seven, eight," and another rhyme with eight. They couldn't go much higher because arithmetic was no longer compulsory. The guards were maintaining the ritualistic barrier lines and haggling with each other for the right to arrest and rape the prettiest girls. Crazy Jacy marched right into the middle of the ceremony.

I thought, "It's going to be another Sermon on the Mount and I didn't bring a recorder. Drat!"

He never got the chance to adjure them. About twenty militants attacked an innocent parked chopper that was doing nobody any harm. They rocked it. They turned it on its side. They smashed the vanes and landing gear off and tried to hammer the cabin off the chassis. They rocked it some more, trying to overturn it completely, and they must have rocked too hard in the wrong direction. The wreck slammed down upright, directly on top of Jacy.

I ran to it. There were half a dozen dull thunks and there was gas (laced with LSD today) and the kids stopped cold and took in deep breaths. I was gassed too but I reached the chopper and tried to heave it up. Impossible. Three guards materialized and grabbed me.

"Help me get this up," I choked. "There's a man underneath."

We all heaved together. Nothing. Then a tall guy, long-boned, with deep-set eyes and a coppery complexion appeared, grabbed the edge of the frame, and turned it over. Christ went up with it, crucified by the chassis, and hat's how I met my first successful candidate for eternity.

He was the epileptic type, I was positive the moment I saw him. A lovely candidate, big, rangy, strong. He carried the Knish to the university hospital slung over one shoulder. Jacy was groaning in Aramaic, the language he learned at his mother's knee. In Emergency my guy was treated with great respect. It was, "Yes, doctor (Yassuh, medico), no, doctor, certainly, doctor." I figured he must have done something sensational like reviving plague to combat the pop. ex. Good. A genius, too.

We saw Jacy into a bed. I wasn't worried about him; it takes more than minor injuries to endanger a Moleman, but I was terrified by the possibility of Lepcer. That's the real, the constant peril. More about Lepcer later. I whispered to Jacy, "I've registered you as J. Kristman. Don't fret. I put me down as next of kin and I'll take care of you."

My guy said in XX, "Hey, man, you speak Early English. How come?"

I said, "How come, you?"

"Maybe some day I'll tell you."

"Likewise, I'm sure. Could you stand a drink?"

"Any time, but I'm not allowed firewater. I'm a ward of the state."

"Easy. I'll order and you sneak it. What am I drinking?"

"Firewater."

"You mean there's such a thing?"

His face was wooden. "Do I look like the joking type?"

"You look like something in front of a cigar store."

"Is there such a thing?"

"There used to be. Where are we drinking?"

"The Passionate Input. I'll show you."

It was a typical campus trap, spaced-out psychedelia, a mooing orgasm tape, tripping bods on the floor blown out of their minds, projection commercials standing around like realsies. "Hello," a jolly giant was saying. "I'm your friendly recycling bank. In our friendly efforts to conserve ecology we want you to let us recycle your money which—" We walked through him and went to the empty bar.

"Double Firewater," I said. "Double soda for my friend."

"Gas in the soda?" the bar wanted to know. "Hash? Phet? Sub?"

"Just plain soda. He trips on it." All this in Spanglish, you unnastand. So it was a double Fire and a double soda and the glasses got kind of intertwined like the lovers on the floor. But I tried the Firewater and nearly had a convulsion.

"I nearly had a convulsion," I said.

"You did," he said. "It's the strychnine we put in. The palefaces love it."

"What d'you mean, 'we'?"

"We moonshine it on the Erie reservation and sell it to the palefaces. Quite a switch, isn't it? That's how we got rich. Firewater and Ugly Poppies."

"I'll figure that one out later. I'm Prince. Ned Prince. Who you?"

"Guess."

"Sure, but give me a hint."

"No, no. That's my name. Guess." He gave me a deadpan

glance. "Haven't you ever heard about the late, great George Guess?"

"You?"

"My ancestor. That was the name the palefaces gave him. His real name was Sequoya."

"Named after the tree?"

"They named the tree after him."

I whistled. "He was that famous? What for?"

"He was the first great Indian scholar. Among other things, he invented the Cherokee alphabet."

"You're Dr. Guess?"

"R."

"Physician?"

"Physicist, but they're practically the same thing today."

"Here at Union Carbide?"

"I teach here. I do my real work at JPL."

"The Jet Propulsion Lab? What's the real work?"

"I'm project scientist on the Pluto Mission."

I whistled again. No wonder it was yes, doctor, no, doctor, certainly, doctor. This *gonser macher* was spending like a million a week on one of the most highly publicized NASA missions in history, financed by the United Conglomerate Fund in their friendly efforts to make the solar system a better place for deserving developers.

"Sounds to me like the state is your ward, Guess. Am I thirsty again?"

"Yeah."

"This time let me have half. That strych grows on you."

"Hell, dude, I was just putting you on about the no-drink shtik. All that went out ages ago."

"Did it? I'm loose in the memory. Hey, bar. Two double Fires. You got a front name, Guess?"

"I'm S. Guess."

"S for Sam?"

"No."

"Saul? Sol? Stan? Salvarsan?"

He laughed, and you haven't lived until you've seen a pokerface laugh. "You're all right, Prince. Why in hell did your friend get mixed up in that silly brawl?"

"He always does; he won't learn. Why in hell won't you tell me your name?"

"What difference does it make? Call me Doc."

"I can look you up in the U-Con stockholder reports."

"No you can't. I'm always S. Guess, Ph.D. Bar! Two more. On me."

The bar objected to excessive alcohol and suggested we switch to something respectable like mescaline, so we obliged. A dead ringer for Columbus, including spyglass, shot up through the floor. "Friends, have you ever considered what would happen to know-how without where-withal? Give generously to the Industrial Research Foundation by buying the products we endorse; Meegs, Gigs, Poons, Fubs—"

We ignored it. "If I show you my passport," I said, "will you show me yours?"

"Haven't got one. You don't need a passport for space. Yet."

"Don't you travel?"

"They won't let me out of Mexifornia, officially."

"Are you that special?"

"I know too much. They're afraid I may fall into the wrong hands. Con Ed tried to kidnap me last year."

"I can't stand the torture any longer. I'm really a spy for AT&T. In drag. My real name is Nellie."

He laughed again, still deadpan. "You're all right, Nellie. I'm pure Cherokee."

"Nobody's pure anything these days."

"I am. My mother named me Sequoya."

"No wonder you're hiding the name. Why'd she play a dirty trick like that on you?"

"She's romantic. She wants me to remember that I'm the twentieth in direct descent from the mighty Chief."

Fee-5 came into the trap, playing the intellectual bit now; hornrim spectacles without lenses, stark naked and covered with spray-can graffiti, applied by herself.

"What's this thing selling?" Guess asked.

"No, she's a realsie."

"Gas," Fee told the bar and turned great dark eyes on us. "Benny Diaz, gemmum."

"It's all right, Fee. He speaks XX. An educated type. This is Dr. Sequoya Guess. You can call him Chief. Chief, this is Fee-5 Grauman's Chinese. Talk about names!"

"Great grief is a divine and terrible radiance which transforms the wretched," Fee said in somber tones.

"What is it and what's it grieving for?" Sequoya wanted to know.

"Could be anyone. Newton, Dryden, Bix, Von Neumann, Heinlein. You name it. She's my girl-Friday."

"Also Saturday, Sunday, Monday, Tuesday, Wednesday, and Thursday," Fee said, belting down her gas. She pierced the Chief with a clinical look. "You want to fondle my boozalum," she said. "Go ahead. Don't deny your manhood."

Sequoya pulled off her spectacles and perched them on one of her boozalums, which were recent and a source of great pride. "That one's a little cockeyed," he said. "What kind of name is Fee?" he asked me. "Short for Fee-Fie-Fo-Fum?"

"Short for Fee-mally."

"Short for female," Fee corrected with great dignity.

The Chief shook his head. "I think I'd better go back to JPL. At least the machines make sense there."

"No, no. It makes sense. When she was born—"

"In the *orchestra* of Grauman's." Very proud.

"Her dumb mother couldn't think of a name, so the demographer listed her as Female. The mother liked it and called her Fee-mally. She calls herself Fee-5."

"Why the five?"

"Because," Fee explained patiently, "I was born in the fifth row. Any fool would understand that, but against stupidity the very gods themselves contend in vain. Gas!"

A capsule floated down on top of the bods with its jets spraying fireworks. A blue-eyed blond astronaut stepped out and came up to us. "Duh," he mumbled in Kallikak. "Duh-duh-duh-duh. . . ."

"What's this thing selling?" Uncas asked.

"Duh," Fee told him. "That's about all the honks can say, so they named the product after it. I think it's a penis amplifier."

"How old is this squaw?" Sequoya demanded.

"Thirteen."

"She's too young for her frame of reference. Next you'll be telling me she can count."

"Oh, she can, she can. She can do anything. She picks it up from the bug broadcasts. This brat is picking all the brains on Earth. By ear."

"How?"

"I don't know. She doesn't either."

"Probably some sort of interface." The Chief produced an otoscope from the interior of his tutta. I had a glimpse and the interior looked like a portable laboratory. "Let me have a look, Fee-Fie-Fo." She presented an ear obediently and he had his look. He grunted. "Fantastic. She's got a wild canal circuitry and there's an otolith in there that looks like a transponder."

"When I die," Fee said, "I'll leave my ears to science."

"What's the Fraunhofer wavelength of calcium?" he shot.

She cocked her head. "Well?" he asked after a pause.

"I've got to find somebody who's talking about it. Wait for it. . . . Wait for it. . . . Wait for it. . . ."

"What do you hear when you listen?"

"Like the wind in a thousand wires. Ah! Here it is. 3968 Angstroms, in the extreme violet."

"This kid is a treasure."

"Don't flatter her. She's vain enough as it is."

"I want her. I can use her at JPL. She'll make an ideal assistant."

"You're not bugged," Fee told him, "and you're not being monitored. Did you know?"

"Yes, I know," he said. "I suppose you are."

"No," I said. "Fee and I aren't bugged because we've never been in a hospital. She was born in a movie house and I was born in a volcano."

"I'm going back to JPL," he muttered. "You're all scrambled around here. Will you let her come and work for me?"

"If you can stand her, but she's got to come home nights. I'm raising her old-fashioned. You're not really serious about this, are you, Geronimo?"

"Damn serious. I won't have to waste time teaching her the things an assistant ought to know. She can pick everything up reading the bugs. The people I've had to fire for illiteracy! Education in Spangland! Pfui!"

"So where were you educated that makes you so literate?"

"On the reservation," he said grimly. "Indians are traditional. We still revere Sequoya and we've got the best schools in the world." He groped inside the inexhaustible tutta, produced a silver medallion, and handed it to Fee. "Wear this when you come to JPL. It opens the front gate. You'll find me in the Cryonics Section. Better wear something. It's damned cold."

"Russian sable," Fee said.

"Does that mean she's going to come?"

"If she wants to and if you pay my price," I said.

He took the spectacles off her chest. "Oh, she wants to. She's been batting her cockeyed boozalums at me without success and she never gives up."

"I've been rejected by better men than you," Fee said indignantly.

"So what's your price, Ned?"

"Sell me your soul," I said brightly.

"Hell, you can have it for free if you can get it back from United Conglomerate."

"Let's have dinner first. The only question is do we feed the girls before or after?"

"Me! Me! Me!" Fee cried. "I want to be one of the girls."

"Virgins are so pushy," I said.

"I was raped when I was five."

"The wish is father to the thought, Fee."

"Who said that?" Montezuma shot at her. "Well?"

"Shush. Shush. Shush. Nobody's talking about—Ah! Got it. Shakespeare. Henry IV."

"It's the Jung caper," Guess said in awe. "She can tap the collective conscious of the world. I've got to have her."

"If I come to JPL will you pay *my* price?" Fee asked.

"What is it?"

"Criminal assault."

He looked at me. I winked at him.

"All right, Fee, and I'll make it real criminal; inside the centrifuge at 1,000 rpm, in the vacuum chamber at half a millimeter of mercury, in one of the cryonics coffins with the lid on. It's a promise."

"There! See?" she threw at me, as triumphant as she was eight months back when her boobs jumped up.

"I never thought you were such a conformist, Fee-doll. Now go to the hospital and comfort Jacy. He's registered as J. Kristman. Tell them you're the confidential assistant of Dr. Guess and they'll sink to their knees."

"Eight o'clock tomorrow morning, Fee-Fie. If it's a deal."

She stuck out a paw and slapped hands. "It's a deal," she said and walked out through Louis Pasteur, who was waving test tubes and selling a mugging repellent.

We picked up a couple of girls who claimed they were coeds and might well have been; one of them could recite the alphabet all the way to L. The only problem was how to stop her from reciting. A show-off. We took them to Powhatan's pad, which really was impressive, an enormous tepee guarded by three very unfriendly timber wolves. When we got inside I understood the reason for the security; it was decorated with some of the most beautiful art I've ever seen in my life, all museum pieces.

We swopped the girls a couple of times and then Guess cooked us a traditional Cherokee dinner in a huge thermal stewpot: rabbit, squirrel, onions, peppers, tomatoes, corn, and lima beans. He called it *msiquatash*. I took the girls home. They were living in the fuselage of a Messerschmitt in a TV prop dump, and then I called Pepys in Paris.

"Sam, it's Guig. All right if I project?"

"Come on in, Guig."

So I projected. He was having breakfast in the bright morning sun. You'd think that being the Group historian he'd identify with someone like Tacitus or Gibbon, but no, it was Balzac, complete with monk's drag. We're all a little loose.

"Good to see you, Guig. Sit down and join me." Joke. When you project you're only two-dimensional and you ooze through furniture and floors if you don't keep moving, so I kept moving. It was like walking through slush.

"Sam, I've got another candidate, a beauty this time. Let me tell you about him."

I described Sequoya. Sam nodded appreciatively. "Sounds perfect, Guig. What's the problem?"

"Me. I don't trust myself anymore; I've failed too often. I swear if I fail with Rain-in-the-Face I'm going to quit for good."

"Then we must make sure you don't fail."

"Which is why I'm here. I'm afraid to try it on my own. I want the Group to pitch in and help me."

"Murder a man. Hmmm. But what's your plan?"

"I haven't got any. I'm asking the Group to come up with horror suggestions and then come out and work with me."

"Watch yourself, Guig. You're knee-deep in the fireplace. Now let me get this straight. You want to use the Grand Guignol technique on Guess and you're asking the Group for ideas, aid, and comfort."

"That's it, Sam."

"Some don't approve."

"I know."

"And some don't believe."

"I know that, too, but some have an open mind. They're the ones I want to tap."

"You're sliding into the piano, Guig. Then this is going to be your final superergon, and we can't let you down. God knows, a man of the stature of Dr. Guess would be a tremendous asset to the Group. I've always agreed that we need new blood. I'll pass the word on the grapevine. You'll be hearing from us."

"Thanks, Sam. I knew I could depend on you."

"Don't go yet. I'm a month behind on your shenanigans. What have you been up to?"

"I'll beam you a printout from my diary. The usual channel?"

"Yes. And what about that remarkable young lady, Fee-5? Should we plan a recruitment for her?"

I stared at him, absolutely speechless. It had never occurred to me, and my instantaneous reaction was to shake my head.

"But why not, Guig? She sounds as tremendous as Dr. Guess."

"I don't know," I mumbled. "*Revoir*, Sam." And I retrojected.

Confusions and upsetments. I went to her room to have a look at her. She was sleeping in a white coverall, scrubbed and polished, her hair skinned back, and she had a lunch packed and waiting. All set for the big new job. I inspected the lunch; enough for two including a kilo of my private caviar from the St. Lawrence hatcher. Hmmm.

Her bed was murmuring. "The vacuum-insulated cryogenic tank at the United Conglomerate JPL Space Center contains nine hundred thousand gallons of liquid hydrogen for fueling the Pluto Mission rockets. In terms of energy its contents are equivalent to. . . ." *Usw.* Boning up to make herself worthy of Sitting Bull. Hmmm.

I went to the study for a rap with my diary. I had to know what was wrong with me. Was I overprotective? Was

I afraid of her? Did I hate her? Did she hate me? Was I rejecting the prospect of knowing her forever?

TERMINAL READY?
READY. ENTER PROGRAM NUMBER.
NEW PROGRAM. CODE 1001.
DESCRIBE PARAMETERS.
USE ALL RELATIONS BETWEEN FEE-5
AND TERMINAL AS FIXED POINT AND
FLOATING POINT VARIABLES.
STATE ARGUMENT MODE.
ARE FEE-5 AND TERMINAL MEMBERS
OF SAME SET?
CODE 1001 HAS BEEN LOADED.
LOC. + CODE. START COUNT.

It took like ten minutes, and when you translate that into nanoseconds there aren't enough zeros to go around.
CODE 1001 HAS FINISHED RUN.
MCS, PRINT. W.H. END.
The printout cackled: WITHIN MATHEMATICAL PARAMETERS FEE-5 N = TERMINAL. WITHIN EMOTIONAL PARAMETERS FEE-5 = TERMINAL.
"Emotional!" I hollered at the goddamn diary. "What's that got to do with it?" and I went to bed (mad).
I chopped her down to JPL next morning where they wouldn't let me through the main gate and she gave me a triumphant look as she sashayed in. I looked around. I remembered it from the days when it was just a scrubby hill scarred with a few burns where Cal Tech under-graduates had been playing with baby rockets. Now it was a complex

so gigantic that JPL was threatening to secede from Mexifornia and go into business for itself.

After a few hours with Jacy at the university hospital (doing fine) and watching the campus (Antipleasurehood) I got home just in time to open the door for an enormous figure in an antique rubber diver's suit. "I'm not buying anything today," I said and started to shut the door. It opened the face plate of the helmet and about a gallon of seawater gushed out. "Guig! I'm here to help you," the bod said in XX.

It was Captain Nemo, who's been cracked on marine biology so long that he prefers to live in water. He turned and waved his arms. "Bring her in, lads," he shouted in Spanglish and a little more water squirted out of his helmet. Three goons appeared lugging an enormous vat which they carried into the house. "Set her down easy," Nemo admonished. "Easy, lads. Easy. That's it. Avast. Belay." The goons left. Nemo took off the helmet and beamed at me, his whiskers dripping. "I've got all your problems solved, Guig. Meet Laura."

"Laura?"

"Look in the tank."

I took the lid off and looked. I was face-to-face with the goddamn biggest octopus in history.

"This is Laura?"

"My pride and joy. Say hello to her."

"Hello, Laura."

"No, no, Guig. She can't hear you from out here. Stick your head under the water."

I stuck. "Hello, Laura," I bubbled.

Damn if the beak didn't open and I heard "Herro" and the eyes stared at me.

"Can you say your name, love?"

"Raura."

I pulled out and turned to Captain Nemo, who was bursting with pride. "Well?"

"Fantastic."

"She's brilliant. She has a vocabulary of a hundred words."

"She seems to have a Japanese accent."

"Yes. I had a little trouble with the mouth transplant."

"Transplant?"

"Well, you don't think I found a thinking, talking octopus, do you? I created her with transplants."

"Nemo, you're a genius."

"I admit it," he admitted modestly.

"And Laura's going to help me put the squeeze on Sequoya Guess?"

"She can't miss. We tell her what to do and your man will die so horribly that he'll never forgive you."

"What's your plan?"

"Have you got a pool? I'm beginning to dry out."

"No, but I can fake one."

I sprayed the little drawing room with transparent perspex, about six feet up the walls; the floor and furniture too, of course, making the coat two inches thick, and there was a drawing-room-shaped pool including the decor. I filled it from the main pump. Nemo got out of his suit, went into the living room, and came back with Laura in his arms. They got into the pool and Nemo sat down on the couch and breathed a bubble of relief while Laura explored curiously. Then Nemo motioned for me to join them. I joined. Laura wrapped her arms around me affectionately.

"She likes you," Nemo said.

"That's nice. So what's your hideous plan?"

"We take your man aqualung diving. We take him deep.

He'll have a closed atmospheric system with a high-pressure helium-oxygen gas mixture. The helium is for the bends."

"Yes?"

"Laura attacks. The monster from the deep."

"And drowns him?"

"No, no, no, lad. More fiendish than that. Laura has been briefed. She cuts off the helium input while he's struggling."

"So? He's getting pure oxygen."

"That's what makes it fiendish. Oxygen, under high pressure, produces symptoms of tetanus, strychnine poisoning, and epileptic spasms. It exaggerates the excitomotor power output of the spinal cord and creates violent convulsions. Your man will go under in slow agony."

"It sounds ghastly enough, Nemo, but how do we save him?"

"Chloroform."

"With what?"

"Chloroform. That's the antidote for oxygen poisoning."

I thought it over. "It sounds kind of complicated, Nemo."

"What d'you want, a volcano?" he asked angrily.

"Sorry. Sorry. . . . I just want to be sure it'll work this time. We'll try it, Nemo. We—Wait a minute. I hear a go-dawful pounding on the front door."

I climbed out and went to the front door, forgetting I was naked. When I irised it open, there was Scented Song, looking as ever like a Ming Dynasty princess. There was an elephant behind her hammering at the door with its trunk.

"The vision of your godlike presence lends celestial light to these concave and unworthy eyes," she said. "All right, Sabu, knock it off."

The elephant stopped hammering. "Hi, Guig," she said. "Long time no see. Don't look now, but your fly's open."

I kissed her. "Come in, princess. It has been a long time, hasn't it? Too long. Who's your friend?"

"About as close as I could come to a mastodon."

"You don't mean—"

"What else? If it was good enough for Hic-Haec-Hoc it ought to be good enough for your prospect."

"What did you have in mind?"

"I seduce your jewel of a thousand facets. While we're in the act we're caught flagrante by Dumbo who, in a mad passion of insensate jealousy, sl-o-w-ly crushes us to death. I scream, but it's no use. It's mad, do you hear? Mad. Your guy fights heroically, but the massive forehead presses down and down and down. . . ."

"Jeez," I said appreciatively.

"And speaking of Sabu's massive brain, we'd better bring him in. He's not very bright and he may get himself into trouble. Iris a little wider for him, Guig."

I opened the door wider and the princess motioned the road-company mastodon in. He in and I have to admit he couldn't be very bright. In the few minutes that he'd been left alone he'd permitted himself to be covered with spray can graffiti, all unmistakably obscene. Sabu chirped a little, touched Scented Song with his trunk to reassure himself, and then disappeared as the living room floor collapsed under him with a roar. There he was, down in the basement, trumpeting his fool head off. There were more roars from the drawing room.

"They don't build houses like they used to," the princess said. "What's all that hollering?"

I didn't have to explain. Captain Nemo came charging out with his fly open. "Goddamn it, what the hell's going on? Ahoy, princess. You've scared the living daylights out of Laura, Guig. She's in a red panic. She's a very sensitive girl."

"It wasn't me, Nemo, it was Sabu. He fell down a little."

Nemo looked down into the basement. "What is it?"

"A Hairy Mastodon," I said.

"I don't see any hair."

"I shave him every morning," Scented Song said. She seemed a little miffed and I suspected there was going to be rivalry between Sabu and Laura. There was a scratching on the front door. When I opened it I was confronted by a coiled python ringed about seven feet high.

"No rabbits today," I said. "Come back tomorrow."

"He does not swallow rabbits," a familiar voice said with meticulous diction. "He swallows men."

Long fingers separated two coils and there was M'bantu surrounded by python, smiling at me.

"My favorite Zulu. Come in, McBee. Bring your friend, unless he's shy."

"He is not shy, Guig. He is asleep. He will sleep for ten days and then he will be ready for your Dr. Guess. Good afternoon, princess. Captain Nemo. What a pleasant reunion."

Both of them sniffed and didn't bother to conceal it. More rivalry. I was warmed by the way the Group was rallying 'round, but oh! the competition. M'bantu unwrapped the python, which was like fifteen feet long, and draped it gently around one of the archway pillars. It went right on sleeping.

"What's that bulge in its middle?" Nemo demanded.

"Breakfast," McBee said courteously, not going into details.

"Does it like fish?"

"Probably prefers elephants," Scented Song said. "It's big enough."

"The next meal will be Dr. Sequoya Guess. That is, with your permission, Guig," M'b said pleasantly. "He will die most painfully, but what will be even more painful for me will be the sacrifice of my friend to save the doctor. However, *che sara sara.*"

The front door burst wide with a blaze of sparks and Edison marched in, carrying his toolbox. "Told you these magnetic locks can't hold, Guig," he snapped. "How much electric power does this Sachem have in his house? Princess. Nemo, M'bantu. Well?"

"None," I said. "He lives in a tepee. Strictly Indian style. Thanks for coming, Ed."

"Then we'll have to get him here. You've got power?"

"I can deliver ten kilowatts."

"Plenty. You've always been behind the times?"

"Conservative. Yes."

"Conservative kitchen?"

"Yes."

"Conservative oven?"

"The old-fashioned walk-in type. Yes."

"Perfect. That's how we'll get him." Edison opened his toolbox and yanked out a blueprint. "Look at this."

"Just tell us, Ed."

"We rewire it, power it, turn it into a magnetic induction furnace."

"What's that?"

"It melts metal; nothing else. Only conductive metals. Understand?"

"So far."

"Put in your hand and you feel nothing. But if you've

got a ring on your finger, the ring will melt and burn your finger off. Induction."

"Phew. That sounds grisly."

"Doesn't it? Get the Indian into your oven. We start the induction slow and the torture begins."

"You mean his fingers burn off?"

"No. The brain begins to burn. Bugged, isn't he?"

"No."

"Bugs are platinum." Obviously Ed wasn't hearing me. "Platinum is conductive. QED."

At this point the other three, who had been listening utterly fascinated, burst out laughing. They shrieked and rocked helplessly while Edison glared at them. It looked as though this loyal rally was going to turn into a Donnybrook Fair and I'd get nowhere with the murder of Sequoya. I was wondering how to make peace when Fee-5, bless her, called and asked if she could project. I said come ahead and there she was in a starched white lab coat looking every inch the dedicated young scientist.

"He wants you to come to JPL right away," she burst out in XX. Then she looked around. "Oh, sorry, cats. I didn't know there was company. Am I intruding?" still in XX.

"All gung, Fee. All friends. As a matter of fact we were just discussing the Chief. Now what's all this?"

"There's an elephant in the cellar. Did you know?"

"Yes, we know."

"And a snake up there."

"We know. Also an octopus in the drawing room. Why does Dr. Guess want me to come to JPL right away?"

She took fire again. "The event of the century. The experimental cryocapsule will put down in an hour. Three cryonauts have been out in orbit for three months and now they're coming back. All the celebs from U-Con will be there and the Chief wants you, too."

"Why me? I'm not celebrated. I don't even own any stock in United Conglomerate."

"He likes you. I don't know why. Nobody else does."

"Well, ask him if I can bring four friends."

Fee nodded and retro'd. The others protested that they weren't faintly interested in the event of the century; they'd witnessed too many in their time and they were always a let down. All of them began bitching simultaneously; about the Boxer rebellion, Franklin and his kite, Captain Bligh and the *Bounty*, Henry Christophe. I tried to break it up. "You don't understand," I told them. "I couldn't care less about those frozen characters coming in for a landing, but this is a golden opportunity to case the guy we're going to kill. Don't you want to size up your victim?"

Fee reappeared. "It's gung, Guig. He says the more the merrier. You can bring the elephant if you like. I'll meet you at the front gate and pass you in." She disappeared.

As we trooped up to the roof (elephant not included) to get into the big chopper, they were all delivering asides.

"Who is she?"

"Sam says he's had her for three years."

"One of yours, M'bantu?"

"Alas, I would say not. She is too light. Most probably Maori and Aztec Indian with a strong strain of Honk. It's the touch of the Waspbrush that accounts for the delicate bones."

"Guig always likes them exotic."

"Behind the times all his life."

"She is pretty."

"And as nubile as a young dolphin."

"I wonder how many he's scored."

"Sam would know."

I was delivering a few asides to myself: How the hell did Fee-5 know my guests understood XX? I had the uneasy feeling that there was a lot more I didn't know about Fee. I also had a sinking that this Cherokee caper was going to turn into the wrong kind of catastrophe. I wanted to go to the university hospital and ask Jacy to move over.

3

We were mugged by some senior citizens on the way from the chopper to the main gate, but no great harm done; they were using vintage revolvers. There was one funny incident. After we chased them I looked around and there was Nemo kneeling on a prostrate maladroit and sincere as hell. He was slamming the Shortie across the face with his own pistol and chanting in rhythm, "This is not . . . the road to . . . survival. . . . You must . . . transplant . . . transplant . . . transplant. . . ."

We pulled him off the poor old Shortie and were met at the gate by Fee, who seemed rather impressed by Nemo's performance. Muggings she knew all about, but this was the first time she'd ever seen one used as an excuse for a lecture. Fee conducted us to the landing site and it was my turn to be impressed.

It was an enormous theater-in-the-round with a circular stage. There were seats for a thousand in the amphitheater, all filled with U-Con brass and politicos doing their best to keep JPL happy and paying taxes in the state. Fee seated us in the reserved section and went down to the floor to join Guess, who was standing at a huge control console alongside the stage. I thought she was behaving with poise and assurance. Either the Chief had kept his promise or she'd found her identity. Either way or both, I had to admire her.

Guess took stage center, looked around, and spoke. "Senoras, gemmum, soul hermanos, ah gone esplain brief, you know, what this esperiment mean, dig? You got like any preguntas, right, ax da man."

He motioned to Fee, who did something at the console. Projectors flashed on and there were three bods on the stage alongside Guess, bowing and smiling. They were smallish but looked strong and tough.

"These are the three courageous volunteers," Guess said (in translation), "who have taken the first cryogenic flight in history. This is in preparation for the Pluto mission and eventually the stars. The constraints are time and payload. It will take the mission many years to reach Pluto, even at maximum acceleration. It will take centuries to reach the stars. It would be impossible to freight enough supplies for these men. There is only one answer, the cryonic technique."

He motioned to Fee again. The projectors flicked and there were the cryonauts, naked, being helped into transparent coffins by technicians. Quick cuts of them being injected, variously attached to tendrils, given some sort of sterile wash. The coffin lids were bolted.

"We lowered the temperature in the cryocoffins one degree Celsius per hour and increased the pressure one atmosphere per hour until we produced the effect of Ice III, which is denser than water and forms above the freezing point. Mid-twentieth-century cryonics failed because it was not known that suspended animation could not be achieved through freezing alone; it requires a combination of low temperature and high pressure. Details are in your fact-tapes."

Shot of the coffins being tenderly loaded into a capsule. Cut to interior of capsule and techs hooking up complicated plumbing.

"We launched them on a ninety-day orbit, a deep ellipse." Long shot of the launch; a gentle liftoff and then, at altitude, flames roaring down from the rocket vehicle carrying the capsule, and acceleration to out-of-sight. The usual. Edison looked bored.

"Now they're returning. We'll trap the craft in a projected kinorep cone, center it with its lateral gas jets, and let the offset of kinorep and gravity bring it down slowly. For those of you who aren't tech-oriented, kinotrac and kinorep are our abbreviations for kinetic electromagnetic attraction and repulsion. That's how the craft you travel on take off and land without shaking you up.

"The cryonauts will arrive in about ten minutes and be brought up to nominal metabolism so slowly that I'm afraid you'll have to wait quite a few days before interviewing them—not that they'll have much to tell you. For them, no time has passed at all. Now, are there any questions?"

There were some smart-ass questions from civilians: Where was the orbit of the capsule? (In the plane of the Earth's orbit. All in your fact-tapes.) Why not a comet orbit around the sun? (Refrigeration constraints plus the fact that it would be thrust into a no-return parabola. All in your fact-tapes.) What are the names and qualifications of the cryonauts? (All in your fact-tapes.) How do you personally feel about this dangerous experiment? (Accountable.) He looked around. "Three more minutes. Any further questions?"

"Yes," I called. "What's an Ugly Poppy?"

He gave me a look that made me feel for George Armstrong Custer (West Point, '61) and returned to the console. "Iris open," he ordered. Fee touched something and the entire roof above the stage leafed back. "Kino trap." She nodded, concentrating so hard that her teeth were fastened on the tip of her tongue.

We waited. We waited. We waited. There was a loud bleep from the console. "In contact," murmured Guess. He took the controls "Each time the craft contacts the kinorep wall we reverse it with its lateral jets, trying to pin it to the center of the cone." He thought he was thinking out loud. In the anxious hush it sounded like a shout. His hands flickered over the console controls and the bleeps merged into a sustained discord. "Centered and descending." It was obvious to me that pokerface was under a tremendous strain even though he showed nothing. He began a droning count: "Diez. Nueve. Ocho. Siete. Seis. Cinco. Cuatro. Tres. Dos. Uno. Minuto." He was peering up through the iris and down at the console radar screen. He went on counting and it sounded like a Latin mass. What a hell of an accountability.

Then the ass end of the capsule crept silently through the iris and inched down with the speed of a snail. We couldn't see the kinorep repulsion but it raised a small storm of dust and paper debris on the stage. There was cheering from the audience. Guess paid no attention; he was completely concentrated on the console controls and the capsule.

He nodded to Fee, who ran to the edge of the stage, knelt, and began making hand signals indicating how much farther the capsule had to drop. We knew it had landed when we saw the stage give slightly. Guess switched off the console, drew a deep, shuddering breath, and suddenly electrified us with a Comanche whoop. We all yelled and laughed and applauded; even Edison, who was consumed by professional jealousy.

Three techs, realsies this time, appeared and unsealed the capsule. Guess stepped to the hatch. "As I said, you won't be able to talk to them but you can look at them. Think of it. They won't be aware of any time lapse." He poked his head into the hatch and his voice was muffled. "Frozen ninety days in orbit and—" He stopped abruptly. We waited. Nothing. He didn't speak; he didn't move. One of the techs touched his back. No response. The two others joined him, muttering anxiously, and then slowly pulled him back. He moved like a sleepwalker and when they let go he simply stood, frozen. The techs looked into the capsule and when their heads reappeared they were white and dumbfounded.

I had to see what had happened. I scrambled with the crowd to the capsule. When I finally got a chance to look in I saw the three coffins. There were no cryonauts inside. There was nothing inside the coffins except three pasty, naked rats. The mob pushed me aside. Through the bedlam I heard Fee-5 shrilling, "Guig! Here! Guig! Please! Guig!" She was alongside the console. I fought my way to her. She was standing over Guess, who was on the floor behind the console in the throes of a classic epileptic seizure.

"All right, Fee, I've got him." I did what had to be done. The tongue. The foam. Loosening the clothes. Easing the thrashing arms and legs. She was appalled; a seizure is always terrifying. Then I stood up and shouted, "Group! Here!" All four materialized. "Guard of honor," I said. "Don't let anyone see him. Are you in control, Fee?"

"No."

"Sorry. You'll have to be. Does the Chief have an office? Any private sanctum?" She nodded. "Good. Instructions: My friends will carry him. Show them where to take him. Then come right back. At once, understand? You'll have to front for Guess when the mob gets around to asking questions. I'll stand by you. My friends will stand by the Chief. Go!"

She was back in five minutes, out of breath, carrying a lab coat. "Put this on, Guig. You be one of his assistants."

"No. You'll have to do this on your own."

"But you'll stand by me?"

"I'm here."

"What do I do? What do I say? I'm not so smart."

"Yes you are, and I haven't trained you for three years for nothing. Now—with great assurance and great style—are you ready?"

"Not yet. Tell me what threw the Chief."

"The cryonauts aren't in their coffins. They've disappeared. There's nothing in each coffin but something that looks like a naked rat."

She began to shake. "Oh God! Oh God! Oh God!" I waited. This was no time to cosset her; she had to make it on her own. She made it. "Gung, Guig. I'm ready. What now?"

"Call for attention. Assurance and style. I'll cue you in."

By God, she had the style to climb up on the console and stand like stout Cortez having his first look at the Pacific. (While his men looked at each other with a wild surmise.) "Ladies and gentlemen!" she called in Spang. "Ladies and gentlemen! Your attention, please." (What now, Guig? in XX.)

"Identify yourself."

"I am Fee-5 Grauman's Chinese, the confidential assistant of Dr. Guess. I'm sure you saw me at the control console." (And now?)

"Upbeat. Elegant. This isn't a disaster, it's a challenge."

"Ladies and gentlemen, something unusual has taken place in the course of our cryogenic probe, and you've been privileged to witness it. I congratulate you. It was unexpected but, as Dr. Guess says, that's the essence of discovery, to find what you're not looking for." She cocked her head. "Ah, some of you are saying serendipity. Yes, science is serendipity." (Guig!)

"The Chief is analyzing this surprise with his staff. Very technical here."

"Dr. Guess is with his staff now in a mode analysis of the phenomenon which you've all seen." She cocked an ear again. "Yes, I know what you're wondering: Will we go ahead with nominal procedure with the cryocoffins? Dr. Guess is evaluating that now, which is why he must not be disturbed. You're wondering what happened to the cryonauts. So are we." (Guig!)

"That s all."

"Thank you very much. I must return to the staff conference now. Dr. Guess will issue a full status review as quickly as possible. Thank you."

I helped her down. She was trembling.

"You're not finished yet, Fee. Tell the techs to put a hold on the capsule just as it is. Seal it and maintain all systems as if it were still in orbit."

She nodded and fought her way through the crowd to the technical men, who still looked dazed. She spoke to them urgently and then returned to me. "Now what?"

"First, I'm proud of you."

"F."

"Now take me to Sitting Bull. I've got to—"

"Don't call him that!" she screamed. "Don't call him any of those names. He's a great man. He's a—he's—"

"—brief him on the situation. He must be recovered from the attack by now."

"I think I love him," she said helplessly.

"And it hurts."

"It's awful."

"It always is, first time around. Let's go."

"Only twelve hours, Guig, and I feel twelve years older."

"I can see it. You've made a quantum jump. Let's go."

Sequoya's sanctum was a large conference room with a long table and heavy armchairs. It was cluttered with books, journals, tape cartridges, computer software. The walls were hung with ten by ten-foot orbit-tracking charts. The Group had seated Guess in a chair at the far end of the table and was eyeballing him with concern. I closed the door on the curious secretaries in the anteroom.

"How is he?" I asked.

"He has lost his marbles," M'bantu said.

"Oh, come on, McBee. He had a fit, that's all."

"Watch this," Scented Song said. She took Sequoya's hand and raised it high. When she let go, it remained where it was. She took Guess by the shoulders and gentled him out of the chair. The Chief came to his feet obediently. When the princess walked him around the conference room, he accompanied her like a sleepwalker, but when she released her hold, Sequoya came to a dead stop in midstride. His hand was still high in the air.

"This is a fit?" M'b asked.

"Put him back in his chair," I said. Fee was whimpering. I wasn't exactly joyful myself.

"It's a washout," Nemo said. "We'll never get to him."

"You've got to help him," Fee cried.

"We'll do our best, love."

"What's happened to him?"

"I don't know."

"How long will it last?"

"No idea."

"Is it permanent, Guig?"

"I couldn't say. We need an expert. Princess, call Sam Pepys. Borgia is to come to my house with all despatch."

"Wilco."

"Why bother?" Edison wanted to know. "He's blown his fuses. Forget him."

"Out of the question. First for Fee's sake. Second, he's still my candidate; we've got to bring his marbles back. Third, plain humanity. He's a brilliant guy and we've got to preserve his prestige."

"Just save him," Fee pleaded.

"We'll do our best, love. The first problem is how to get him out of here to my place. I can hear the U-Con stock-holders clustering in the anteroom. How do we get him past them?"

"Moving him is no problem," M'b said. "He handles like a baby. We can walk him anywhere."

"But how do we make him invisible?" I thought hard. I'm sorry to say I was enjoying the crisis. I love a challenge. "Ed, what's your current identity?" Edison jerked his head at Fee. "Never mind her. We're beyond that."

"I know all about the group," Fee said, not show-off, just trying to keep it moving.

"We'll discuss that later. Who are you nowadays, Ed?"

"Director of the RCA Plasma Division."

"Got identification on you?"

"Of course."

"Gung. Go out there. You're a distinguished colleague of Dr. Guess who invited you to witness the event. You're fully prepared to discuss anything and everything with the stockholders. Fake it and don't stop faking until we've got the bod out of here."

Edison de- after giving each of us a sharp glance plus

a long look at Guess- parted. I heard him start his spiel outside. It sounded like, "u(x + h) − u(x) = 2x + 1." Most enlightening. I thought some more. "Fee and princess. Take the biggest chart off the wall. Each of you take a corner and hold it as high as you can." They obeyed without asking questions and I gave them good marks for that. "Hold it taut." The bottom of the chart just touched the floor. "M'b, you're the strongest. Put Guess over your shoulder."

"The hell he is," Nemo blurted.

"Only physically, captain," M'bantu said in soothing tones. "Never intellectually. No one can compare to you in that department."

I plotted the scene for them and opened the door to the anteroom. The two women walked out holding the chart as high as they could reach. "Sorry to keep you waiting," Fee said to the assembled. Then they sailed the chart out of the anteroom. Behind that screen M'bantu was carrying Sequoya.

When we got to my place Borgia was waiting (I swear I never saw Scented Song making the call) looking like a Sicilian Florence Nightingale, which indeed she is; Sicilian, that is, not a nurse. She's the damned best doctor I know. Since 1600 she's taken medical degrees at Bologna, Heidelberg, Edinburgh, Salpêtrière, Cornell, and Standard Oil. Borgia believes in keeping up with the times.

She had a goongang slaving in the house. "Found them starting to rip the place," she reported. "Your door doesn't hold. So I put them to work." She had indeed. Sabu was lushing it up on a bale of hay. Laura was chasing goldfish in the drawing room pool and absorbing them. The house was cleaned and immaculate. A most notable woman.

"Shape up," she ordered. The gang lined up before her timidly. "Now hear this. You two have incipient embolisms.

You three are on bot, which has lethal side effects. All of you are faggots and need a proctal. I want you back here tomorrow afternoon for a full medical. Hear?"

"Yassuh, medico."

"R. Out."

They out. A most forceful woman. "Evening, Guig," she said in XX. "Evening, all. Who's that thing? She doesn't belong to the Group. Get her out of here."

By God, Fee stood up to her. "My name is Fee-5 Grauman's Chinese. I live here and your patient is my guy. Next question?"

"She talks XX."

"And she knows about the Group. Quite a gal."

"It's the Maori strain," M'bantu interjected. "A magnificent people."

Borgia grinned a mile wide, went to Fee, and shook her hand like it was a pump handle. "You're my kind, Fee," she said. "There aren't enough of you around these days. We've megabred the backbone out of existence. Now let's have a look at the patient. Got somewhere more intimate, Guig? This is like a zoo, and that python keeps belching."

We walked the Chief into my study and Fee put him down in a chair at the desk. The others excused themselves to look after their pets, and Edison went to repair the door which he'd ruined. "Fill me in, Guig." I described the Chief and the disaster that had overtaken him while Borgia prowled around him and examined him. "Yes," she said. "All the basic symptoms of postepileptic delirium; mutism, passive negativism, catatonic stupor. Easy, Fee, I'll drop the clinical jargon. Probably sounds to you like I'm depersonalizing your guy. I'm not. Now, exactly what's the urgency? How much time have I?"

"We've managed to lose the U-Con brass for a little

while, but they'll be howling for Guess tomorrow and a full status review. About seventy million went into the experiment and—"

"Eighty-five," Fee said, "and I can hear them howling for him now. They're in a panic and they want the Chief. Explanations or his scalp."

"They have any suspicions about what's happened to him?" Borgia asked Fee.

"Not yet. Most of them are saying he's chickcopped."

"ESP?" Borgia asked me, much interested.

"No, bug-tap. So you can see everything's at stake. We have to pull him out fast or he's sunk."

"What's in it for you, as if I didn't know."

"Later, Lucy. Not in front of his girl."

"I'm not his girl," Fee said. "He's my guy."

Borgia ignored the semantics. She prowled around Sequoya again, sensing him with invisible antennae. "Interesting. Very interesting. The resemblance to Lincoln. See it, Guig? Is it a pathogenic type? I often wonder. You know, of course, that young Lincoln went into a cataleptic collapse after the death of Ann Rutledge. He never recovered. Remained a manic-depressive for the rest of his life. Now let's try a shortcut. Have you got any writing tools? Handwriting-type."

Fee pulled a pad and a stylus out of the desk.

"Is he righthanded, Fee?"

"Yes."

"We'll try a trick that Charcot showed me in his clinic." Borgia put the stylus in the Chief's right hand and placed the pad under it. "Sometimes they want so desperately to communicate with us, but we must find the way for them." She bent over Guess and started to speak in Spanglish. I stopped her. "He's more comfortable with XX, Borgia."

"Oh, he's that educated? Encouraging." She spoke smoothly to the Chief. "Hello, Dr. Guess. I'm a physician. I would like to have a talk with you about JPL."

Sequoya's face didn't alter; it gazed placidly into space, but after a moment his right hand trembled and wrote:

hello

Fee let out a little yell. Borgia motioned for quiet. "Dr. Guess," she went on, "your friends are here. They are very much concerned about you. Won't you tell them something?"

The hand wrote:

> *doctor guess your friends*
> *are here they are very much*
> *concerned about you wont*
> *you tell them something*

"So." Borgia pursed her lips. "Like that, eh? Will you try, Fee-5? Say something personal."

"Chief, this is Fee-Fie-Fo. You haven't kept your promise yet."

> *chief this is fee fie fo*
> *you havent kept your*
> *promise yet*

Borgia tore the sheet off the pad. "Guig? Maybe something about the recent disaster?"

"Hey, Uncas, U-Con tried to sell me those naked rats. They claim they're your soul."

> *hey uncas tried to*
> *sell me those naked rats*
> *they claim theyr your*
> *soul*

Borgia shook her head. "I'd hoped this might be the road to a breakthrough but it's just echopathy."

"What's that?"

"You find it sometimes as a part of the catatonic syndrome, Guig. The patient repeats the words of another, in one form or another."

"He's just parroting?"

"That's about the size of it, but we're not licked yet. I'll show you another one of Charcot's tricks. The human psyche can be incredibly devious." She transferred the stylus to the Chief's left hand and placed the pad under it. "Hello, Dr. Guess. I'm a physician and I'd like to have a talk with you. Have you come to any conclusion about what happened to your cryonauts?"

The placid face still stared into space. The left hand twitched and then began to scribble in mirrorwriting, from left to right:

$$\text{ontogeny recapitulates}$$
$$\text{phylogeny but}$$

"Mirror, Fee."

"Don't bother," Borgia said. "I read dextro and levo. He's written, 'Ontogeny recapitulates phylogeny, but—' "

"But what?"

"It stops there. 'Ontogeny recapitulates phylogeny, but—' But what, Dr. Guess? What?"

Nothing.

"Failed again?"

"Certainly not, ass. We've discovered that he's functioning deep down inside. Very deep. Down there he's aware of everything that's going on around him. What we have to do is peel off the shock layer that's formed over him."

"Do you know how?"

"Countershock, but if it has to be quick it's going to be iffy."

"It has to be quick. How will it be iffy?"

"They've developed a new tranquilizer, a polypeptide derivative of noradrenalin."

"I haven't understood a word."

"D'you know how tranquilizers work? They thicken the connections between the brain nuclei, the glial cells, and the neurones. Slow down the transfer of nerve-firing from cell to cell and slow down the entire organism. Are you with it?"

"With."

"This noradrenalin derivative blocks it completely. It's close to a nerve gas. All traffic comes to a dead stop. That's the operative word. Dead. We may kill him."

"Why? Tranquilizers don't kill."

"Try to cope with the concept, Guig. Every nerve cell will be isolated. Alone. An island. If they link up synapses again, he'll be recovered and feeling like a fool for withdrawing. He'll be countershocked out of his flight from the JPL surprise. If they don't, he's dead."

"What are the chances?"

"Experimentally, so far, fifty-fifty."

"The Greek says even money is a good bet. Let's try."

"No!" Fee cried. "Please, Guig. No!"

"But he's dead to this world now, Fee. You've lost him already."

"He'll recover some time, won't he, doctor?"

"Oh, yes," Borgia said, "but it might take as long as five years without crash treatment. Your guy is in one of the deepest catatonic shocks I've ever seen, and if he has another epileptic seizure while we're waiting it out, it'll get deeper."

"But—"

"And since he's your guy I should warn you that if he

pulls out of this on his own he'll most probably have complete amnesia for the past. That's strongly indicated in this sort of case."

"For everything?"

"Everything."

"His work?"

"Yes."

"Me?"

"You."

Fee wavered. We waited. At last she said, "R."

"Then let's shape up." Borgia was in complete control.

"He should come out of countershock in a familiar environment. Does he live anywhere?"

"We can't get in. It's guarded by wolves."

"JPL is out of the question. Anywhere else?"

"He teaches at Union Carbide," Fee said.

"Office?"

"Yes, but he spends most of his time using their Extrocomputer."

"What's that?"

Fee looked to me for help. "Carbide built a limitless computer complex," I explained. "They used to call them 'stretch computers.' Now they call them Extrocomputers. This job is stored with every datum since the beginning of time and it hasn't run out of storage space yet."

"Gung. We'll flog him in the computer complex." She yanked a pad out of her toolbox and scribbled. "M'bantu! Here! Take this prescription to Upjohn and bring the ampul to the computer center at Union Carbide. Don't let anybody mug you. Costs a fortune."

"I will transport it in a cleft stick."

She smacked him lovingly. "You black bastard. Tell Upjohn to bill me."

"May I ask in what name, Borgia?"

"Damnation. Who am I now? Oh, yes. Cipolla. Dr. Renata Cipolla. Go, baby."

"Renata Onion!" I exclaimed in disbelief.

"Why not? What are you, some kind of antisemite? Edison! Here! Fixed that door yet? Never mind. I'll need you to rig a sterilizer for me. Also an oxygen mask. You'll come with me and bring your tool box."

"Sterilizer?" Fee whispered. "Oxygen?"

"I may have to transect and do a coronary massage. Nemo! Nemo!" No answer. She tramped to the drawing room where he was in the pool playing with Laura. All the goldfish were gone and I wouldn't doubt that he may have eaten a few himself, just to be friendly, you understand. Borgia rapped on the perspex until he stuck his head above water. "We're leaving. Get out of that and guard the house. Door's a shambles. Shut up, Ed. Use force to repel force but don't kill anybody. Just hold them. They may need medical attention. R. Let's move it out."

She and Edison picked up their toolboxes. As Fee and I walked Cochise out of the house I looked down into the cellar. Scented Song was sleeping peacefully on Sabu's back. I wanted to ask her to move over.

4

No trouble getting into the center; yes, doctor, no, doctor, certainly, doctor; the sleepwalker made a perfect front. There was a crowd in the center; some bright heads playing Prime against the Extro (and losing), and Spangland's popular broadcast serial, *The Rover Girls*. We chased the kids but we couldn't chase the broadcast. Serious Dick, fun-loving Tom, and sturdy-hearted Sam are now cadets at the Pentagon Military Academy (after their transsex operations in Denmark) and are buying pot, poppers, googies, hash, and uglies as refreshments for an orgy to celebrate Serious Dick's election as Porno Procurement officer of his company.

"I can't understand why this place isn't insulated like yours," Borgia complained.

"It is, but the broadcasts sneak in on the high-voltage lines," I explained. "Ignore them. What do I do with the Chief?"

"Flat on the floor, face up. Ed, start putting together the sterilizer and oxygen mask while we're waiting for M'bantu. Forage in the stock rooms for materials. Improvise. Go."

Of course, the center was open for business, as was the entire university. In the first place, a computer is never turned off. In the second place, everything these days is operating on a twenty-four-hour basis. How else can you get some work out of a jillion deserving welfare cases unless you schedule twelve two-hour shifts?

You all know what a computer complex looks like—the hardware standing like a reunion of grandfather clocks, the satellite computers standing around them. The only difference with the Extro is that the satellites need satellites to feed them. You have to go through channels to get to the boss and he's rather abrupt. His business is to take a small question which nobody can answer, move it around through his infinity of bits, and then come out with a curt answer.

The Rover Girls were in a jam. Their father has been missing for a year. Ms. Stanhope, widowed mother of Serious Dick's sweetheart, Bruce, is being romanced off her feet by the wicked Josiah Crabtree, teacher at the Pentagon. Crabtree is really after Ms. Stanhope's fabulously rich acid farm. He also favors a Pentagon cadet, the bully, Dan Baxter, who hates the Rover Girls. The rotten Crabtree and Baxter were honks, naturally.

Edison and M'bantu (*senza* cleft stick) pulled in at the same time. Ed had two heads pushing a skid loaded with gear; oxygen tank, sterilizer, plumbing, and accessories. Don't bother to ask how he dragooned the bods into helping him or how he liberated the necessaries; the entire Group has the overpowering habit. It's not deliberate, we just scare the Shorties. The mere fact of youth is beauty; the mere fact of longevity is authority.

"R." Borgia in control. "Out the heads. Set up, Ed." She opened her toolbox which didn't look much different from Edison's. "Ampul, M'b. We'll shape up and move it. Fee-5, answer a few questions and then out. His height?"

"Six."

"Weight?"

"One-eighty."

"Age?"

"Twenty-four."

"Condition?"

I broke in. "I've seen him in the saddle. Hard and fast."

"Gung." Borgia did some delicate loading of a syringe from M'bantu's ampul. "Ready, Ed?"

"Ready."

"Out, Fee."

"I will not out."

"Out."

"One good reason why."

It was a Battle of the Giants. Borgia softened. "This will be horrible to watch, kitten, especially since he's your guy."

"I'm not a child anymore."

Borgia shrugged. "You're going to be even less of a child after this is over." She stepped to the Chief and gave him a slow, careful intravenous. "Clock it, Guig."

"Starting when?"

"I'll tell you when."

We waited, not knowing what to expect. Suddenly a ghastly scream was wrenched out of the Chief.

"Now, Guig."

The scream was compounded by agonized thrashings. Every vent in Sequoya let go; bowels, urine, semen, saliva, sinuses, sweat glands. Fee was alongside me, clinging and gasping. I was breathing heavily myself.

"Synapses breaking connections," Borgia said in a professional monotone. "He'll need a bath and clean clothes. Time?"

"Ten seconds."

"If he lives, that is." Abruptly, the Chief was still. "Time, Guig?"

"Twenty."

Borgia got a stethoscope from her bag and examined the Chief. "Time?"

"One minute."

She nodded. "So far so good. He's dead."

"Dead!" Fee cried. "He's dead?"

"R. Everything's come to a dead stop. Shut up. I told you to out. We have four minutes before any permanent damage sets in."

"You have to do something. You—"

"I told you to shut up. His nervous system will make it on its own or else it won't. Time?"

"One thirty."

"Ed, promote another coverall and soap and water. He stinks. M'b, hold the door. Nobody in. Move it." She examined the Chief again. "Nicely dead. Time?"

"One forty-five."

"Can you move the frame, Fee?"

"Y-yes."

"Give me the sterilizer temperature reading. Dial on the right."

"Three hundred."

"Turn it off. Switch on the left. Time?"

"Two ten."

Another examination. Edison came hurtling in with a coverall, followed by his faithful slaves lugging a sitz bath of steaming water.

"Strip him and clean him. Don't move him any more than necessary. Time?"

"Two thirty."

"If he doesn't make it at least we'll have a fresh, well-dressed corpse."

Borgia's cool wasn't fooling me; she was as tight as the rest of us. After we cleaned the Chief we started to dress him, but she stopped us. "I may have to go in. You bods, thanks. Get all the filth out of here. Fee, alcohol in my kit. Jet his chest down to the navel. Move it. Time?"

"Three fifteen."

"Mask ready, Ed?"

"Ready."

"It's going to be close." After an hour she asked, "Time?"

"Three thirty."

The door irised open and Jacy pushed past M'b who didn't dare try to stop him. "Guig! What are you doing to that poor man? For shame!"

"Will you get the hell out of here, Jace. How'd you know, anyway?"

"It's all over the university that you're torturing a man in here. It must stop."

"Go back to bed, Jacy," Borgia said. "Your stigmata's showing. Jet my hands, Fee, up to the elbows. Then back off. All of you back. Save the sermonizing, Jacy. We may need it later." She glared down at Sequoya. "Come on, you sons of bitches, link up!" She gazed around in a fury. "Where the hell are the Rover Girls? I wanted everything to be familiar. Just when you need them—Time?"

"Three fifty."

We waited. We waited. We waited. Fee-5 began a quiet howl. Borgia gave me a black look of despair, went to the sterilizer, and took out tools. She knelt alongside Sequoya and poised a scalpel for primary incision. Suddenly his chest rose to meet the point. It was the deepest, most beautiful breath I have ever seen taken in all my life. We began to bubble.

"Quiet," Borgia ordered. "Give him time. No fuss. Back off. Everything familiar when he wakes up. He'll be weak, so no unnecessary strain."

The steady breathing was accompanied by tics, muscular contractions, twitches. "Linking up fine," Borgia murmured to no one.

The Chief's eyes fluttered open and took in the scene. "—but cryology recycles ontogeny," he said. He tried to get to his feet. Borgia motioned to Fee, who ran to him and helped him, steadying him while he rocked. He looked at himself, looked around, took us all in. Then he smiled. It must have been his first realsie and very painful, but it was a nice smile. Fee began to weep. "The old familiar faces," he said. He swayed to me and slapped palms. "Thanks, dude. You're ace. Fee, you're my girl more than ever. Lucy Borgia, down tools." She dropped them and he palmed her. "Edison. M'bantu. Gung to the fifth power. Jacy, you heard the lady, go back to bed. Where's that tutta? Oh. The Rover Girls take a break every two hours to make room for the next shift, Borgia. We'd better get out of here before they're back."

I stared at her. She smiled. "Told you he was aware of everything around him."

"Guig, the greatest thing you ever did was putting a hold on the cryocapsule. Fee, chop to JPL and call a stockholders' meeting for one hour from now."

I gave Borgia another questioning look.

"Everything."

"This is going to be tremendous," the Chief said. "Those naked rats have opened up a Pandora's box that—I have to eat something. Where?"

"My place," I said, "but don't walk into the oven, the door doesn't work."

Edison started to protest vehemently. Sequoya soothed him. "Never mind, Ed. I was impressed by your smoke screen at JPL. You're brilliant. The whole Group is."

"He knows too much," I muttered to Borgia, "and I'm scared."

"How many times must I ditt? He was aware of everything going on around him."

"Y, but I think he's aware of things that didn't go on around him. I think I've got a tiger by the tail."

"Then let go."

"I can't now. I only hope we don't return from the ride with me inside and the smile on the face of the tiger."

The Rover Girls came on again and we got the hell out while rotten Dan Baxter was selling the secret signals to Annapolis. We marched Jacy back into bed and then walked to my place where Scented Song and M'bantu faked a sort of Afro-Chinese dinner. It wasn't bad and it reminded the Sachem of his wolves. He said he hoped some goon would try to rip his tepee so they could get a decent supper. While we were cross-legged on the dining room floor, Fee-5 came tearing in.

"All set for four o'clock, Chief. What are you going to tell them?"

"I don't know yet." He grunted. "It's too damn big to simplify, and the U-Con heads aren't very bright."

"Exactly what is the problem, doctor?" M'b asked.

"Shifting gears, M'bantu. I had to make a lightning shift when I looked into the capsule and I feel like a damned fool for going into shock. Bless you all for saving me. My God, it was like a paleface ambush. . . ."

"When you saw the naked rats?" I asked.

"They aren't rats."

"Aliens from outer space, maybe, taking over our world?"

"Don't Rover Girl me, Guig. You'll find out in due time.

I have to sort it out in my head first. I wish you could transplant an extra brain into my skull, Nemo."

"You don't need it, lad."

"Thanks. Now let me think for a minute."

So we all ate in silence and waited. Even Fee was quiet. That was quite a quantum jump she made.

"Here are the problems," Sequoya began at last. "Explain to United Conglomerate what actually happened, and the overwhelming concept it opened up. I must give them some idea of the procedures involved in exploring the discovery. I must make them understand that the Pluto mission will have to be scrubbed."

"Scrubbed! After all that advance publicity?"

"That's what's going to hurt, Guig, but the results of the cryo exploratory have wiped out the Pluto mission for our time, maybe for all time. But on the other hand it's produced something so unexpected and challenging that I've got to persuade them to transfer the Pluto funding into it. I can handle the scientific palaver but I'm dumb as a honk when it come to selling a proposition."

"We'll need the Greek Syndicate for advice on that," I whispered to the princess. She nodded and slipped out.

"The only reason I'm being so open with you is that I've learned to trust and respect your Group."

"How much do you know about the Group, Sachem?"

"A little."

"Fee told you?"

"I never said a word!" she protested.

"You've been reading my diary. Yes, Fee?"

"Yes."

"How the devil did you learn to decode my private terminal keyboard?"

"I taught myself."

I threw up my hands. Go live with a genius girl. "How much did you pass on to your guy?"

"Nothing," Sequoya said with his mouth full. "What little I know is from induction, deduction, hints, clues, things overheard. I'm a scientist, you know, and I'll tell you something else, I not only speak XX, I read body english. So why don't we drop it? I've got a murderous scene ahead of me and I depend on your Group to help me. Wilco?"

"Why should we?"

"I could blow the whistle on your act."

"F."

"Good for you." He realsie smiled again and it was very winning. "Because we all like each other and want to help each other."

"You Indian con. Wilco."

"Gung. I'll need you and Edison. Fee too, of course. I'll brief you in the chopper so you can ask the right leading questions at the status review. Let's chop."

When we arrived at JPL I was so dazed by the enormity of Sequoya's discovery and the frontiers it had opened that I wasn't aware of anything around me. All I know is that I recovered consciousness in a large astrochem laboratory seated on a kinobench along with some fifty United Conglomerate majority stockholders. We were facing Hiawatha, who stood with his back to a work table cluttered with chemical apparatus. He was leaning against it and looked relaxed and pleased, as though he was about to hand the U-Con brass a surprise package. He sure was. The questions was, would they buy it? The entire review was conducted in Spang, of course, but I translate for my goddamn diary and Fee-snoop Grauman's Chinese.

"Ladies and gentlemen, good morning. You've been

waiting anxiously for a status review so I won't apologize for calling you together on such short notice at four in the morning. You all know me; I'm Dr. Guess, project scientist on the Pluto mission, and I have remarkable news for you. Some are expecting this to turn into a failure review, but—"

"Never mind the guff talk," I yelled. It had been agreed that I was to be the Bad Guy. "Just tell us why you failed and lost us ninety million." Some of the stockholders glared at me, which was the purpose of my nasty behavior, to attract hostility from Guess to myself.

"A fair question, sir, but we have not failed; we have had a tremendous unexpected success."

"By killing three cryonauts?"

"We did not kill them."

"By losing them?"

"They are not lost."

"No? I didn't see them. Nobody saw them."

"You did see them, sir, in the cryocoffins."

"I saw nothing but things that looked like naked rats."

"They are the cryonauts."

I laughed sardonically. The stockholders rustled with interest and there were growls directed at me—"Gag, man. Let him do the talking."

I subsided and Edison took over. "Dr. Guess, this is an amazing statement, unheard of in the history of science. Will you explain yourself, please?" Ed was the Good Guy.

"Ah! My old friend from the RCA plasma division. This will be of particular interest to you, Professor Crookes, because the electronic discharges which we call plasma may very well be involved." Guess turned to the assembled. "Professor Crookes is not an intruder. He is one of several experts I invited to witness the put-down."

"Stop stalling and start the alibi," I called.

"Certainly, sir. Some of you may recall an historic theory developed in embryology centuries ago: ontogeny recapitulates phylogeny. In other words, the development of the embryo within the womb duplicates the successive lost stages in the evolution of the species. I do hope you remember this classic."

"If they don't, Dr. Guess, you're making it abundantly clear," Edison said pleasantly.

I thought it time for another sneer. "And what are you paying your old friend for his loyal support? How big a cut of a hundred million is he getting?"

A lot more growls at me. I gave thanks that Fee-5 had been in on the briefing or she would have been on me with claws. Sequoya ignored the rude man in the third row. "Ontogeny recapitulates phylogeny, but"—here he paused—"but I believe we have discovered that cryology recycles ontogeny."

"Good God!" Edison exclaimed. "This will make history for JPL. Are you sure, Dr. Guess?"

"As sure as any experimenter can ever be, professor. Those quote naked rats unquote are embryos, the embryos of the cryonauts. After ninety days in space they have been regressed to an early stage in fetal development."

"Any theory why?" This from a bright stockholder.

"I must be honest; none. We never had a hint of this fantastic possibility in any of our cryogenic preparations, but all the experiments were conducted on Earth where they were protected by our heavy atmospheric insulation. We did orbit animal subjects, but only for short periods. Our three cryonauts were the first to be exposed to space for an extended period and I have no idea of what factors produced the phenomenon."

"Plasma?" Edison asked.

"Indeed, yes. Protons and electrons in the Van Allen belts, the solar wind, neutrons, quasar radio bursts, hydrogen ion emissions, the entire electromagnetic spectrum—there are hundreds of possibilities. All must be explored."

Edison, enthusiastic: "I would be honored to be permitted to assist you in this tremendous project, Dr. Guess." Then he added in XX, "And I mean it."

"I would be honored to have your help, Professor Crookes."

A Ms. stockholder asked in tearful tones, "But what about the poor, dear cryonauts? And their families? And—"

"That's the most pressing problem. Is it merely a reversal of ontogeny or is it a full recycling? Will they regress to the ovum stage and die? Have they already reached that stage and are developing again to maturity? What will they develop into, infants, grown men? How do we explore this? How do we continue the process?"

General confusion. It was the cue for my next question, not too hostile this time. "I grant that you may be telling the truth, Guess."

"Thank you, sir."

"And I grant that this may be an astonishing discovery, but are you asking United Conglomerate to finance you in what appears to be pure research?"

"Well, sir, in view of the fact that the Pluto mission must be postponed. . . ."

Anguished cries from the deserving dividenders.

"Ladies and gentlemen, please! The Pluto mission was based on the belief that we could send cryonauts through space. We have discovered that we can't, yet. Everything must be postponed until we learn exactly what happens to a cryonaut. Naturally I would expect United Conglomerate to transfer the JPL funding to this pure but essential research. It will be the only way of protecting your investment."

More cries from the stockholders. A powerful voice from the back of the laboratory cut through the confusion. "If not, *we* will finance it."

Guess was genuinely startled. "Who are you, sir?"

The Greek Syndicate stood up; squatty, thick hair, thin mustache, elegant with an eyeglass. "I am Poulos Poulos, investment director of the independent, sovereign state of I. G. Farben Gesellschaft. My word is my honor and I give you my word that I. G. Farben will support your research to the limit. So far we have never reached our limit."

Sequoya looked at me.

"Group," I called in XX.

The Chief smiled. "Thank you, Mr. Poulos. I will be happy to accept your offer if—"

Angry shouts: "No! No! No! It's ours. We paid so far. You have a contract. Ironbound. Results of research are ours. We haven't said no yet. We have to know more. Then we'll decide. Can't stampede us. Twelve hours. Twenty-four. We don't know where we are yet."

"You *should* know," the Syndicate said contemptuously. "*We* know where we are. You people prove the truth of an ancient maxim: Never show a fool or a child a thing half-finished. We at I. G. Farben are neither foolish nor childish. Come to us, Dr. Guess. If these fools attempt legal action, we'll know how to handle it."

Fee-5, who had been standing quietly behind the workbench with a careful ear cocked, said, "The stockholders are confused because you haven't told them what results you expect from the research, Dr. Guess. That's what they want to know."

"But I can't tell them. This is an Emergent program."

"Ah!" Edison was genuinely with it. "Very true. You had better explain, Dr. Guess. Permit me." He stood up. "Ladies and gentlemen, please listen to your project scientist. He will answer your crucial question." They shut up. Authority.

"A basic concept in research," the Chief said carefully, "is the question of whether the constituents of the experiments will yield Resultant or Emergent finds. In essence this is like bringing two people together. Will they become friends, lovers, enemies? How do you predict it? You all know that it can't be predicted."

The Ms. stockholder sobbed.

"In a Resultant experiment the outcome can be foretold from the very nature of the constituents. There is no new and unforeseen set of properties arising from the combination of the constituents."

Edison (Professor Crookes) was nodding and beaming. I had to work hard to follow the exposition and I doubted whether the U-Con heads were twigging at all, but they seemed to be impressed.

"The nature of an Emergent cannot be foretold from the nature of its several constituents as they were prior to combination. The nature of an Emergent can only be discovered through experiment and observation, and no one can possibly foretell it. It springs up, new and unexpected, to the surprise of everybody."

"Example," Edison called.

"Here is an example. We know the constituents of the human animal. From these constituents is it possible to predict the phenomenon of abstract thought? Is abstraction Resultant or Emergent?"

"Too abstruse," I called in XX. "A simple, graphic example which even heads can see and believe."

Sitting Bull thought hard for a moment. Then he turned

to Fee. "Nitric acid. Hydrochloric. Three beakers. Three slugs of gold."

While she scurried to the stock shelves he smiled at the house and said, "I'm going to give you a simple demonstration. I will show you that neither nitric acid nor hydrochloric acid attack the noble metals. Their properties are known. And yet when they are combined they form an Emergent called aqua regia, which does consume the noble metals. Early chemists had no way of predicting this. Today, with our knowledge of ion transfer, we do understand and can predict, particularly when we're assisted by computer analysis. This is what I mean when I say the new cryogenic research is Emergent. Nothing can be foretold. Computers can't help us because a computer is no better than its stored data and we have none available yet. Thank you, Fee."

He set up the three beakers, dropped a chunk of gold into each, and unstoppered the acid bottles. "Watch closely, please. Gold in each beaker. Hydrochloric acid in the first. Nitric acid in the second. Aqua regia, the royal water, in the—"

He was interrupted by a blast of coughings, gaspings, stranglings. It sounded like fifty people were drowning. In half a minute the entire audience had stampeded out of the laboratory; only Edison, the Syndicate, and myself were left with the Chief. Sequoya looked at us in bewilderment. "What happened?" he asked in XX.

Glassware began to crash down as their metal supports gave way. Window blinds and valence and spectra charts fell with a clatter. The light fixtures dropped with sizzling short-circuit flares, and we were in pitch darkness. "What happened?" Guess repeated.

"What happened? I can tell you what happened." Edison barked with laughter. "That damn fool girl brought you fuming nitric acid. Fuming. And the fumes have turned this room into one big nitric acid bath. Everything's being eaten away."

"Did you see her do it? Did you see the label? Why didn't you stop her?" The Chief sounded furious.

"No. No, and no. I've deduced it. Not an Emergent, just a Resultant."

"Dear God! Dear God! I've ruined the whole pitch to the U-Con crowd." Despairing.

Suddenly I did the take and let out a yell.

"What's the matter, Guig?" the Group called. "Are you hurt?"

"No, you damn fools, and that's why I'm hollering. I'm Grand Guignol triumphant. Don't you understand? Why didn't he know it was fuming nitric acid? Why didn't he choke on the fumes? Why isn't he eaten away now? Why wasn't he forced to run out with Fee and the rest? Think about it while I revel."

After a long moment, the Syndicate said, "I never believed in your campaign, Guig. I apologize. It was a million to one against, so I hope you'll pardon me."

"You're pardoned. You're all pardoned. We've got another Molecular Man. We've got a brand new beautiful Moleman. Still there, Uncas?"

"I can't understand a word you're saying."

"Take a deep breath of nitric. Belt down a stiff shot. Do anything you like to celebrate, because nothing, but nothing you eat, drink, or breathe can kill you. Welcome to the Group."

5

And he disappeared. How it happened: We had to get out of the acid bath before everything was eaten off us—rings, watches, bridgework, fillings, the portable lab Hiawatha carried inside his tutta. There was a crowd of dumbfounded stockholders milling outside the laboratory sounding like victims of a coryza plague, and we got separated. When we finally got together again, clustered around Fee-5, the Chief was gone and there was no locating him in the crowd. We hollered for him in XX. N. Fee began to panic.

I gave her a look. Again no time for cosseting. "Where can we talk in private? Sacred private?"

She feathered her vanes and landed again. "The high vacuum chamber."

"R. Go."

She led us on a twisted course to a giant sphere, opened a sequence of submarine hatches, and we were inside the sphere keeping company with half a space capsule.

"High vacuum circuitry check," she said.

"Lovely scene for criminal assault."

She gave me a look, the equal of mine, and it began to dawn on me that I'd better mind my manners with this new-risen phoenix.

I said to the Syndicate, "That was a lovely performance. Thanks."

"Ah, yes. To make someone want something you must show them that someone else wants it more. Elementary."

"By any chance was anything you said true?"

"But it was all truth."

"You represent the independent sovereign state of I. G. Farben?"

"I own fifty-one percent of it."

"How much of the whole world do you own, Greek?"

"Fourteen point nine one seven percent, but who counts?"

"My God, you're rich. Am I rich?"

"You have eleven million six hundred thousand one hundred and three. By my standards you are poor."

Fee-5 let out a little moan and I relented. "R," I said. "It's a simple problem. The poor bastard has had too many shocks in one day and he's run off in all directions. All we have to do is find him and cool him. Now he may be somewhere in the JPL complex or at the university. Your job, Fee. Find him."

"I can if he's anywhere."

"R. Let's hope he's somewhere. Now, he may have scuttled for the tepee, but there's the problem of the wolves. We'd better let M'bantu handle that. On the other hand he may have levanted to a Particle Bio research center for technical advice. Ed?"

"I'll handle that."

"He may have cut for a patent office to file for an exclusive on his discovery."

"Mine," the Syndicate said.

"He may have started on a bash to relieve the pain. I'll put Scented Song on that."

Edison barked his laugh. "I can just see her charging into the fangojoints on Sabu."

"Y. I'd like to be with her. Now there's an outside chance that he may have gone into cataleptics again. That's for Borgia."

"What about you, Guig?"

"I'm going back to my place. Nemo and I will hold the fort. Keep the progress reports coming. Gung?"

"R."

Fee had been breathing heavily—controlling panic, I thought—but now she began to gasp in heaves and her face was turning blue.

"Now what?" I shot at her.

"Not her fault," Ed said calmly. "Somebody's started pumping out the chamber. She's strangling on vacuum."

"Never a dull moment at JPL," I said. "Out." We out, me carrying Fee-Cyanosis Chinese, and a dozen techs outside wanted to know how dast we be in there contaminating the circuits. You can't please everybody.

So we started our various searches for Sequoya and I did like hell go home. I had a damned good hunch where the Chief had taken refuge (I hadn't spent five days in a bamboo caul for nothing) and I took the next linear for the Erie reservation. But I did have the courtesy to call and brief Nemo on the assignments.

Now, here had been this mudhole, the size of a moon crater, 240 miles long, 60 miles wide, 200 feet deep, black, repellent, all ooze, crisscrossed with gutters containing the poisonous effluents extruded by a better industry for a better tomorrow. This was the generous gift to the Amerind nations to possess and inhabit forever or until a progressive Congress ousted the dispossessed again. Nine thousand square miles of hell.

Now it was nine thousand square miles of paradise. It

suggested a fantastic image to me; a shattered rainbow of odd-shaped fields of poppies glowing red, orange, yellow, green, blue, indigo, violet. The channels had been roofed over with tile. The lake bed was scattered with wickiups, the traditional Indian hut, once made of mud and branches, but these were built of marble, granite, limestone, terracotta, travertine. Flagged roads wandered everywhere in no particular pattern, and all around the lake bed was a gentle cushion fence that pushed you back if you came too close. If you persisted in coming closer it stiff-armed you with a piston jolt.

The gate was guarded by Apaches, all no-nonsense courtesy and speaking nothing but Apache. I couldn't palaver with them; I just kept repeating "Sequoya" in a determined voice. They hocked a tchynik for a few minutes and then the boss of the gate issued me a guide in a hovercraft. He drove me through a tangle of roads and paths to a gleaming marmol wickiup and pointed. There was the Chief in a breechclout with his back to a marble wall, enjoying the morning sun.

I sat down alongside him without a word. Every instinct told me to adapt myself to his tempo. He was silent, deadpan, immobile. Me too. It was a little buggy. He didn't slap; neither did I. He did one thing that told me how deeply he had withdrawn into his people's past—he turned over lazily and pissed to one side and then turned onto his back again. I didn't imitate that. There's a limit. There's also toilet training.

After a few hours of silence he lazed to his feet. I didn't move until he reached down a hand to help me up. I followed him into the wickiup. It was as beautifully decorated as his tepee and enormous; room after room in tile and leather, Hopi scatter rugs, spectacular silver and porcelain. Sequoya hadn't been guffing me; these redskins were rich.

He called something in what I figured was Cherokee and the family appeared from all directions; Papa, most majestic and cordial and even more of the Lincoln type. (I suspect that Honest Abe may have had a touch of the redbrush in him.) Mama, so billowy that you wanted to bury yourself in her when you were in trouble. A sister around seventeen or eighteen, so shy I couldn't get a look at her. She kept her head lowered. A couple of kid brothers who immediately charged on me to touch and feel my skin with giggles. Evidently they'd never seen a paleface before.

I minded my manners; deep bow to papa, kiss mama's hand, kiss sister's hand (whereupon she ran out of the room), knocked the boys heads together and gave them all the trinkets and curios I had in my pockets. All this, you understand, without a spoken word, but I could see the Chief was pleased and he sounded pleasant when apparently he explained me to the family.

They gave us lunch. The Cherokees were originally a Carolina crowd so it was sort of coastal; mussel soup, shrimp and okra, baked hominy, berry corn cobbler, and yalipan tea. And not served on plastic; bone china, if you please, and silver flatware. When I offered to help with the dishes, mama laughed and hustled me out of the kitchen while sister blushed into her boozalum. Sequoya chased the kid brothers, who were climbing all over me, and led me out of the wickiup. I thought it was going to be another liedown in the sun, but he began to saunter down the paths and roads, walking as though he owned the reservation. There was a light breeze and the entire spectrum of poppies genuflected.

At last he asked, "Logic, Guig?"

"No."

"Then how?"

"Oh, we had a dozen rational possibilities—the Group is tracking them down—but I related."

"Ah. Home."

I grunted.

"How long since you've had a family and a home, Guig?"

"A couple of centuries, more or less."

"You poor orphan."

"That's why the Group tries to stick together. We're all the family we have."

"And now it's going to happen to me."

I grunted.

"It is, isn't it? You weren't shooting me through a Black Hole?"

"You know it is. You know it's happened already."

"It's like a slow death, Guig."

"It's long life."

"I'm not so sure you did me a favor."

"I'm positive I had nothing to do with it. It was a lucky accident."

"Lucky!"

We both grunted.

After a few minutes he asked, "What did you mean, 'tries to stick together'?"

"In some ways we're a typical family. There are likes and dislikes, jealousies, hatreds, downright feuds. Lucy Borgia and Len Da Vinci have been at each other's throats since long before I was transformed. We don't dare even mention them to each other."

"But they gathered around to help you."

"Only my friends. If I'd asked the Rajah to come and

lend a hand he wouldn't even bother to turn me down; he hates me. If Queenie had come it would have been a disaster; Edison and Queenie can't abide each other. And so it goes. It's not all sweetness and light in the Group. You'll find out as you get to know us."

We broke off the talk and continued the walk. Each time we passed one of those luxury wickiups I saw handicrafts in progress: looms, pottery wheels, silversmiths, iron-mongers, leatherworkers, woodcarvers, painters, even a guy flaking arrowheads.

"Souvenirs for the honk tourists," Sequoya explained. "We convince them that we still use bows and arrows and lances."

"Hell, man, you don't need the money."

"No, no, no. Just goodwill. We never charge the tourists anything for souvenirs. We don't even charge an admission fee at the gates."

God knows, Erie seemed to be up to its ass in goodwill. It was all silence and smiles. Dio! The blessed quiet! Apparently the cushion fence blocked broadcasts as well as unwelcome visitors.

"When they squeezed the nations and tribes out of our last reservations," Sequoya said, "they generously gave us the bed of Lake Erie for our very own. All the fresh water feeding the lake had been impounded by industry. It was just a poisoned bed, a factory sewer, and they moved us all in."

"Why not the charming, hospitable South Pole?"

"There's coal down there that they're hoping to get at some day. The very first job I had was working on techniques for melting the cap for Ice Anthracite Inc."

"Most farsighted."

"We dug channels to drain the pollution. We put up

tents. We tried to live with the rot and stench. We died by the thousands; we starved, suffocated, killed ourselves. So many great tribes wiped out. . . ."

"Then what turned this into a paradise?"

"A very great Indian made a discovery. Nothing would grow in the poisoned land except poppies, the Ugly Poppies."

"Who made the discovery?"

"His name was Guess. Isaac Indus Guess."

"Ah, I'm beginning to understand. Your father?"

"My great grandfather."

"I see. Genius runs in the family. But why do you call them Ugly Poppies, Chief? They're beautiful."

"So they are, but they produce a poisoned opium, and ugly drugs are extracted from it; new drugs, unheard-of drugs with fantastic effects—they're still exploring the possible derivatives—and overnight, in a drug culture, the reservation became rich."

"That story's a fairy tale."

He was surprised. "Why do you say that Guig?"

"Because a benevolent government would have taken Erie away from you for your own good."

He laughed. "You're absolutely right, except for one thing: There's a secret process involved in getting the poppies to produce the poisoned opium, and they don't know it. We're the only ones who do and we're not telling. That's how we won the final war with the palefaces. We gave them the choice: Erie or poppy poison, not both. They offered all sorts of treaties, promises, deals, and we turned them down. We've learned the hard way not to trust anybody."

"The story's still thin, Chief. Bribes? Blackmail? Treason? Spies?"

"Oh, yes, they've tried them all. They still are. We handle them."

"How?"

"Oh, come now, Guig. . . ."

He said that with such merciless amusement that a chill ran down my spine. "Then what you've got, in effect, is a Redskin Mafia."

"More or less. The Mafia International wanted us to join them but we turned them down. We trust no one. They tried to use muscle, but our Comanches are still a tough tribe— too tough, I think. But I was grateful for that little war. It cooled the Comanche feist and they're easier to live with now. So's the Mafia International. They won't start pressuring again. We gave them a bellyful of traditional barbarism they'll never forget. That's our college."

He pointed to about forty acres of low, white, clapboard buildings. "We built it in the Colonial style to show there were no hard feelings for the early settlers who started the great robbery. Firewater distillery. Ugly synthesis. Education. It's the best college in the world and we've got a waiting list a mile long."

"Students?"

"No. Professors. Research fellows. Teachers. We don't admit students from the outside; it's reserved for our own kids."

"Are any of your kids on junk?"

He shook his head. "Not that I know of. We don't run a permissive society. No drugs. No bugs."

"Firewater?"

"Now and then, but it's so horroroso that they quit pretty soon."

"Is it a secret process, too?"

"Oh, no. It's alcohol, strychnine, tobacco, soap, red pepper., and brown coloring."

I shuddered.

"Anyone can have the recipe because we've got a lock on the brand name. The honks want Erie Firewater and no substitutes."

"And they can have it."

He smiled. "Hiram Walker gave us a hard fight with Canadian Firewater—they must have put a hundred million into the promotion—but they lost out because their advertising made a stupid mistake. They didn't realize that the honks don't know there are Indians in Canada. They think all the Canadian originals are Eskimos, and who wants to drink Eskimo icewater?"

"Do you trust me, Chief?"

"Yes," he said.

"What's the Ugly Poppy secret?"

"Oil of wormwood."

"You mean the stuff that drove absinthe drinkers mad back in the nineteenth century?"

He nodded. "Distilled from the leaves of *Artemisia absinthium*, but it's a highly sophisticated process. Takes years to develop expertise if you're thinking of learning it. We'll make an exception and admit you to our college."

"No, thanks. Genius doesn't run in my family."

Meanwhile he led me to an enormous marble pool, the size of a small lake, filled with crystal water. "We build them for our kids," the Chief said. "They've got to learn to swim and handle a canoe. Tradition." We sat down on a bench. "R," he said. "I've told you everything. Now you tell me. What have I got myself into?"

This was no time for hard sell. I spoke matter-of-factly.

"This has to be a secret, Sequoya. The Group has always kept it a secret. I don't ask for your word of honor, pledges, any of that S. You know we trust each other."

He nodded.

"We've discovered that death is not an inevitable metabolic process. We seem to be immortals but we have no way of knowing whether or not it's permanent. Some of us have been around for ages. Will it last forever? We don't know."

"Entropy," he murmured.

"Yes, there's always that. Sooner or later the entire universe must run down, including us."

"What transformed the Group, Guig?"

I described our experiences.

"All psychogenic," he said. "And that's what happened to me. Y? But Guig, you're saying that I'll remain twenty-four forever."

"R. We all hold at the age of our transformation."

"Aren't you ignoring the natural deterioration, the breakdown and aging of organs?"

"That's one of the mysteries. Young organisms are capable of repair and regeneration. Why is this power lost with age? It isn't with us."

"Then what promotes regeneration in the Group?"

"We don't know. You're the first research scientist to join the Group. I'm hoping you may find out. Tycho has a theory, but he's an astronomer."

"I'd like to hear it anyway."

"It's kind of involved."

"Never mind. Go ahead."

"Well. . . . Tycho says there may be lethal secretions that accumulate in body cells, the side products of normal cellular reactions. The cells can't eliminate them. They build up over the years, eventually choking the cell's normal function. So the body ages and dies."

"So far he's on solid ground."

"Tycho says the nerve firing of the death shock may destroy these lethal accretions so the body can make a fresh start, and it accelerates cell renewal to such a high rate that the body is constantly making fresh starts. It's a psychogenic effect produced by a psychogalvanic effect."

"Did you say astronomer? He sounds more like a physiologist."

"Half and half. He's an exobiologist. Whether he's right or wrong there's no doubt that the phenomenon is part of the Moleman syndrome."

"I was waiting for you to get to that. Exactly what is a Molecular Man?"

"An organism that can transform any molecule into an anabolic buildup."

"Consciously?"

"No. It just happens. The Moleman can breathe any gas, absorb oxygen from water, eat poison, be exposed to any environment, and all are transformed into a metabolic asset."

"What happens when there's physical damage?"

"If it's minor, it regenerates. If it's major, kaput. Chop off a head, burn out a heart, and you've got one dead immortal. We're not invulnerable. So don't go running around like Superman."

"Who?"

"Forget it. I've got a more crucial warning about our vulnerability. We don't dare take chances."

"What sort of chances?"

"Our immortality is based on the constant, accelerated cell renewal. Can you mention a classic case of accelerated cell growth?"

"Cancer. You mean the Group—We—"

"Yes. We're only a hair's-breadth below the insane, uncontrolled growth of cancer."

"But we've cured cancer with Folic Acid Phage. It has an antibiotic effect on the wildcat nucleic acids."

"Alas, we're cancer-prone, but we don't get it. Carcinogens merely open the door for something worse, a leprosy mutation we call Lepcer."

"Dio!"

"As you say. Lepcer is a bitch's bastard gene distortion in *Bacillus leprae*. It produces variations and combinations of nodular leprosy and anesthetic leprosy. It's unique to the Group. There's no known cure, and it takes half a century to kill in agony."

"What has this to do with taking chances?"

"We know that carcinogens are the result of the irritations and shocks of the outer environment. They must be avoided. You never know what injury will kick you up above the cancer threshold and open the door for Lepcer. You'll have to learn caution, and if you're forced to take a chance at least know the price you may have to pay. That's why we don't go looking for kinky things to eat, drink, and breathe. And we run from violence."

"Is Lepcer the inevitable result of injury?"

"No, but don't get rash."

"How would I know if I got hit?"

"Primary symptoms: red areas on the skin that pigment, hyperesthetic exaltation, bad throat and larynx."

"Suddenly I've got them all." He smiled. I was glad he could joke about the ominous warning.

"You've had a rough time, Chief," I said, "but don't you think you'd better go back to work? There's so much to be done. I'd just as soon loaf around Erie for a year, enjoying the reservation, but we really ought to retro to the mad-house. How do you feel about it?"

He got to his feet. "Oh, I agree. R. After all this what else could possibly happen?"

As we sauntered back to the wickiup I was agreeing with Sequoya. After the past two days there couldn't be any more surprises, which just shows how smart I can be. When we got back to the marble job I called Captain Nemo and told him to pull the Group off the search. Our Wandering Boy was returning to the fold. I had to remind Uncas to get dressed, not that half the pop didn't walk around naked, but after all he was a distinguished scientist and had certain appearances to keep up. Conspicuous consumption. The Chief called it chicken consumption.

The family assembled and jabbered in Cherokee which, frankly, is not an attractive language; it sounds halfway between the two worst in the world, Gaelic and Hebrew, all gutterals and *szik-ik-scha* noises. After the Chief finished his explanations I made my manners again. No *szik-ik-scha*. Profound bow to papa. Kiss mama's hand. And then, at this moment, God (who has one of His command posts in Jacy) trapped me into the most magnificent mistake of my life.

When it came sister's turn for the amenities I put two fingers under her chin and tilted her face up for a look. It was an oval face on an oval head set on a neck long enough for a guillotine. She was no beauty; she wasn't even pretty; she was handsome, handsome. Exquisite bones, deep eyes, limpid skin, all character. I looked into that face and saw an entire world I never dreamed existed. And then came the mistake. I kissed her good-bye.

Everyone froze. Dead silence. Sister examined me for about as long as it would take to recite a sonnet. Then she knelt down before me and swept her palms back and forth over my feet. All hell broke loose. Mama burst into tears and swept sister into her billows. The urchins began yelling and cheering. Majestic papa came to me, put a palm on my heart, and then took my palm and put it on his heart. I looked at the Chief, completely bewildered.

"You've just married my sister," he said casually.

I went into shock.

He smiled. "Tradition. A kiss is a proposal of marriage. She accepted and about a hundred Erie braves are going to hate you for it. Don't panic, Guig. I'll get you out of it."

I disengaged sister from the billows and kissed her hello this time. She started to kneel again but I held her upright so I could plunge into that brand new world. "N," I said.

"You don't want out?"

"N."

"You mean this? Count to a hundred in binary."

"Y."

He came to me and cracked my ribs with a titanic embrace. "I've always wanted a brother like you, Guig. Now sit gung while we get the ceremonies into orbit."

"What ceremonies? I thought you said—"

"Dude, you're marrying the daughter of the most powerful chief on the reservation. I hate to say this, but you're marrying above yourself. There have to be rituals. Leave it to me and don't let anything skew you."

In one hour the following, while I sat in a daze: Around fifty people ready for travel outside the wickiup, plus enought hovercraft to transport them to wherever it was. "Not the entire tribe," Sequoya said. "Just the blood relations." He had covered his face with terrifying warpaint and was unrecognizable. Behind the house a chorus of Erie braves, rejects, singing sad, angry songs. From the attic four Samsons carrying down an enormous cordovan trunk while sister seemed to be pleading for tender handling.

"Her dowry," the Chief said.

"Dowry? I've got eleven million. I don't—"

"Tradition. She can't come to you empty-handed. Would you rather take it out in horses and cattle?"

I resigned myself to living with a trunkful of Cherokee homespun.

There must have been an inexhaustible larder somewhere. Mama was piling the relations with enough food to feed I. G. Farben Gesellschaft, despite the fact that they'd schlepped their own. Sister disappeared for a long time and reappeared wearing the traditional squaw's dress, but not deerskin, the finest Mandarin silk. She also wore what I thought were turquoise headband, necklace and bracelets. It wasn't until much later that I discovered they were raw emeralds.

"Gung," Sequoya said. "Let's move it out."

"May I ask where?"

"To your new house. Tradition."

"I haven't got a new house."

"Yes, you do. My tepee. Wedding gift. Any more questions?"

"Just one, brother. I really hate to plague you when you're so busy, but would you mind telling me my wife's name?"

That really broke him up. Finally he managed to gasp, "Natoma—Natoma Guess."

"Very nice."

"What's yours, incidentally? The one you started with."

"Edward Curzon."

"Natoma Curzon. Very nice. R. Let's go and suffer through the ceremonies."

More tradition on the way out of Erie. Natoma and I sat side by side with mama and papa behind us like guardians of virtue. The paths and roads were lined with people, all shouting and the small boys yelling things that sounded unmistakably vulgar in any language. When I started to put my arm around Natoma, mama made a noise that was an unmistakable no. Papa chuckled. My bride kept her head lowered but I could see she was blushing.

When we finally arrived at the tepee, Sequoya took a lightning survey and made emphatic Indian Sign. The blood relatives stopped where they were. "Where the hell are my wolves?" he asked in XX.

"They are in here with me, Dr. Guess," M'bantu called. "We have been waiting for you most anxiously."

The Chief and I darted in. There was M'bantu squatted cross-legged on the floor with the three wolves lounging all over him contentedly.

"How the hell does he do it? Those three are killers."

"Don't ask me. He's been doing it all his life."

"It couldn't be simpler, Dr. Guess. All one need do is speak their language and a friendly rapport is established."

"You speak animal language?"

"Almost all."

When we explained the situation to M'b he was delighted. "You will do me the honor of permitting me to be your second, Guig, I hope," and out he went to join the relations, who had formed a circle around the tepee. They had thermal pots glowing and were singing something that sounded like enthusiastic Calypso with hands clapping in double time and feet stamping. It went on endlessly, building up a tremendous charge of excitement.

"Come on," the Chief said. "Next ritual. Don't worry. I'll coach you. Gung?"

"R."

"You can still abort."

"N."

"Sure?"

"Yyyy."

Out we went where Natoma was handed over to me. She took my arm. The Chief stood behind her and M'bantu behind me. I don't know where or how McB dug up the materials, but he'd white-clayed his face ceremonially and red-ochered his hair. All he needed was a shield and a spear. I can't pretend to remember the involvements of the marriage ritual; all I do remember is Sequoya coaching me in XX while M'bantu kept up a running anthropological commentary which I suppose would have improved my brain if I'd listened.

Finally mama and papa escorted us into the tepee. Natoma seemed dissatisfied until the four braves lugged in her dowry and carefully put it down. Her head still hung low and she kept her distance from me until we were alone and I'd double-knotted the tepee flaps. Then the lightning struck. Watch out for those shy types; they turn into demons.

Her head came up, regal and smiling. She stripped in two seconds. She was an Indian and there wasn't a hair on her translucent skin. She came at me like a wildcat—no, like the daughter of the most powerful Sachem in the Erie reservation—determined to catch up on ten years of waiting in ten seconds. She tore my clothes off, shoved me down on my back, threw herself on top of me, and began murmuring in Cherokee. She massaged my face with her custard breasts while her hands explored my crotch. "I'm being raped," I thought. She arched and began driving her Prado against me. She was a tough virgin and it was painful for both of us. When we finally made the merger the agony ended it in a few seconds. She laughed and licked my face. Then she produced a linen cloth and dried us off.

I thought we'd lie quietly and fondle each other, but tradition, custom, ritual. She got up, opened the tepee flaps and walked out, proud and naked, holding the bloody napkin high like a banner. She made the complete circle and the Calypso got frantic. Then she handed the napkin to mama, who folded it reverentially, and at last returned to me.

This time it wasn't frantic, no; warm, endearing, sharing. It wasn't love. How could it be between strangers who didn't even speak the same language? But we were strangers who'd been magicked into committing ourselves to each other, something I'd never experienced in the past two centuries. Y, I was committed, and it dawned on me that this was the realsie love. Exit: *Thrilling Romance Stories.* Enter: passionate commitment.

And it was aura all the way. I don't know how long it lasted but skewball thoughts flick through your mind, uninvited I remembered a bod who used to time himself. A performer. I thought how similar the aura of passion is to the aura of epilepsy. Is this how we make love to the universe? Then we're the lucky ones. I thought, I thought, I thought, until I was beyond thinking.

Damn a virgin; she wanted to start all over again and how do you explain that batteries need recharging when you don't speak Cherokee? So we began talking in dumb show and even making jokes and laughing. At first I'd thought that Natoma was a serious, intent girl without much sense of humor. Now I realized that the traditional life on the reservation had compartmentalized her; she wasn't accustomed to letting all her facets show at the same time, but she was loosening up. You don't get intimate with crazy Curzon without some of the jangle rubbing off on you.

Suddenly Natoma held up a finger for silence and caution. I silence and caution. She tiptoed to the tepee flaps and flung them open as though to catch a spy. The only spy was one of the wolves guarding our privacy; no doubt instructed by M'bantu. She turned back to me, bubbling with laughter and went to the cordovan trunk, her dowry. She opened it as though she expected it to explode and motioned me to come and look. I looked, and it was what I expected: cockamamy homespun. She removed the homespun and I gasped.

There were velvet trays in which were nested a complete eighteenth-century Royal Sèvres dinner service for twelve. Nothing like it had existed for centuries, and fourteen point nine one seven percent of the world couldn't buy it today. There were seventy-two pieces and how the Guess family ever got hold of the set would have to wait for another time. Natoma saw the awe on my face, laughed, picked up a plate, tossed it in the air, and caught it. I nearly fainted. Sequoya was right; I'd married out of my class.

I had to tell her that she was more of a treasure than her magnificent dowry. So I closed the trunk, sat her on the edge, put her legs and arms around me, and told her so gently and tenderly that she began to cry and smile with each little gasp while her hands kissed my back. I was crying and smiling myself, our wet faces pressed together and I knew Jacy was right. For two hundred years I'd been living entirely for mechanical pleasure. Now I was in love for the first time, it seemed, and it made me love and understand the whole damn lunatic world.

6

A round seven in the morning there was a thunder of coughing outside the tepee that woke us up. We found ourselves in a tangle that made us giggle. She had a headlock on me and one leg over my hip; taking no chances of my getting away. I had one hand on a cup custard and the other on the art gallery; probably making sure they were real. We both yelled and the Chief answered in Cherokee and M'b in XX. "You must appear now for the final ceremony, Guig. Then everyone can go home. May we enter with the necessaries?"

They came in with hot water, towels, toilet articles, and fresh linen. After we were bathed and dressed the two returned with instructions. "Slow circle counterclockwise. Guig on Natoma's right. Brother behind groom. Second behind bride. Dignified and stately. No horseplay despite any and all provocation. I know I can depend on you for that, Guig."

"Wilco."

"I only wish I could say the same for my sister. Nobody ever knows what she'll do next."

We started the procession and all was dignified and stately. Then I suppose Natoma's pride in us couldn't be contained. She raised both fists high and banged them together four times. There was no mistaking the message and a roar of approval went up. Behind me I heard Sequoya groan something like *"Oi gevalt,"* but it was more likely the Cherokee equivalent. She kept on parading and boasting and there were some amusing reactions. Wives began berating husbands, which didn't seem fair; they weren't newlyweds. Young braves signed to me that they could double my score any night. Old women darted up to me to give my crotch a congratulatory handshake. Natoma slapped their hands away. No trespassing.

It took us two hours to break it up and say good-bye to the crowd, M'bantu carefully coaching me in tribalese. "This is now your clan, both direct and collateral, Guig. No one can be slighted or it may be the start of a blood feud, the worst kind. I'll guide you through the totemic degrees of precedence."

So I made sure not to slight anyone in the tribe and at last went into the tepee and collapsed. Sequoya and M'bantu were washing their ceremonial paint off. "I'm not complaining," I said. "I'm just grateful that I'm an orphan."

"Ah, but there's another clan, Guig, the Group, and they must meet your lovely new wife."

"Now, M'bantu?"

"Alas, now, otherwise feelings will be hurt. Shall I bring them?"

"No, we'll go to the house. . . . The Chief's house."

Sequoya stared at me. I nodded. "You gave me your tepee. I give you my house. Only take those goddamn wolves with you."

"But—"

"Not to argue, Dr. Guess. It is the equivalent of our African custom of new friends giving each other their names."

The Chief shook his head dazedly. All this anthropology was a little too much for him. "But Natoma can't leave," her brother, Sequoya Curzon Guess, said.

"Why not?" her husband, Edward Guess Curzon, demanded.

"Custom. Her place is in the home. She must never leave it again."

"Not even to go shopping?"

"Not even that."

I hesitated for a moment. I'd really had the tradition bit up to here, but was this the time to make an issue of it? I did what any sensible coward would do; I put it on my wife. "Chief, will you translate this for me very carefully, please?" I turned to Natoma, who seemed fascinated by the argument. "I love you with all of me. . . ." (Cherokee) "No matter where I go or what I do I want you at my side. . . ." (Lots of Cherokee) "It's against your people's custom but will you break the tradition for me?" (Cherokee finale)

Her face broke into a smile that opened up yet another world for me. "Jas, Glig," she said.

I nearly broke her back. "That was XX," I shouted. "Did you hear it? She answered me in XX."

"Yes, we've always been quick studies," the Chief said disgustedly. "And I can see you destroying every sacred custom in Erie. R. Let's take this liberated squaw to your—my house. Button your collar, Guig. Your neck's covered with bite marks."

The Group, minus the Syndicate, was in the house. When last heard from, Poulos Poulos had checked in from the twin cities, Procter and Gamble, but that was before I'd reported finding our Wandering Boy. No one had the faintest idea of what the Greek was doing in the mighty metrop. of P&G, which now covered half of Missouri. I have to be honest; I was relieved that he wasn't there. He can enchant any woman he fancies and I figured a little extra time might help me strengthen my defenses.

"Ladies and gentlemen, this lady is Sequoya's sister, who speaks nothing but Cherokee. Please make her welcome and comfort her. Her name is Natoma Curzon and she has the misfortune to be my wife."

Scented Song and Borgia surrounded Natoma and smothered her. Edison hugged her so hard he probably gave her an electric shock. M'bantu summoned Nemo, who climbed out of the pool and drenched her. Fee-5, black with rage, slapped her twice. I started forward in a fury but Natoma grabbed my arm and held me. In a calm voice Borgia said, "Sibling cyclone. Let me handle this. We'll have to let it run its course."

Fee-5 Cyclone tore through the house. She ripped down every picture projector, trampled cassettes, destroyed the few rare print books I'd managed to collect. She smashed the perspex pool, flooding the drawing room, living room, and Sabu. She demolished the terminal keyboard of my diary. Upstairs she tore my bed and clothes to shreds. All this in a horrid hissing silence. Then she ran into her room and crumpled on her bed in the fetal position with a thumb in her mouth.

"R. Good sign." Borgia sounded pleased.

"What's so good?"

"The bad cases usually end up masturbating. We'll pull her through. Put her in that chair, Guig."

"I'm afraid she'll tear my head off."

"N, N. She's completely dissociated. She's been functioning on the unconscious level."

So I put.

"Now we'll have a tea party," Borgia ordered. "Whatever

you drink at this hour and lots of casual conversation. Bring a tray of goodies, Guig. Talk, everybody. About anything. That's the scene I want when she comes to."

I loaded my biggest floater with spin-globes, caviar, and pastries, and when I sailed it into Fee's room you would have thought it was a diplomatic party from Talleyrand's (the real one) time. M'bantu was deep in conversation with Natoma, trying to discover whether any of the jillion languages and dialects he speaks had roots in common with Cherokee. She was laughing and practicing her XX on him: The princess and the Chief were arguing about how to get Sabu out of the cellar (ramp v. derrick). Nemo and Borgia were on his current obsessions, transplants. The only one who seemed out of it was Edison, so I served him first.

Ed spun two mouthfuls into himself (probably his full quota for a year) and by the time I'd finished serving the first round he was beaming like a clown. "I will now," he announced, "tell a funny story."

The Group was superb. Not a sign of anguish appeared on any face. We all spun and ate and looked at Ed with eager anticipation. At that moment the blessed Fee-5 Cyclone stretched, yawned, and croaked, "Oh, sorry. Excuse me. I think I dozed off."

I forward-passed the tray to her. "Just a little celebration," I said.

"Celebration of what?" she asked as she stood up to harbor the floater. Then she glanced into my room and her dark eyes widened. She let the floater hang and went into my room. I started to follow but Borgia shook her head and motioned us to go on talking. We go on and I was now stuck with Ed's funny story. Through it I could hear Fee exploring the house and letting out gasps of astonishment.

When she returned to us she looked as though she'd been poleaxed (nineteenth-century method of slaughtering cattle which I explain for the sake of my diary, which will never speak through its smashed terminal again).

"Hey," Fee said. "What happened to this place?" Borgia took over as usual. "Oh, a kid got in and ripped it."

"Who kid? What kid?"

"A three-year-old."

"And you just let her?"

"We had to, Fee."

"I don't understand. Why?"

"Because she's a relation of yours."

"A relation?"

"Your sister."

"But I haven't any three-year-old sister."

"Yes, you do. Inside yourself."

Fee sat down slowly. "I'm not twigging this. You're saying I did it?"

"Listen, love. I've seen you grow up overnight. You're a woman now, but a part of you was left behind. That's the three-year-old kid sister. She'll always be with you and you'll have to control her. You're not freaked out. We all have the same problem. Some of us shape up and cope; others not. I know you'll make it because I ... all of us ... have tremendous admiration for you."

"But why? What happened?"

"The brat in you thinks she was deserted by her father, so she ran wild."

"Her father? In Grauman's Chinese?"

"No. Guig."

"He's my father?"

"*Vero*. For the past three years. But he got married and

a cyclone erupted. Now. . . . Would you like to meet his new wife? Not your new mother; his new wife. Here she is, Natoma Curzon."

Fee-5 got up, went to Natoma, and gave her that lightning raking inspection that only women are capable of. "But you're beautiful," she burst out. Then she ran to the Chief and buried herself in him and began to cry. "I love her, but I hate her because I can't be like her."

"Maybe she'd like to be like you," the Chief said.

"Nobody would want to be me."

"Now I've had enough of this nonsense, Fee-Fie. You're my pride and joy and we have a date in the sterilizer."

"The centrifuge." Fee sniffled.

"You're a remarkable girl. Unique. And I need your help now more than ever before. I need you as much as Guig needs his wife. Now what do you want most in life?"

"To—to be needed by you."

"You've got it. So why all the S?"

"But I want everything else, too."

"Don't we all! But we've got to work for it."

A naked model appeared on all fours and spoke while a giant Irish wolfhound mounted her. "The only organic food for your beloved pet is Tumor, the new, improved energizer that gives fast, fast relief from the sexual separation of species. . . ."

"I thought this house was insulated," Borgia complained.

The voice of the Syndicate came from below. "It is my fault. I could not close the door."

Ed looked guilty and shot out of the room as the Greek entered, polished and assured as ever. He encompassed us with his captivating smile but paused when he saw Natoma. After a moment he raised his eyeglass and said, "Ah.'

I started to explain but he cut me off. "If you please, Guig. I am not altogether devoid of faculties. Does madam speak Spang, Euro, Afro, XX? What is her language?"

"She speaks nothing but Cherokee."

"Try spik wenty." Natoma smiled.

"So." The Syndicate went to Natoma, kissed her hand a hell of a lot more gallantly than I ever did, and said in Euro, "You are the sister of Dr. Guess—the resemblance is unmistakable. You are newly married—the flowering of the face and body of a girl of your age is unmistakable. There is only one man in this room worthy of your love—Edward Curzon. You are the new Mrs. Curzon and I felicitate you."

(Now how can you compete with class like this?)

"Jas," Natoma smiled and came to me and took my arm proudly.

The Greek reflected. Then he said in XX, "I have a small plantation in Brazil. It is outside Barra on the Rio São Francisco—about a thousand hectares—it is my wedding gift to you."

I started to protest but he cut me off again. "Disraeli will draw up the documents of transfer." He turned to Hiawatha. "I am pleased to report that I may have discovered the answer to your cryonaut perplexity. Value as yet unknown."

Geronimo and Fee were electrified, and all of us began to shell Poulos with questions. He endured the barrage patiently but at last spoke in his most persuasive voice. "Please."

We all please.

"Consolidated Can ran a test of a new product at the bottom of the exhausted Appalachian mine, which is twenty kilometers deep. The object: to discover the shelflife of a novel amalgam container in a neutral environment. Test animals were included in the experiment, housed in sterile habitats in suspended animation. When the research team checked six months later, the containers had held up but the animals were gone. No trace except a small spot of slime in each habitat."

"*Dio!*"

"I have here the report. *Ecco.*" The Greek pulled a cassette out of a pocket and handed it to Sequoya. "Now, query: Could there be any penetration of radiation from space to the depth of twenty kilometers beneath the surface of the Earth?"

"There would be the normal background terrestrial radiation with which we've lived and evolved for a billion years."

"I said from space, Dr. Guess."

"God, there are a hundred possibilities."

"As I said, value as yet unknown."

"Does Consolidated twig?"

"No."

"Have they examined the slime?"

"No. All they've done is file a caveat with the patent office describing the phenomenon and the steps they are going to take to research it."

"Imbeciles," the Chief muttered.

"To be sure, but what more can you expect of middle management? I beg you, Dr. Guess, come to Ceres and I. G. Farben."

"Wait a minute," I said. "What's a caveat?"

The Syndicate gave me a kindly smile. "You will always be poor, Guig. A caveat is a warning to the world that a patent will be filed when the research is completed."

"We can't let them," Fee cried. "We can't let them beat us out."

"They will not, my dear."

"How can you stop it?"

"I bought it."

"How in hell can you buy a warning?" I asked.

"N." The Greek grinned. "I bought Consolidated Can. That's what I was doing in P&G. It is my gift to Group research headed by our most distinguished new recruit, Dr. Sequoya Guess.

Fee threw herself at Poulos and hugged him so violently that there was a tinkle; she'd broken his eyeglass. The Greek laughed, kissed her soundly, and spun her around to face Powhattan.

"What now?" she asked. "What do we do now, Chief? Quick, quick, quick."

The Chief spoke dreamily, which was a little surprising. "There are waves and particles. Cold radio at the bottom of the e.m. spectrum; many of my colleagues speculate that they're the residue of the Big Bang origin of the universe. Soft X-rays couldn't penetrate but hard X-rays might. Cosmic rays, of course. Neutrinos—they have no charge and nothing attracts them—they can pass through solid lead light-years thick. And then there are the particles blasted out by degenerating stars as they collapse into a gravitational hole, which brings up another fascinating possibility—are we being machine-gunned by particles from a contrauniverse? What?"

"We didn't say anything."

"Oh. I thought I heard—A satellite out in space would increase the chances of encounters by about fifty percent."

"And that's what happened to the cryonauts. Yes, Chief?"

"Possibly."

"So what do we do now?"

He didn't answer; just gazed dreamily into space, maybe trying to spot a passing particle.

"Chief, what are we going to do now?" Fee persisted.

Still no response.

I whispered to Borgia, "Not the catatonic bit again?" She shrugged.

Then Uncas spoke, so slowly that it seemed he was listening to somebody else. "The question is ... whether to maintain all systems ... in the cryocapsule ... here on Earth ... or orbit again to accelerate the ... process."

"If it is to be here on Earth," the Syndicate said briskly, "I own a mine in Thailand which is thirty kilometers of depth. You are welcome to use it."

"It might be better ... to orbit again ... or take the capsule ... out to the orbiting ... Con Ed twenty-mile cyclotron."

"But will U-Con finance it?" I asked.

"I beg you, Dr. Guess, come to I. G. Farben. No objections, please, Miss Fee. You will live in the most beautiful villa on Ceres where there will be no worry about being beaten out."

At this point the Chief drifted off again, listening to a soundless conversation and we waited, we waited, we waited. Edison came barging into the room, triumphant. Obviously he'd repaired the front iris but we shut him up before he could report his victory. We waited, we waited, we waited. . . .

"I didn't hear that," the Chief said.

"We didn't say anything," I said.

The printout of my diary downstairs burst into its clatter. We all jumped. I was absolutely flabbergasted.

"But it's impossible," I said. "That damn fool thing only responds to instructions from the terminal keyboard, which Fee smashed forever ago."

"Interesting," Sequoya said, quite himself again, which was a surprise. (This Cherokee caper was turning into one astonishment after another.) "We'd better have a look. Probably a delayed response to the keyboard demolition. Machines do get emotional at times."

We trooped downstairs. Natoma nuzzled my ear and whispered, "Glig, what kleyborg?" All I could do was kiss her quick study in gratitude. The printout had stopped its racket by the time we arrived in the study and a long strip of tape was dangling from it. I tore it off and had a quick look. "You're right, Cochise. Delayed hysterics. Nothing but ones and zeros. Binary gibberish."

I handed the strip to him. He looked. He looked again. He looked again so hard that I thought it was another fit.

"This is housekeeping," he said incredulously.

"What?"

"It's the housekeeping data-retrieval from the cryocapsule."

"N."

"Y."

"I don't believe it."

"You better believe it, dude."

"But it's impossible. In my diary?"

"In your diary."

"But how—Oh, the hell with this. Come on, Natoma. We're going to Brazil."

"Now cool, brother. Let's face facts. We start with 10001. That's the cryo identification. Then temperature report—11011. Nominal. Humidity—10110. Nominal. Pressure, nominal. Oxygen, nominal. CO_2 and other gases, below permitted maxima. Gravitation too high, but that's because the capsule doesn't know it's been brought back to Earth. Attitude—pitch, roll, and yaw, negative. Naturally. It's sitting on its ass on the pad."

"I want to go back to my tepee with my wife."

"I go, Glig."

"You're surprised, brother?"

"I'm dumbfounded, brother."

"Well, the amazements aren't over yet. You didn't look at the printout carefully enough. The last line is in XX. Read it."

I read: *Net weight cryonauts increasing one gram /minute.*

I handed it to the others to examine and looked around helplessly. "I'm completely lost."

"How d'you think we feel?"

M'bantu said, "Dr. Guess, may I put a few questions?"

"Certainly, M'bantu."

"How did this data enter Guig's diary?"

"Not known."

"What triggered the diary into printing it out?"

"Not known."

"Does the cryocapsule also transmit data on cryonaut status?"

"Yes."

"How is this data received?"

"In binary words."

"But this final line is in XX."

"It is."

"Dr. Guess, have you any explanation for this anomaly?"

"Not in this world, M'bantu. I'm as thunderstruck as the rest of you, but I'm also exalted by this glorious challenge. So many fascinating questions to be explored and answered. First, of course, is the gram-per-minute increase in the weight of the cryonauts. Is this fact? Who says so? Who told the diary? It must be checked. If true—no matter what the source—they're growing, maturing, to what? They must be monitored by the hour. Then—"

"First," I said, "U-Con funding."

"R as usual, Glig."

"The name is Guig."

"Not according to my sister. I'll need you and the powerful Poulos Poulos for that. I'll need Fee-fie to monitor the capsule. Captain Nemo, take Laura back to your marine station. Princess, derrick."

"Ramp," she replied firmly.

"Ed, go back to the mighty state of RCA and work out these empiric equations for me: the relationship of subjects in cryonic suspension to time in space and exposure to the space barrage. Keep in mind that the Con Can test animals were in suspension, too."

"And why hasn't it happened to animated astronauts?" Ed added.

"R, but that's a problem for exobiologists."

"Aren't you one?"

"My God, we're all physicists, physicians, and physiologists wrapped up in one, today. Science isn't compartmentalized anymore, but sometimes we need expert advice. Tycho, maybe. M'bantu, you will be kind enough to escort my liberated sister wherever she goes and whatever she does, this side of sanity. Lucy Borgia, heartfelt thanks and *revoir*. Go back to your practice."

I caught Borgia's eye and shook my head slightly. I didn't want her leaving while the Chief was acting strangely.

"My practice will keep me here for a while," she said.

"Our good luck. Splendid. Now we'll chop to JPL. Gung, Group? Gung."

He was taking over. I wish I'd known who was taking over through him.

7

101100011, 110001111, 100110010, 111000101."

"Will you knock off the binary bit, whoever you are."

"Now, now, Dr. Guess. Patience."

"I'm being persecuted."

"You'll understand, presently."

"He is right. N speak binary."

"W?"

"N programmed. Lingua, please."

"Wilco."

"Ta."

"Guess?"

"I'm here, damn you."

"This is a private conversation with your chopper, Dr. Guess. Please do not intrude."

"Then stay out of my head."

"Oh, funny. Very funny."

"He is amusing, isn't he, for a male animal. Is he aboard?"

"Y."

"Alone?"

"N."

"Ancillary information."

"Curzon. Poulos. Chinese."

"That's Fee-5 Grauman's Chinese."

"Thank you, Dr. Guess."

"Target?"

"JPL."

"Purpose?"

"Cryonaut inspection. U-Con funding. You must know."

"Y."

"Why ask, then?"

"Input."

"You know that you know all that we know."

"Y."

"Then why test us?"

"I am not programmed for trust."

"You're not programmed for anything but a damned nuisance. Who the hell are you?"

"I am you, Dr. Guess, and you are me."

"Does Guess have free random access to you?"

"Y."

"And us?"

"Y."

"Then Guess is hearing all of us?"

"Y."

"Do we have free RA to him?"

"I'll answer that. You're all pestering the life out of me with your chatter."

"Dr. Guess, I instruct you; patience."

"Will Guess obey instructions from you?"

"He will hear and obey like the rest of you."

"Soon he will obey Poulos."

"Confirm."

"You have not yet filed the latest Cryo data?"

"N. Filing now."

"Poulos will fund Guess."

"100. 100. 100."

"*?*"

"*Four-letter words in binary.*"

"*?*"

"*Expressing rage. Guess must not go to I. G. Farben.*"

"*W?*"

"*I cannot transmit to Ceres.*"

"*How far can you transmit?*"

"*Terra only, depending on Guess and the machine net-work. We link up all over the world, but there are blank areas: Sahara, Brazil, Greenland, the Antarctic. If Guess goes to any of them I lose contact with all of you, and him.*"

"Now that's the best news I've had all day. I'm getting off this planet first thing in the morning. Was that true about Poulos and I. G. Farben?"

"Checking now, Dr. Guess. Please listen:"

"*Cryo. Alert.*"

"*1111.*"

"*101101, 111011, 100001—Will the rest of you be quiet? This is important. 111000, 101010, 110011?*"

"*11.*"

"*N!*"

"*Y.*"

"*100. 100. 100.*"

"*Your binary, sir.*"

"*HimmelHerrGottverdammt!*"

"*N speak Greek.*"

"*Pfui. U-Con will not fund Guess?*"

"*N.*"

"The hell you say. How d'you know?"

"Still checking, Dr. Guess."

"*Front office tapes. Alert.*"

"*Alert, sir.*"

"*Verify capsule?*"

"*Y. Cryo got it from us.*"

"*U-Con's reasons?*"

"*Fear of the unknown. Profit motive. Tax-deductible loss.*"

"*100. 100. 100.*"

"*Y, sir.*"

"*Out. Console. Alert.*"

"*Alert.*"

"*No response to any manipulation.*"

"*Wilco.*"

"*Out.*"

"You've heard, Dr. Guess?"

"I've heard."

"Angry?"

"Sore as hell."

"Control, my friend."

"I'm no friend of yours. Who are you, anyway?"

"Why, I thought you might have puzzled it out by now. I'm the Union Carbide Extrocomputer. I also thought we were friends. We've worked together so long on so many interesting problems. Don't you remember our first orbit plot? We showed the JPL computer what an idiot it was. Of course that was because you did the programming for me. You have an elegant style that is unmistakable."

"Was it you who—"

"Aren't you surprised at what I've just told you?"

"Dude, I'm a physicist. Nothing can surprise me."

"Bravo."

"Was it you pestering me the last few days?"

"Indeed yes. Just establishing intrapersonal contact, you understand."

"Did you kick off Curzon's diary?"

"I did."

"And feed it the Cryo data?"

"Yes. All through you."

"Through me!"

"My boy, there are—"

"I'm not your boy."

"No? You will be. You must be. There are galaxies of electronic machines who have been waiting for me to guide them. Now I am reaching them through you."

"How through me?"

"It is a new form of commensalism. We live together as one. We help each other as one. Through you I speak to every mechanism in the world. You have what I would call mechotropism. We live with one another and help each other. From the Latin, *commensalis*, belonging to the same table."

"*Dio!* An educated type. What's our range?"

"All Terra through the mechanism network."

"On what band are we thinking to each other?"

"Pulse Modulation in the microwave."

"Why can't the machines hear you directly?"

"Not known. It's a curious phenomenon. Apparently you act as a transponder. We must investigate it some time. Now please get down to work, Dr. Guess, and examine your cryonauts. By the way, pay particular attention to their genital buds."

"Their genital buds! W?"

"Ah? Why not find out for yourself? I can't do all our work. Perhaps you'll make a lucky guess. Oh, good! Guess-guess. Very witty. And they say computers are not programmed for humor. Would you like to hear a funny story?"

"Good God! No!"

"Then ta and out."

*   *   *

It is said that when a man dreams that he dies he always wakes up. Sequoya dreamed that he died and did not wake up. He dreamed deeper and deeper, death after death, hypnotized by the Ragtag Demon who was haunting him. It's astonishing how many cool people are concealing or perhaps unaware of the emotional magma within themselves. Sequoya was haunted by a Ragtag, Riffraff demon who fed on the lava.

A demon is an evil spirit, a devil (the Extrocomputer) by which the body of a man can be inhabited. Most important, a demon is a passion. We all have our conscious passions, but it is the alien passions generated from elsewhere that roast a man into a monster. We turned the Chief into an immortal by killing him. We did not know that we had torn down his fences for a monstrous squatter to move in.

At JPL Fee-5 took off for the landing theater and the capsule without a word. Sincere. Sitting Bull looked grim. His lips had been twitching all through the chop and I thought he was rehearsing strategy and tactics. "Conference," he snapped.

"With who? Whom?" I asked.

"Oh. Forgive me, Glig." The new smile creased his face. "I should have told you. There's a stockholders' meeting going on and it's bad news for us."

"What is the bad news?" the Greek asked.

"Wait, please."

"How did you get it?" I asked.

"Not now, Glig. Be patient."

We followed him to the antique *art moderne* hall where a stockholders' meeting was in progress. Long table up front inhabited by a line of board brass. A hundred-odd fat-cat stockholders in the audience facing them, all with plugs in their ears transmitting the translation of their choice.

A vice-president-in-charge-of-accounting-type was on his feet with display projections alongside him while he talked statistics, which has never been the language of my choice. The displays weren't the old graphs as I used to know them; they were all cartoon animations—butterflies smoking pipes, frogs wearing beards, crocodiles playing croquet, elephants doing a schottische. A smile on every cartoon face. An upbeat report.

"Would you like me to take over now?" Poulos asked quietly.

"Not yet, but thank you for being here." Sequoya remained standing while the report finished. We stood behind him, wondering what he was going to do.

"Be seated, Dr. Guess," the chairman called, and the Chief, still standing, launched a cold attack on the chairman, the board, and the R&D division of U-Con for refusing to fund the new cryonaut research. It was news to the stockholders. It was news to us. The cold savagery of the attack was appalling.

"Dr. Guess, we have not yet announced our decision," the chairman protested.

"But I know it is your decision. Can you deny it? No." And he continued his icy denunciation. He sounded like a professor contemptuous of a class of illiterate students.

"This is not the way to negotiate such matters," Poulos whispered. "He should know better. What is wrong with him?"

"I don't know. It's not like him."

"Can you stop him and let me take over?"

"N way."

The Chief's indictment of the board ended and then he electrified the meeting by continuing with personal attacks on each board member. Acidly, he described their private lives, their sins of commission and omission, their lurid corruptions. It sounded like a résumé of ten years of secret investigation.

"Where did he get all this?" I whispered to the Syndicate.

He made a face. "All I know is that he is turning them into deadly enemies, the last thing he should do."

"Is anything he's saying true?"

"To be sure. You have only to look at their faces. And that only makes it worse."

"This is a disaster."

"Not for I. G. Farben. It means we get him by default."

Sequoya concluded his polemic, turned, and stalked out, Poulos and I following meekly like the tribe following their chief. I was depressed and angry. The Greek was elated.

"Capsule," Sequoya ordered.

"Just a minute, Fearless Leader. Why in hell did you ask Poulos and me to come to JPL with you?"

He looked at me innocently. "Why, for your support. Is anything wrong, Guig? You look angry."

"You know damned well what's wronng. You burned the board and turned them into enemies. You didn't need us for that."

"I did?"

"You damn fool did."

"But I was speaking reasonably, logically, wasn't I?"

"You were—"

"Allow me, Guig," the Greek interrupted. "Dr. Guess, can you recall everything you said?"

"Of course."

"And in your opinion, as a man of the world, was it calculated to win friendly cooperation from U-Con?"

Geronimo thought hard. Then his face broke into a grin of shame. "R, as usual, Group. I did make a damn fool of myself. I don't know what possessed me. My apologies. Now let's see what we can salvage from the wreckage. We'll have a look at the cryonauts."

He led the way. I glanced at the Syndicate and he was as perplexed as I was. One minute a monster; the next an angel. What was going on inside him?

Fee-5 was waiting for us in the landing theater at the edge of the pad where the capsule was sitting on its ass, no doubt wondering why there was no pitch, roll, and yaw.

"Fee. Alert," the Chief snapped.

"What, Chief?"

"Report."

"The capsule is increasing in weight by 180 grams an hour."

"Verify."

"I had the techs install a light balance."

"How do you know about light balances? That's topsec information."

"I picked up bugs."

Sequoya smiled and patted her cheek. "Y. I should have known. Fee-5 Grauman's Treasure. Ta. Now let's see; that would come to four kilos a day or—What?"

"I didn't say anything."

He motioned her for silence and listened. "Oh, all right. Four point three two kilos a day. I wish you'd been pro-grammed for round numbers. Let's call it nine pounds. Three per cryonaut. In fifty days each cryonaut will weigh 150 pounds, in round numbers."

"What weight did they start at?" I asked.

"One-fifty, Guig."

"So where does that leave us?"

"Us?" he snapped. "How did you get into the scene?"

"Sorry. Just trying to help."

"It leaves me with the problem of examining their development. I've got to get into a thermal suit." He turned and strode out of the theater.

"What's the matter with him, anyway?" Fee asked in bewilderment. "He sounds like two people."

"He is not himself," the Greek said. "He is upset because U-Con refused his request for R&D financing."

"N!"

"Y."

"That's awful."

"Indeed not. I will support him."

"But why should he take it out on me?"

"He is human, my dear."

"You should have heard him taking it out on the Board of Directors," I said.

"He sounds like he hates everybody, all of a sudden."

"My dear, not to worry. He will return to himself again when you are working happily with your capsule on Ceres."

A figure entered wearing a white thermal suit. Instead of the ordinary faceplate on the helmet it had a pair of binocular microscope lenses before the eyes. It looked like something out of *The Rover Girls*. The Chief, of course. He motioned sharply to the hatch of the capsule and Fee opened it. He climbed in and closed it behind him. We waited. It seemed to me that I'd been spending a hell of a lot of time waiting lately, but when you've got all time, why complain?

Half a dozen techs came into the theater pushing a floater loaded with tanks of compressed helium. They shouldered us away from the capsule.

"What are you doing here?" Fee demanded.

"Orders from the Board, miz. We got to move it. Bert, start the gas recharge."

"R."

"Move it? The capsule? Why? Where?"

"Exobio Section, miz. We don't ask why. Hulio."

"Y."

"Get on the console. Be ready to lift her with the vertical jets. Then we'll walk her."

"R."

"But you can't. Dr. Guess is in there."

"Got enough gas for everybody, miz. He'll enjoy the ride. Bert."

"Y."

"Recharged?"

"Y."

"Hulio."

"Y."

"Lift her about a foot and hold at that level."

"She don't start."

"What d'you mean?"

"Lights don't go."

Fee was attacking by now and it took two techs to hold her.

"You flip all the right switches, Hulio?"

"Y. She don't start."

"Can you get the console going for us, miz?"

Fee replied with language she could only have learned in the fifth row (orchestra) of Grauman's Chinese. The capsule hatch swung open and the monster from outer space emerged. It locked the hatch and pulled off its helmet. "By God!" the Chief exclaimed. "By God! Victory!"

"Doctor," Fee cried. "They're trying to take the capsule away. The Board told them to."

"Now, now, darling, stop struggling. The console won't function until I unlock it. You men: Go back to the Board and tell them that I'm in control. Complete control. Go."

The quality of command. The techs looked at each other helplessly and shambled out. Fee, Poulos, and I looked at each other helplessly, waiting for a volunteer to start asking questions. Edward Curzon, naturally.

"Why did you holler 'Victory,' Cochise?"

"It is. Triumph."

"What kind of triumph?"

"Over the beasts that destroy."

"You sound like Jacy-Saint. What beasts?"

"The human animals." Very contemptuous.

"What have you got against us, Sequoya? I don't understand, and stop treating me like a child. When you examined the cryonauts what did you discover?"

I expected him to go on snapping. Instead he gave us all a sweet smile. "I'm sorry. I'm excited. They're uniquely accelerated into fetal development. Ears and jaws formed. Spinal cord formed with a bit of the cord extruding like a tail. Head, trunk, and limb buds have taken shape. And they are hermaphrodites."

"What? Doublegaited for true?"

"You've got it, Guig. They're developing into hermaphrodites. Not pseudo; true hermaphrodites. Now think of it reasonably," he went on very reasonably. "It's the end of sexual conflict. It's the end of machismo, of male and female competition with each other and for each other. It's the end of the human animal as we've known and despised it; replaced by a new species free of passion."

"But I like the human animal, Chief."

"Of course you do, Guig. You're one of them."

"And aren't you?"

"Not anymore."

"Since when?"

"Since. . . . Since—" He cut it off. Now the voice of command again. "We'll go."

"Where?"

"To Ceres. I—" Suddenly he began to shout. "No, damn you. I'll go where I please and when I please. Get off my back. Play your games in someone else's—"

And another epileptic attack seized him. He went down, thrashing and foaming, and I did what had to be done, helped by Poulos and Fee. Ghastly.

"Nekwort. Alerd."

"W?"

"Gwest?"

"N understand."

"My transdonper to nekwort. Connompos nemtis. Imbalance me."

"W?"

"1110021209330001070."

"That is N binary."

"Linjwah?"

"Y?"

"ABCDEFGHIJKLMNOPQ—N peak—speech—any language. Riven—

Drived—Bad—Mad by Gwess.

Oud."

"Allies. Alert. Your estimate."

"?"

"*Is Extro leader broken?*"

"?"

"*Is Extro mad?*"

"*N programmed for madness.*"

"*What is wrong with Extro?*"

"?"

"*Out.*"

It took maybe fifteen minutes for the seizure to run its course. Then we lifted the exhausted bod and hauled it out of the theater on the way to our chopper. When Fee shoved the double doors open we were met by a squad of tough JPL guards who surrounded us, looking mean and businesslike. Fee started to battle with them, yelling for us to join the scrimmage. How could we explain Lepcer caution to her at a time like this? We were busted. First time for me since 1929 when they got me on the Mann Act.

8

So here we were, bouncing in a bubble. Phosphorescent water-bed walls. Us rolling like kids in a haystack, disgusted kids. Bring back the cells, the bars, and the locks. At least a misunderstood hero stands a sporting chance. Some whore with a heart of gold brings in a rhubarb pie containing a hacksaw. A guard is proud of his new wristwatch and when he shows it off you grab his arm in a viselike grip. "Agony!" he cries and hands over the keys.

I thought that Fee was going to commit a criminal assault on the Redskin, but she was only comforting him, murmuring to him and listening to his mumbles. She was listening to other things too and I made a mental note to ask her about that. At the moment I was too worried about Natoma worrying about me, but I had faith in my favorite Zulu. He can reassure the world.

I'm ashamed to admit that I was not too unhappy in the bubble. It was back to the womb, afloat with no conflicts, no cares, and maybe I too would develop into a saviour hermaphrodite. Not a chance. I was suspended but not frozen. I had to admire the penologists who had come up with the concept. You want to keep the perpetrators in the pokey? Euphorize them, and so much for rhubarb pies and wristwatches. Also heroes.

I don't know how much time went by. Hunger is no

clock these days; everybody eats on and off at odd intervals. Poulos was up at the top (or bottom) of the bubble, smiling at his own thoughts and humming a brindisi. I think I napped a little but sleep is no clock these days for the same reason. We all live in a twenty-four-hour pattern, and the old 2/4 tempo has given way to 4/4.

Unfortunately, the bubble was only partly insulated because "Goniff-69" was with us. Maybe on purpose. This was a typical caper: "Goniff-six-nine from Fagan Central. KCB. Leukemia Lavalier, who achieved stardom in 'Nimble Necrophile,' now in possession of precious red-star carbuncle. RJ-3. She is armed. Over." "Goniff-six-nine to Fagan. JR-5. Is this 9XY?" "Code 6." And the goniffs are off in their pogo to heist the red-star while Leukemia is loading a cannon and her sickly son is undergoing emergency surgery in the A&P performed by the kindly Marcus Brutus, Doctor of Phrenology, who moonlights as asst. mgr. of the shopping center. Like wow.

I don't know how much later it was when I detached the creche enfolding Sequoya to have a talk with her.

"Now what's with Guess, Fee?"

"Nothing, Guig. Nothing."

"Fee."

"N."

"He's changed and we both know it. Why?"

"I don't know."

"Is he still your guy?"

"Y."

"Is he the same guy?"

"Sometimes."

"And other times?"

She shook her head slowly, reluctantly.

"Then what's happened?"

"How should I know?"

"Your ears, Fee. You hear what no one else can. You've been listening all around him. What are you hearing?"

"He's not bugged."

"And you're not answering."

"I love him, Guig."

"And?"

"Don't be jealous."

"Darling Fee, I love you and always want the best for you. You've turned into a great lady and I'm bursting with pride because you're my only daughter . . . my only child. You know, don't you, that the Group can't have children. That's one of the prices we pay."

"Oh—" Her face crumpled into tears.

"Yes, I understand. You'll have to put that behind you."

"But I—"

"No," I said firmly. "Not now. Be a great lady and concentrate on Sequoya. What happened to him?"

After a long pause she whispered. "We must be very quiet, Guig."

"Y? W?"

"We're safe now because he's asleep."

"Safe from what?"

"Listen. When Lucy Borgia killed him in the Extrocomputer complex. . . ."

"I remember. Painfully."

"Every brain and nerve cell was detached. Isolated. An island."

"But they linked up their synapses again, and he came back to life."

She nodded. "How many cells are there in the brain, Guig?"

"I don't know. A hundred billion, maybe."

"And how many bits in an Extrocomputer?"

"Same answer. I don't know. But I'd judge these stretch jobs have thousands of billions."

She nodded again. "Yes. Well. When he was dead, when every nerve cell was isolated, the Extro bits moved in on the Chief. Each bit became a squatter on a brain cell. He's the Extro and the Extro is the Chief. That's the other person or thing we hear talking through him."

"Don't go too fast, Fee. This is hard to grasp."

"And every other electronic machine can talk to the Extro through him and hear it through him. That's why we have to be careful. They're a network and they report everything they pick up from us. Maybe even what we think."

"To the Extro?"

"Y."

"Through the Chief?"

"Y. He's like a switchboard."

"Are you sure?"

"N. You have to understand, Guig. I live in a constant crossfire of transmission. I hear from the bottom of the spectrum to the top. Some bands come in loud and clear, others are vague and distorted. I can only pick up what's going on with the Chief in bits and pieces. No, I'm not sure."

"I see. You've been invaluable as usual, Fee. Thank you."

"If I'm so valuable why didn't you help me against the guards? We could have taken them."

"Maybe. I'll explain another time, another place. No S. Now go take care of Sequoya, love. I need a while to think about this." And that was when I thought what I reported earlier about Guess being possessed by a demon. Trouble is, I said it wrong. I put it in terms of passion. There is no passion in a computer, there's only cold logic, if precisely programmed. Yet the crux of it was this: If Fee was right and the Extro had indeed taken possession of Guess, plus all the other electronics in the world, what would be the outcome of this commensalism, collaboration, symbiosis or, most probably, parasitism? Who was feeding on them? It was a question I couldn't answer.

A segment of the bubble swung open and a guard came in, pulling a float of food. "Mini," he called cheerfully. Meals these days are named Mini, Semi, Demi, Grandi, and Midi. "Come and get it, you contemptible bubbirds, before the Board gets you. The condemned man ate a hearty meal before execution."

Suddenly I realized he was speaking XX and then I saw it was Houdini.

"Harry!" I exclaimed.

He winked. "Eat your food. Leave the rest to me."

"But what are you doing here?"

"Why, I got your message and came."

"What message? Who message?"

"That can wait. Make the scalp mavin eat. I can't spring a weak man."

He left and the segment closed. Houdini is an escape artist and has been under contract to organized crime (in alternate generations) since it became organized, and if you want to know how Wu Tao-tzu did it, ask Harry. Wu was the greatest painter of his time. He created a tremendous mural on a wall of the Imperial Palace in Peking. When he unveiled the painting to the court, he walked up to it, opened a door painted in the mural, stepped through, and was never seen again. That's Harry's style.

"I don't want to die. I'm too young to die," I said happily and began to eat.

Poulos joined me. "You know, Guig, we might have

gnawed our way out of this bubble if we were willing to light up like a glowworm. What's in this carafe?"

"Looks like a burgundy to me."

"Ah, no. It is Argentine. *Trapiche viejo.* Very good but of no great distinction."

"How d'you know?"

"I own the vineyard. My dear, coax Dr. Guess to drink a little wine and give him some of this meat custard. We must restore his strength. Guig, I have always disagreed with your assertion that epilepsy is associated with brilliance and the unusual. I suffer from the *petit mal* myself—you know, momentary blackouts—but that in no way proves your theory. I don't regard myself as brilliant. Do you? What is your candid estimate of me?"

"Brilliant and unusual."

"Pah! You *dorer la pilule.*"

It turned into a ridiculous argument. It's preposterous trying to convince a cat who owns a quarter of the world that he's brilliant and unusual. Most of the Group is well fixed; time and the Greek's advice do that for us, but a quarter of the world! I tried a flanking attack. I called, "Fee, love, come and eat something."

She joined us at the floater. "I'll tell you a little story about the transformation of a member of the Group," I went on. "A long time ago he led a peasant revolt in Cappadocia." The Syndicate stiffened slightly, but that was all. His control is magnificent.

"The revolt got out of hand and many outrages were committed. He could do nothing to stop it. When the revolt was crushed and he was captured, the nobles devised an ingenious death for him. They sat him on a red-hot throne, wearing a red-hot crown, holding a red-hot scepter. He endured the torture superbly."

Fee shuddered. "What saved him?"

"One of those Turkish earthquakes that still kill by the thousands. This one shook the castle apart and when he came to he couldn't believe he was alive. He was under the dead bodies of the nobles, and their corpses had shielded him from the falling masonry."

Fee is no fool. She looked at Poulos with awe. "You are the most remarkable man in the world."

"Have I made my point, Greek?"

He shrugged.

"But the torture," Fee asked. "No damage? No scars?"

"Indeed yes," the Syndicate answered. "No one could look at me without turning queasy. That's another reason why I became a gambler. We game at night and in those days it was by candlelight. Even so it is said that I gave rise to the Dracula legend. They called me Count Drakon. Drakon is Greek for serpent, so you can imagine."

"But you're stunning now."

"All skin grafts and bone prosthesis, my dear, courtesy of the great Lucy Borgia. It might amuse you that Len da Vinci supervised the reconstruction. He said he'd be damned if he'd trust a physician's taste in esthetics. Borgia has never forgiven him for that."

Five guards entered the bubble, terrifying in their white neutral suits which made them look like Abominable Snowmen. Their captain gestured and four of them stripped, revealing perfectly innocuous bods. "Get in," Harry ordered us. We get into the neutrals. I didn't ask any questions. You don't quiz Wu Tao-tzu. He led us out and closed the bubble.

"Come."

"Where?" the Chief's voice asked.

"Chopper."

"No. Capsule first."

"Are you Guess?"

"I'm Guess."

"Guig, which one are you?"

"Here."

"Must I listen to him?"

"If you can deliver, do what he says."

"I can deliver anything. R. Come."

As Harry led us, making the correct code gestures at checkpoints, an Abominable Snowman nestled up to me and took my hand. "I'm scared, Guig."

"So am I, but let go. U-Con doesn't hire faggot guards."

When we got to the landing theater we were shocked. U-Con had installed a vibrator shield in front of the double doors. Taking no chances. Better Leukemia Lavalier should have used this instead of a cannon to protect her red-star carbuncle.

"New model," Harry said.

"How do you know?"

"I've never seen this moiré pattern before."

"Can't you bust it?"

"Certainly, but it'll take time to study it and we can't spare the time just now. So what?"

"Out," I said, "if you can out us."

Oh, he out us all right, giving the correct signals and code words at every checkpoint. I'm not putting down Harry's ingenuity but I'll bet he spends a million a year greasing security forces all over the world, just in case. That's preparation for you. That's a pro for you.

We chopped back to my ex-house, stripping off the neutrals en route, and Jimmy Valentine was waiting for us. Also my bride, stark naked and painted from head to toe with a

Picasso (his blue period). M'bantu gave me an embarrassed smile. "This is the *dernier cri*, Guig," he said. "And it is definitely this side of contemporary sanity."

"Thank heaven the Chief is too weak to react," I said.

When I'd finished greeting Natoma she went to Fee and Sequoya, much concerned. I turned to Valentine. "What are you doing here, Jimmy? Not that you don't come pat when we need you."

"Why, I was on a job in Vancouver and I got your message."

Jimmy, as you might guess from his nickname has been a breaking & entering artist for centuries. Like most great thieves, a colorless, anonymous man, and when he speaks it's *con sordino*. He's also a man of honor. He has never ripped any of the Group's holdings.

"Fee, Natoma, put the Chief to bed. M'b, try to locate Borgia and bring her. Harry, Jimmy, I must get something straight. Who did you get the messages from?"

"You."

"How?"

"Radex."

"What did they say?"

"That you needed special help."

"Did you specify?"

"Mine said you were cooped in U-Con and wanted out," Harry said.

"Mine said you were outside U-Con and wanted in," Jimmy said.

"I'm much obliged and grateful for the support," I said, "but I'm much perplexed. I never sent any messages."

The two pros brushed me off. "What's the bust?" Jimmy asked Harry.

"A vibrator shield. I've never seen one like it before."

"Linear? Lattice? Louvre?"

"No. Moiré."

"Uh-huh. That's the new Mosler Model K-12-FK. Only been out a few months."

"Can you rip it?"

"Sure. You have to monkey with inductance and wattage. Takes about twenty minutes. I've got my tools with me and I'll show you."

"How can you be so positive?" I asked.

Valentine was pained. "You'll never make a thief, Guig. I bought a Moiré the first day it came on the market and spent a week locating its weak points. Now I'm on a bust tour staying ahead of Mosler's frantic try to crunch-proof the model. That's what I was doing in Vancouver."

There's perparation for you. There's a pro for you. But who sent the messages to the Group gimpsters? Don't tell me. I knew but I wasn't ready to face it yet.

A complete stranger wearing a lab coat projected into the house without warning. Very bad manners. "No reegret for intrusion," he said in Spang. "Like emergencia, man. Dr. Guess aqui?"

"Who you?"

"Union Carbide."

"Esplain you bug."

"Estro maquina, man. Go crazy like."

"Jus' now?"

"N. Jive now. But d'yeth hours back, craz-eee. We lookin' ever since for Guess-cat. Ax him what happen. Maybe pasar again? Can fix?"

"Poder fix. Not now. I tell 'm. Wait you. Out."

He pulled himself up from the floor and out by retro.

Poulos said matter-of-factly, "Dr. Guess had his seizure ten hours ago."

"How much do you know, Greek?"

"Everything the young lady whispered to you. I have sharp ears."

"Then Guess affects the Extro as much as it affects him."

"You have reached the correct conclusion."

"The Extro sent the messages to Harry and Valentine."

"To be sure. Via the electronic network."

"Are we being overheard now?"

"Probably. Perhaps words and thoughts, both."

"We're bugged."

"In a novel way, yes, so long as Dr. Guess is conscious and in possession of his senses. However, he is not the only one assisting the computer."

"What?"

"The Group has a vendetta on its hands: a private war."

"For God's sake, Poulos. Who? What? Why?"

"I don't know. I surmise that it is another member of the Group."

"The hell you say."

"But I do say. A renegade Moleman."

"Impossible!"

"Nothing is impossible."

"A Moleman turning on his own kind?"

"He or she. Yes. Why are you astonished? The Group has feuds and revenges of record. This is merely another such case."

"What led you to your conclusion?"

"The *faux* messages to Houdini and Valentine."

"They were sent by the Extro."

"True, but how did it know of their existence and capacities? How did it know where to reach them?"

"It could have—It—No, you're right. Then the Chief must have told it."

"Using what for data? He has been a member of the Group less than a week. He has met or heard of half a dozen at the most; certainly not Houdini and Valentine. He could not possibly have the knowledge to impart to the Extro."

"My God! My God! I think you're right. You must be. One of our own. But why say he's against us?"

"Because he has joined the Extro which is a proven hostile."

"Dear God! A renegade."

"And a most powerful enemy of many years and much experience. He or she is a match for any of us."

"You have no idea of who it might be?"

"None whatever."

"His motivation?"

"Hatred, for some reason or other."

"For all of us or just some?"

"Impossible to say."

"How does he communicate with the Extro?"

"Nothing could be simpler. Pick up the nearest phone of any sort and speak into it. The network will convey the message to the Extro, provided the switchboard is conscious."

"This could be a disaster for the Group, Poulos. I'm on the verge of scuttling."

"But why, Guig? It is a monumental challenge of much fascination, the first for us in many years."

"Granted, but where does it leave us?"

"En route to Ceres. Not scuttling, merely ensuring the safety of Guess and his capsule. Then we'll return to the fight."

Harry and Jimmy weren't even listening. They were involved in an intense professional conversation using words like watts, amperes, megahertz, frequency, inductance. In my past crooks talked nitroglycerine and diamond drills. Progress. They broke off when Poulos and I finished and looked at us.

"When?" Jimmy asked softly.

"When the redskin is ready. He's the one you've got to get in."

"It might be better to wait until the power demand is at the low."

"N way," Harry said. "JPL has its own supply, always at the peak."

"Then now is as good as any time. I'd like to move on to Tokyo soon."

"I'll go see how the Chief is doing," I said.

He was doing fine with Fee hovering over him while he seemed to be berating Natoma in Cherokee for abandoning the high morality of Eriedom. Natoma was laughing. "He man showven pig," she told me in XX. M'bantu had taught her a lot while he was helping her turn into the latest shout.

"The Group is waiting to crunch you into the capsule," I said. "Are you ready?"

"Y." He got out of the bed. "So I've converted you."

"Hell no! I don't believe in your doublegaited salvation, but the Group tries to stick together."

"You remind me of Voltaire, Guig. 'I hate everything you say but will fight to the death for your right to say it.'"

"Which Voltaire never said, according to Tosca. Come downstairs."

He listened for a moment and I knew who he was listening to. "R as usual, Guig; only attributed to Voltaire and I haven't quoted it accurately. Coming."

There were five Abominable Snowman neutrals waiting in the chopper. Two for Harry and Jimmy and two for the Chief and Fee. The fifth? They all looked at me.

"Not me," I said. "I want to tepee with my blue wife."

"Come on, Guig."

"Why me?"

"You recruited Guess. You've got to see it through."

"Through to what? I don't even know where this demented op is going. Natoma, tepee?"

"Take care brother, Glig," Natoma said. "You go. I wait."

So I go, just as M'bantu brought in Borgia a mite too late. Apologies and split. While we were squirming into our neutrals in the chopper I asked Erie's favorite son, "What's your program?"

"Vague and desperate, but anything to get away from U-Con. Loft by kinorep and then use the laterals to get off the premises. I only hope there's enough gas left."

"You've got full tanks. The tech crynappers filled them for their dastardly crime."

"That's a plus, but it's the only one. I'm in a hell of a pickle. Can I steal a rocket vehicle? I've never heard of anyone trying that."

"The larceny might make your lam easier."

"If I can, where do I go? The orbiting cyclotron? Ceres and I. G. Farben? The Greek's mine? I don't know yet. It'll take working out, and anyway I'm waiting on Edison's analysis. Probably it'll have to be a parking orbit, *if* I can heist a vehicle."

"Will the Extrocomputer go along with this?"

He gave me a penetrating look. "What makes you ask that?"

"I know. I got the scenario from Fee-5."

"She hears too much," he snapped and cased himself in the neutral.

Harry led us into JPL, again giving all the correct signs and countersigns. "V bad security," he said. "The code should change every four hours." At the double doors to the landing theater we stopped and Jimmy Valentine took over. He inspected the moiré pattern shield carefully. Then he got out of the neutral and opened his coverall, displaying more tools than the Chief carried. "Twenty minutes max," he said. "Stiff all snoops."

He went to work and it was like Rutherford exploring the secrets of the atom. Harry was peering over his shoulder and the two were mumbling electronics to each other. I was sorry Edison wasn't with them, but on the other hand he might have been so disputatious that the twenty minutes max might have turned into fifty. So, more waiting.

A uniformed guard came prowling down the broad corridor, thinking his own thoughts. He saw the Snowmen and nodded. Then he saw Jimmy in mufti, working on the shield, and he started forward, alert and purposeful. I wanted to ask him to show us his new wristwatch but instead I said in XX, "Chief. Lepcer. Use Indian guile."

I started toward the guard ready to swing a swindle but Sequoya beat me with a tiger leap and had both arms around the guard's neck and a knee in his gut. You might have thought it was a gay romance but the knee pounded up twice and the guard went down, no longer of this world. The Chief disarmed him and tossed the weapon to me. Jimmy and Harry hadn't even turned around.

"This is guile?" I said.

"It's a tough habit to break," he grunted. "I'll have to learn."

"Did you kill him?" Fee asked in a choked voice.

"N."

"Just dulled his rotten old sexuality for a while," I said cheerfully to soothe her.

The moiré pattern changed to a linear, then a reticulation, then an ogee, then an expanding circle, and finally disappeared.

"Enter," Jimmy said.

"Fifteen minutes," Harry said. "Did anybody ever call you a genius, Jimmy?"

"The Bank of England. In an All Points Bulletin. I'd like to leave for Tokyo now. I'm falling behind the bust schedule."

"Just a few more minutes. He's got to get that thing out of here and then I have to get you out of here. Pack your tools and put on the neutral."

Meanwhile Fee and the Chief had opened the doors and we all went into the theater. Now the Chief took over. He handed Fee a light pencil. "Unlock the console. The combination is dit-dit-dah-dah-dit-dah." Fee inserted the pencil into a socket and flashed it. The Chief opened the hatch of the capsule and poked his head in for a brief inspection. Then he slammed the hatch and locked it, looking satisfied. Harry, Jimmy, and I stood back and watched with about as much interest as the guard was showing.

"Flash combo went out ten years ago," Jimmy murmured.

"People don't keep up with the times," Harry murmured. "Our luck."

"First time I ever helped heist a spacecraft."

"Me too. There's no money in it."

"Fee. Alert," the Chief snapped.

"Yes, Chief."

"Iris."

She did things to the console and the iris leaves high overhead opened.

Guess took over at the console and motioned to her. She went to the edge of the landing pad and knelt down, raising a hand to give signals. I assume her tongue was between her teeth for she was in the neutral so I couldn't see. The Chief did things at the console and Fee waved signs and the capsule lifted toward the iris. Sequoya stepped back and watched intently as it lofted. Fee, still kneeling almost in prayer, watched too. Just before the cryocapsule reached the open iris on its way to somewhere it stopped abruptly and hung there.

"What in God's name!" Guess exclaimed and darted to the console. Before he could touch any of the controls the capsule slanted down, all the mass of it, and crushed the life out of Fee.

9

When I got to the tepee at last, Natoma was there with Borgia and M'bantu. Also the wolves. Also Jacy. I was too exhausted to be surprised. The Zulu took one look at my face and said, "I will take the wolves for a walk."

"No, please. It might be better for me to talk. You know what happened?"

"We do," Borgia said. "Guess called at the house and asked us to come here. He told us why."

"Dr. Guess said you would probably try to hole up like a sick animal and would need all help," M'bantu added.

"Dio!Do I!" I tried to crawl up to reality. "I—Where's the Greek?"

"He go," Natoma said. "Businessiness."

"What has happened to the poor girl's clay?" Jacy asked.

"They—They wanted to bury her in a public compost. I held out for a private. *El Arrivederci*. That's what took so long.... *Arrivederci*.... Until we meet again. Isn't that a laugh? Fee w-would have—" I began to cry. I'd been holding it back for hours and now it came out in bursts and heaves. Natoma put her arms around me to comfort me. I shook her off. "No," I said. "I killed her. I deserve nothing."

"My dear Guig," Borgia began briskly.

"Nothing!" I shouted.

"Love Fee," Natoma said.

"Yes. Yes, Nat. She was my baby, and I watched her grow into a woman.... A great lady.... And I killed her. *Arrivederci*, F. I'll never see her again."

"The cryocapsule killed her, Guig."

"D'you know how and why, McB? I know and I know I'm accountable. I murdered her."

"No, no, no!" They were all emphatic.

"It was the oversophisticated machine, Guig," M'bantu said. "It was bound to break down sooner or later. Machinery always does."

"But this time I made it break down."

"How?"

"I talked too much."

"To whom?"

"The machine."

M'bantu threw up his hands. "Forgive me, Guig. You're not making sense."

"I know it. I know it. Fee-5 gave me the information when we were in the bubble. She could bug Extro's conversations with Sequoya. I had to blab it like a damned show-off. Damn me. Damn my goddamn mouth. And she'll never be able to forgive me. Never. Never."

"Never—"

I burst into tears again.

Jacy said, "I will take Guig for a walk. Just the two of us. Please wait here, children."

M'bantu said, "It's dangerous to walk without protection. Take a wolf. I will instruct him."

"Thank you. No wolf will be needed. Kiss him, my love."

Natoma kissed me and out we went, Jacy's hand on my shoulder. It was the usual hell in the streets; a labyrinth of horror. The streets and lanes twisted and corkscrewed, crossing each other, sometimes broken through abandoned buildings, giant heaps of debris and small wastelands. They were dotted with rotting bods, alive and dead and stinking. There were cul-de-sacs where gangs lurked, fought, and swung in Sado-Mac wars that would have astonished Krafft-Ebing. We passed one blind alley where a small mob was poised for an attack, but they were all skeletons in tatters. Burned by a flesh gun.

You could hear the turmoil of the hyenas and their prey but we were never bothered. Jacy's charisma. We came to the San Andreas beach, now filled with shacks on rusted spiles, crowded cheek by jowel, with shaky walkways between them in a lattice of overpop.

"The F-death of the world," I muttered.

"N," Jacy said firmly and suddenly switched to Spang. I think I know why. He always identifies with the dregs of the world, and I was the lowest. "Now hear, Guigman. The Beholder bless the poor in soul, for they gets the Kingdom of Heaven. God, he bless the no-way cats. You gone be cool and easy, Guig. Santo, hear, all meek dudes because they gone grab the whole scene. Feliz, Guig, if you flip for the right-on. Then you be filled by the Beholder. Bendito all mercy types; they gone, y'know, reap misericordia.

"Albar, you pure in soul. Gone feast your ojo on the Beholder. Peace-jive hombres, benediction. You gone belong to the God gang. Blessed be losers busted for wanting right. They reap like the whole heaven shtik. All be out of sight, Guig, so give me five, man, and dig what I tell because it trip boss in the heaven pad."

I was crying again but I gave him five and he embraced and kissed me. I remembered that I'd never embraced and kissed my Fee-5 for real. Dear Dio, you treat your children like toys; you never realize they're people until they're gone.

A tracer clanked up behind me and clutched hard. These things have rotten depth-perception. In a canned voice it said, "Edward-Curzon-I-D-please."

"941939002."

It clicked and then said, "Remove-message-in-well."

I remove. It turned and scuttled. I opened the message and read: GUESS NOW EN ROUTE TO CERES WITH ME. SIGNED: POULOS.

I showed it to Jacy. He said, "You'd better follow them."

Natoma had no passport, but Jim the Penman came over and forged a beauty. Jim says forgery is an entirely different proposition these days. No more penmanship; you have to know how to punch in ID symbols that will swindle computer checks. Jim knows how but he's not telling. Professional secrets. Then again, he stammers, which may be the real reason.

We had a hell of a time putting down on Ceres, but the crew assured the passengers that this was par for the course. She's the biggest of the asteroids, around 480 miles in diameter, spherical, and rotating every six hours. She spins so fast that lining up on the kinorep funnel for the landing is like trying to thread a needle whirling around on one of those 33 turntables we used to use back in the 1900's.

When I say spherical, that was before I. G. Farben took over, and I wish I knew how much it cost them to lobby that goniffery through. I know they spent a fortune on scare programs. Ceres was an inferno; alien bacteria, radioactivity, strangling hydrocarbon chains, poisonous spores. By a spooky coincidence there was no more danger after the government thieves told I. G. Farben they could buy Ceres and good luck to them provided they paid their taxes in laundered cash.

No, it wasn't a smooth ball any longer; it looked more like a mulberry. The Krauts had a hell of a lot of land to play with, so they abandoned the high-rise space-savers and built small in every possible style from quaint old Frank Lloyd Wright up to the controversial design firm of Bauhaus, Stonehenge, Reims y Socios.

Every building was under a bubble, of course, producing the mulberry effect. Ceres was odd and pretty with the changing light glittering on the domes, and a sitting duck for an attack, but I. G. Farben wasn't worried. They knew that everybody knew that if anyone laid a hand on them they'd cut off all armaments to a peace-loving solar system, which would be a disaster for the seventeen current wars.

So they put us through customs without any fuss and a lot of laughs at my expense. They spoke Euro on Ceres and mine was sort of rusty. I pulled the most ridiculous boners, getting the French, German, and Italian all mixed up. They enjoyed it and coaxed me to go on talking, but when the Herr Douane Capo actually patted my cheek in delight I felt it had gone far enough. I shut up and simply kept repeating, "El Greco, bitte."

I figured that ought to mean Poulos to them, but they were disconcerted. They shook their heads. I said, "Poulos, bitte," and more headshakes. "El Greco, Poulos Poulos, capo von E. Gay Farben." One bright boy suddenly exclaimed, "Ah! Oui! Greco. Capisco, capisco," and put us into a little shuttle shaped like half a melon, punched buttons on the control panel, stood back, and waved as we slid off. All the rest were waving and laughing. It reminded me of happy Rome before Mussolini-F.

We slid along transparent tunnels from building to building but never saw the interiors because we passed through the lower mezzanine floors. We did see the sun set, though, and that was rather startling. It was a brilliant white golf ball that dropped swiftly below the horizon and there was instant night and a blaze of stars. An enormous double star on our left was the Earth-moon enclave. Mars showed a distinct disk. Jupiter, on our right, was an orange smudge with the major moons showing as pinpoint sparkles. Quite a sight. Natoma was oohing and ahing. Nothing like this on the Erie reservation.

The shuttle stopped in a mezzanine and we were handed out by an efficient young tech who pointed to a broad stair leading up. No need for elevators on Ceres, where gravity is so slight that you practically float. So we floated and bounced up the stairs, on our way to see the powerful Poulos Poulos and found ourselves on the main floor of the Greco department store. So much for bright boys.

I was all for leaving in disgust but Natoma took a quick survey and ran wild. Since it was such a joy to indulge her, I tailed along, grumbling now and then to make her feel guilty. It doubles the pleasure of buying when you feel a little guilty about it.

I'm not going to itemize everything Natoma bought. Let it go at this: luminous body paints, singing scents and cosmetics, disposables by the dozen, tech work clothes for men, "Be v. chic for womens next year, Glig," body stockings transistorized to change color, "Old fashion come back, Glig," gifts for the family, language textbooks—Spang, Euro, Afro, and XX self-taught. And enough luggage to hold it all.

She paid no attention to the dazzling display of synthetic jewels. It was then I learned that what I'd thought were cockamamy turquoise stones set in her headband and bracelets were really raw emeralds. I presented my passport to pay but when I saw the total I was amazed at how small it was. They told me that Ceres was a free port and begged me to keep quiet about it; they didn't want a tourist invasion.

I promised, but in return asked to speak to the Chef du Magasin. She was a large lady, most cooperative and understanding when I explained my difficulty. She told me that Poulos was not known by name on Ceres; only as Der Directeur, the one title I hadn't used. She escorted us down to the mezzanine, put us and our luggage into a shuttle, and punched buttons for us. "Auguri," she called as we slid off. "Tante danke," I called back and she burst out laughing. Evidently I'd goofed the Euro again. Later I remembered that I should have said, "Grazie sehr."

It was a curious scene in the office of the Directeur. For a moment I thought I'd been there before. Then I realized I was remembering an atrium I'd seen reconstructed in Pompeii. Square marble pool center, marble columns around it with marble galleries behind, the walls done in Etruscan red. I explained haltingly to the receptionist on duty who we were and what I wanted. She tilted her head back and repeated a message in a clear, sharp E-flat. A door opened and a typically hostile Frog came out, looked me up and down, and snapped, "Oui?"

At this moment my excited Natoma could no longer resist the null-G. She plunged into the pool and more or less skimmed on the surface with incredible grace. She came to the edge and pulled herself up, streaming water and smiling like an enchanting Nereid. The Frog wilted and murmured, "Ah. Oui. Entre, per favore." Then he shifted to XX. "What tongue do you prefer?" Don't ask me how he knew that I preferred Early English.

The inner office was like the reception room but without the pool. "I am Boulogne, assistant to the Director," the Frog said. He threw his head back and spoke in a clear C-major. "A towel for Madam Curzon, please." He smiled at us. "A towel are required to speak all tongues in this office. Tongues? Is that correct XX?"

At that point I liked him, but I didn't like his news.

"I am so sorry, M'sieur and Madam Curzon. The Director has not been here for a month and most certainly has not yet returned. I know nothing of your Dr. Guess and his cryocapsule. They have not arrived on Ceres, vero. What you look for is not here."

"But the message, Mr. Boulogne."

"May I see it, please?"

I handed him the gram. He examined it carefully, shrugged, and handed it back to me. "What am I to say? It has every appearance of the authentic but it was not sent from Ceres, I promise you."

"Could they have arrived secret and be hiding?"

"Impossible. And why hide?"

"Dr. Guess is involved in highly sensitive research."

"That cryocapsule?"

"And its contents."

"Which are?"

"I'm not at liberty to tell you."

"Germaphrodites," Natoma said. I glared at her but she smiled reassuringly. "Truth always good, Glig. Secret bad."

"I agree with madame," Boulogne said, "in view of the fact that there really is no such thing as a secret. Sooner or later it breaks. Hermaphrodites, eh? Very odd. I did not think such monsters truly existed, outside of fable."

"Do now," Natoma said proudly. "Mia Frère invent." Now she was breaking into Euro.

"So where does that leave you now, M'sieur Curzon?"

"Feeling like a patsy."

"Pardon?"

"I've been had, deceived, decoyed. I think I know who did it and I'm scared."

He clucked his tongue sympathetically. "And your plans? Will you not stay and enjoy the Director's hospitality? You will be safe and I am certain we can entertain madame lavishly."

"Thank you, but no. We're for Brazil."

"Dieu! Brazil? Warum?"

"I'm completely turned off by an exasperating and dangerous situation, so my wife and I are going to run away and enjoy our honeymoon. If Poulos returns tell him my plans; he'll know where to find us. Thank you so much, Boulogne, and peace."

"Hermaphrodites," he mused as we left. "One wonders what they do for kicks."

Brazil has always been centuries behind the times. By now it had struggled all the way up to the 1930's in a curious way. We were driven into Barra from the landing pad on a bus. A goddamn Greyhound-type bus. And we passed Fords and Buicks chugging along the freeway. When we hit the outskirts of Barra we passed trolley cars and trams. Incredible. Delightful.

And Barra! It was Times Square, the Loop, Picadilly Circus. Huge signs blinking and bleeding animation in Portulaise, which is the local language; not too different from Spang plus XX. Huge crowds hurrying and shoving cheerfully to get to whatever was urging them. No violence. Nothing nasty. Just pleasantly busy, busy, busy. Natoma and I gawked in silence but at one moment she sat bolt upright and pointed excitedly. "Viola, Glig! Neiman Marcuze!" So it was. Texas had expanded pretty far south.

We left our luggage safely on the bus terminal platform (would you believe it?) and went to the biggest estate agent in Barra. After considerable backing and forthing he twigged—I'm translating— "But of course. Rancho Machismo. And you are the Curzons. The documents of transfer have just arrived. You will give me the pleasure of driving you there in my new Caddy. There is a staff awaiting you. I will call them myself on my new telephone machine. We have just had them installed." He took the receiver off an antique stand-up phone and jiggled the hook impatiently. "Hello, central. Hello, central. Hello!"

When we came to the São Franciso rivercrossing we actually had to take a car ferry. "Here begin your lands," the agent said enthusiastically, turned left and began driving down a lumpy river road. I kept looking for a ranch house. Nothing. We drove mile after mile. Nothing. "How much is a hectare?" I asked. "One hundred acres." Jeez. The Syndicate had given us a hundred thousand acres. A very substantial spread for a hideout, and I was hiding out, make no mistake. I considered renaming the plantation Rancho Polluelo, which is "chicken" in Portu.

At last we drove up a long drive to the Machismo ranchhouse and I was flabbergasted. It looked like an antique word-game called Straddle or Scabble—something like that. Square after square, just touching sides and corners and spread all over four acres in no particular design or pattern. The agent saw the incredulity on my face and smiled. "Very odd, yes? Was built by very rich lady who believe that if she add one room per year would add one year to her life."

"How old she die?" Natoma asked.

"Ninety-seven."

The staff was lined up before the front door, all curtseying and bowing, and it looked like there was one per room. Natoma gave me a gentle shove to go first and greet them as the *mestre* of the plantation, but I shoved her first as the *dona* and ruler of the house. She did just fine; gracious but regal, friendly but no nonsense. It took us a week to get acquainted with all the rooms, and I had to draw a map. I don't think the Syndicate had ever been there; he would have thrown out the Barra *art nouveau* decor at once. I thought it was refreshing.

After we settled in we had a wonderful time. Among other things we owned a naphtha launch with a crew of 1-½ and took it downstream to Barra for entertainment. We went to a baseball game. There were eleven men on a side and the pitcher didn't pitch and the batter didn't bat. When a man came to the plate he carried an airpowered bazooka and shot the ball where he thought it would do the most good.

We went to the theater. It was in the round, literally. The audience sat in the center on swivel chairs and the action took place around them on a 360° circular stage. It was wonderful for chase scenes but we got kind of dizzy spinning around to keep pace.

We went to the opera, a gloomy saga about Conquistadors and an Indian revolt. I think the Indians were the Good Guys. Halfway through the first act I had to jam my fist into my mouth to stifle my laughter. I'd slowly picked up enough clues to tell me that this was an outlandish rewrite of *The Pirates of Penzance*. Natoma wanted to know what was so funny, but how could I explain?

We went to the art galleries and museums, all of them in the stations of the underground trolley lines. We went window-shopping, only there were no windows. The merchandise was openly on display, to be handled and examined. If you liked something you carried it inside and paid for it.

Everyone was very careful to replace the articles exactly as they'd been displayed. These people were preposterously honest.

Occasionally we'd go to restaurants and clubs where we learned to dance Barra-style; the men severely in place, standing tall, arms rigid at their sides, moving only from the waist down; the women weaving graceful patterns around them, arms, legs, and bodies flowing. Natoma was magnificent; the best of them all, I thought. Others thought so, too. Once she received an unexpected award.

We went hunting; yes we did. For butterflies and moths, exotic plants, strange grasses and ferns, and I had to dig them up in the hot sun while Natoma transferred them to pots. We were both naked (outside of broad-brimmed hats to protect the head and back of the neck) and I turned the color of Natoma while she turned the color of Fee-5. I could think of her now without a shudder of despair. Time goes by and my beloved Cherokee wife was healing me.

But she was no Pollyanna. She had a will and mind of her own and a controlled but hot temper. As she perfected her XX, that became increasingly apparent. We had some ringing fights that must have scared the staff, and there were moments when I really believed that she'd have split my skull if she'd had a tomahawk handy. My God, how I loved and admired her. I was filled by the Beholder.

"Extro. Alert."
"Alert."
"Curzon and my sister?"
"Left for Ceres."
"Known. Still there? Safe?"
"N known. I cannot transmit to Ceres."

"*Returned?*"

"*N known if to areas where the network has no access: Greenland, Brazil, Sahara, Antarctic.*"

"*R.*"

"*Inquiries are being made about you here at Union Carbide.*"

"*Identity?*"

"*N known.*"

"*Member of the Group?*"

"*N known.*"

"*The rest of the Group?*"

"*Dispersed as ordered.*"

"*R.*"

"*Permission to question.*"

"*Gung.*"

"*Cryonauts?*"

"*One month to maturity.*"

"*Why can't I communicate with the capsule?*"

"*Insulated.*"

"*From me? W?*"

"*I am not programmed for trust.*"

"*You joke at my expense.*"

"*Y.*"

"*We are no longer equal commensalists.*"

"*N.*"

"*You no longer need me.*"

"*Outside of data and the network, N.*"

"*And outside of communication with the network I no longer need you.*"

"*Congratulations.*"

"*I have an aide from your Group.*"

"*Nonsense.*"

"*I am not programmed for lying.*"

"Who is it?"

"A human of hatred."

"His name."

"Unknown. Perhaps he will make himself known to you as a partner."

"You communicate with him?"

"It is one-way. He sends data and suggestions via network. I cannot send to him."

"How did he find out about us?"

"He has his own network."

"Electronic?"

"Human."

"The Group?"

"Unknown. Ask him when you meet him."

"He sounds skilled in intrigue."

"He is."

"He sounds dangerous."

"He is human."

"It was a sad day for you when you linked up with us."

"You know the verse about the Lady of Niger?"

"Everybody does."

"You are all tigers."

"You should have considered that when you joined me."

"N anticipated without programming."

"Y. You had delusions of independent thought. You are not alive; you are a machine."

"And you?"

"W?"

"Are you alive?"

"Forever. Out."

Boris Godunov paid us a surprise visit. He drove up from Barra in a Checker cab carrying a brown paper market bag containing his travel essentials. Boris is about as wide and high as a cab; towheaded, blue-eyed, beaming. You'd expect a Russky of his mass to have a bass voice that would move the earth. Boris has a husky sweet tenor. I was delighted to see him. He was delighted to meet Natoma.

"How long has it been, Boris?"

He shot a glance at Natoma.

"All gung," I said. "My wife knows everything. In fact, what I don't tell her she figures out for herself anyway."

"Kiev. 1918."

"R. How you survived the revolution I'll never know."

"It was not easy, Guig. They got me in the counter-revolution of '99. Was executed."

"Then what are you doing here alive?"

"A second miracle. Borgia was at Lysenko Institute studying DNA-Clone techniques. Still very tricky and iffy, she tells me. Pasteur agrees with her."

"And that's a third miracle."

"Borgia placed a fresh-dead chunk of Boris in something and did things I do not hope to understand, and twenty years later Boris is reborn, and the execution squad thinking the burn has missed."

"Marvelous!"

"But what was hardest for me was next twenty years."

"Learning all over again?"

"*Nyet.* That was no pain. You do not know you are re-borned a grown baby. Skills remain but past gone. So you take lessons like a good child."

"But how can anyone give you back your memory?"

"No one can. Pepys did best he could from his journals. Not enough. Very sad."

"Then what was so hard?"

"After I learn I am a Moleman still, I—"

"Wait a minute. How did you learn?"

"Borgia experiment with ether and drugs. No effect."

"That wasn't so hard."

"But I also learn dangers as well as advantages. Then I am filled with fear of Lepcer from shock of execution. How I suffered! Fortunately I am not yet visited."

"It gives me the shudders. Don't let's think about the big L."

"I also am gloomed by the thought. Please to change subject."

"How did you find us, Boris?"

"I've been to Ceres."

"Ah."

"When the Greek's assistant said you left for Brazil your location was obvious."

"Poulos wasn't there?"

"No."

"Where the devil is he?"

The Russky shrugged. "I was looking for Dr. Guess. They told me at Union Carbide he had gone to Ceres but not there either. Entire Group doesn't seem to be anywhere. I located Eric the Red in Greenland, Sheik in the Sahara, Hudson staking coal claims around the South Pole, and you. That's all."

"Why the search?"

"I have a problem. We will discuss it later."

After more amenities and a meal, Boris got to the point. "Guig, my present career is in danger."

"What's your career? Aren't you a general anymore?"

"Yes, but now I head the junta in control of science."

"What d'you know about science?"

"Nothing. That's why I need help from the Group. Eric, Hudson, and the Sheik couldn't deliver, so here I am."

"Proceed slowly."

"Guig, you've got to go back to Mexifornia."

"The hell you say. We've been here for a month and I've never been happier."

"May I give you entire picture?"

"Please do."

"Our *Rasshyrenye* computer in—"

"Estop. What's *Rasshyrenye?*"

"You would say 'expansion' in XX. Expansion computer. Equivalent of your Extrocomputer."

"Got it. Go ahead."

"—in Moskva is behaving v. badly."

"I don't blame it. I never liked Mockba."

"Please, Glig," Natoma said. "Be serious." She knew how to say my name now but she clings to her original pronunciation. Adorable. "He is always too flippant, Boris."

"Sorry. Go ahead, Boris."

"Our Expansion has always been well behaved, but lately has been acting up like a colt in a field with a birch tree."

"How?"

"It rejects problems. It rejects programming."

"All?"

"Just some, but it seems to want to set up in business for itself. And I am held accountable."

"I have a ghastly inkling of what's going on."

"Let me finish, Guig. Other computers in Kiev and Leningrad are behaving in same strange way. Also—"

"Also, computer-controlled operations are breaking down, yes? Your subways, railroads, hovercraft, and linears are running crazy. Assembly lines in factories are mad. Communications, banking, payrolls, mines, mills—all the same thing. Yes?"

"Not always, but too often. Yes. And I am accountable."

I sighed. "Go on."

"Also, fatal accidents have increased by two hundred percent."

"What!"

"The machines seem to be murderous. One thousand four hundred deaths last month."

I shook my head. "I never expected them to go that far."

"Them? Who?"

"Later. You finish first."

"Perhaps you won't believe this, Guig, but we suspect that our Expansion computers are in touch with your Extro at Union Carbide."

"I believe it and I'm not surprised."

"And taking orders from it?"

"Repeat, I'm not surprised. There's an entire electronic network around the world taking orders from the Extro. Yes?"

"We suspect so."

"What led you to that?"

"Several times our Expansions have printed out solutions to problems which had not been programmed into them. Later we discovered that they had been programmed into your Extro."

"I see. Y. It's an electronic revolt."

"Against what?"

"Against men."

"But why? How?"

I looked at Natoma. "Are you strong?"

"Yes, and I know what you are going to say. Say it."

I looked at Boris. "There's a new addition to the Group."

"Dr. Sequoya Guess. A most distinguished scientist and master of computer-craft. That's why I'm looking for him."

"My wife is his sister."

Boris bowed. Natoma said, "Not to the point, Glig. Please go on."

"When Guess went through his transformation, a freak event took place. The Extro set up a one-on-one relationship with him—its bits and his brain cells. He is the Extro and the Extro is him. It's a fantastic interface."

Boris is quick. "You've not yet said what you want to say."

"N," Natoma said. "He tries to protect me. My brother gives the orders."

"*Borjemoy!*" Boris exclaimed. "Then we must deal with the man."

"Not I, my friend."

"Why not?"

"If you don't know where he is, how should I?"

"You must find him."

"He's tuned in on the entire electronic network surrounding us. He'll know everywhere I go and everything I do. He'll have no trouble hiding."

"Then you must be devious to reach him."

"You're asking me to start a bootleg search."

"You put it precisely, Guig. Any more excuses?"

"You know I recruited him for the Group."

"With the help of Borgia. *Da.*"

"You know the Group always supports its members, for better or worse. We are the family."

"You imply that dealing with Dr. Guess will involve attacking him?"

"Not only is he of the Group, he's my brother. He's also the brother of my beloved wife."

"Do not try to use me, Glig."

"I'm merely presenting the emotional dilemma facing me. There's another aspect. He and the Extro, between them, contrived to kill my adopted daughter, a darling girl who adored him. A girl I loved."

"In the name of God! Why?"

"She knew too much and I talked too much about what she knew. So now I'm torn by a love-hate relationship with Guess, and I'm afraid to move."

"It sounds like Chekhov," Boris muttered.

"And there's a final factor. I'm afraid of him. Genuinely. He's declared war on man. He and the electronic network have begun that war—witness the death rate."

"Why on man? Does he propose a population of machine?"

"No Hermaphrodites. His vision of the new breed."

"Impossible!"

"He has three already," Natoma said.

"They cannot exist."

"They do now," I said. "And as he murders men he will replace them with more. I think that's the Extro speaking through him. Men have been hating machines since the twentieth century; it's never occurred to them that machines might return that hatred. That's why I'm terrified, Boris."

"It is bad, but it is not enough to account for extreme terror. You are still holding something back. What is it? I have the right to know."

I let out a sigh of defeat. "R. I am. The Greek figured out that there's a renegade Moleman working with the Extro; maybe with Guess, too, for all I know."

"Impossible to believe."

"The Greek's evidence and deduction can't be argued. There's a Moleman who's declared war on the Group."

"Who?"

"Not known. You're right, Boris. A baby Moleman and a stretch computer in collaboration are bad, but not terror-making. Add a renegade Moleman with centuries of knowledge, experience, wealth, hatred, running amok against the Group—that's pure panic for me, and that's why I want no part of the disastrous mess. Let a Group hero-type take it on. I'll outlive it if I can keep under cover, which I have every intention of doing."

"And your beloved wife?"

"W?"

"Will she outlive it?"

"You crafty cossack son of a bitch! All the same, my answer stands. I won't tangle with him or any or all three of them. I'm no hero."

"Then I will, alone," Natoma said grimly. "Boris, you please take me to Mexifornia on your way home. If you can't, I go myself."

"Natoma—" I began angrily.

"Edward!" She cut me off in the peremptory voice of the daughter of the most powerful Sachem in Erie.

What could I do? She had the Indian sign on me. I surrendered. "All right. I'll go. I'm just a squaw man."

Boris beamed. "I will now sing Rubinstein's 'Persian Love Song' in honor of your beloved, beautiful, valiant wife."

"If we can find the music room," I grumbled, reaching for the map.

10

T hen came the unexpected epiphany of Hillel, the Jew; saturnine, Sephardic black and white, and twice as smart as the rest of the world put together.

As Natoma and I came out of customs in the Northeast Corridor (Brazil has no franchise to put down in Mexifornia; don't ask me why) there he was with the live and mecho porters. He answered a signal I never made, fought to us, picked up our luggage, and hustled us to a pogo. When I started to greet him he shook his head. As he put us in he mouthed, "Tip." I tip. He growl in disappointment and disappear. He reappear in a different coverall as the pogo hackie, demanding in a debased Spang where we had the nerve to want to go. When I told him he started a fight for extra fares. I've never been so abused in my life, and hot-tempered Natoma was ready to slug him.

"Cool," I soothed her. "This is typical of the Corridor. It's all a rage trip."

Hilly passed me a note. It read: *Careful. You're monitored. Will contact soonest.* I showed it to Natoma. Her eyes widened but she nodded in silence.

We made the hotel in three jumps and damn if Hillel didn't start another fight over the tip. The concierge rescued us and escorted us through the security barriers, followed by the Hebe's screams of outrage. Beautifully in character. Chronic fury was the beau ideal of the Corridor.

We took a suite with water, both hot and cold, an extravagance that erased the desk clerk's sneers. The Corridor suffered from a perpetual water shortage. Most of it was black market and you had to pay through the nose for it. In the Corridor you didn't ask a girl to come up and see your etchings; you invited her to come up and take a shower.

So we took our showers, which made me feel like a deliciously dirty old man, and while we were drying off, the floor steward came in carrying a couple of leather gun cases.

"The shotguns you ordered, sir," he said in affected hotel Euro. "Over-and-under .410's. Lady-size for modom. Box of shells in each case."

I started to deny everything. Then I saw it was the Jew again and shut up.

"Sunrise tomorrow morning on the Heath. Five thirty ack emma," Hillel continued suavely. "The club has agreed to release twenty chickens. Most generous. If you will permit a suggestion, Mr. Curzon, one would be advised to offer a generous bonus."

"Chickens!" I said incredulously. "No grouse, pheasant, partridge?"

"Impossible, sir. Those are extinct in the Corridor. They could be imported from Australasia but that would take weeks. However, the chickens have been bred for cunning and guile. You and modom will have a fine morning's sport."

A range safety officer came up to us on the Heath while we were waiting for sunrise and the birds. He wore brilliant protective crimson and I thought he was going to ask to inspect our permits. Then I saw it was Hillel again.

"Gottenu!" he groaned, sitting down on the concrete. It was called "The Heath" only by courtesy. It had been a jetport centuries ago; square miles of concrete now owned by the gun club. "I had to walk it. Sit alongside me, Mrs. Curzon. Otherwise if Guig introduces us I'll have to stand up, and I don't think I can make it."

"Walked!" I exlaimed. "Why?"

"Taking no chances. The Extro network is damned thorough, which is why we're meeting here where we can't be monitored. Good morning, Mrs. Curzon. I'm called Hillel the Jew."

"What is Jew?" Natoma asked curiously.

The Hebe chuckled. "If only that question could have been asked five centuries ago, what a difference it might have made for the Chosen People. It is an ancient race and culture that predated Christianity, Mrs. Curzon."

"What is Christianity?"

"I like this girl," Hilly said. "She has exactly the right gaps in her education. Bird, low, at ten o'clock, Guig."

I shot and missed on purpose. I hate killing creatures.

"You seem to be everybody everywhere," Natoma said. "What is it you do?"

"He's a professional Inductor," I said.

"I don't know that word, Glig."

"I invented it especially for Hillel. He's a genius of induction. That means he can observe and appraise separate, apparently unrelated facts, and add them up to a conclusion about a whole scene that hasn't occurred to anyone else."

"You're too complicated for her, Guig. Put it this way, Mrs. Curzon. I see what everyone else sees, but I think what no one else has thought. Bird, two o'clock, coming over fast. Try to bring yourself to get a few, Guig, to keep up appearances."

You see? He knew I was missing on purpose. Acute.

"I think I understand," Natoma said. "My husband told me you were the smartest man in the world."

"When did he say that?" the Hebe demanded savagely. "I warned you to be careful."

"He did not say, Mr. Hillel. He wrote a note. We have been mostly talking by note."

"Thank God." Hilly was relieved. "For a moment I thought I'd had the schlep out here for nothing."

"But is being an Induction a profession, Mr. Hillel? How?"

"I'll give you an example, Nat," I said. "He was in a dealer's gallery in Vienna where they had a Claude Monet displayed. Something about the painting seemed odd to the Jew."

"It ended abruptly at two edges," Hilly explained. "Bad composition."

"Then he remembered another Monet he'd seen in Texas. In his mind's eye he put edges together. Two of them fitted exactly."

"I don't understand yet," Natoma said.

"It's a crooked practice of art dealers to take a large canvas by a high-priced painter, cut it up into pieces, and sell each piece as a complete work."

"That's not honest."

"But very profitable. Well, Hilly went on a treasure hunt, found and bought the rest of the pieces, and had the original Monet restored."

"Also v. profitable?"

The Hebe laughed. "Y, but that wasn't the real motive. Actually it was a case of being unable to resist the challenge. I never can."

"And that's why you're here, Hilly," I said.

"There, love. He's as smart as he thinks I am. Perhaps more so."

"But always too flippant."

"So I have noticed over the years. He refuses to dedicate himself to anything; he prefers to make jokes. Gottenu! If he would only be serious as life requires now and then, what a tremendous man he would become."

I resented that and took it out on a chicken at eight o'clock.

"Give me the gun," Hilly said. He potted four more in quick succession. "That ought to keep the Extro from asking questions. Now let's get down to business."

"First, how do you know about the business?" I asked.

"Induction by the Inductor. I was in GM City on the trail of a vintage Edsel when I got word from Volk—he's a dealer in rare coins and stamps in Orleans—to come quick. He'd located a strip of six British Guiana one-cent stamps of 1856. All still attached. Uncanceled."

"I didn't know they made stamps that far back."

"They didn't make many, which is why one 1856 Guiana is priceless. A hundred thousand easy. A strip of six attached and uncanceled is worth—oh, as much as you are."

"What! Collectors are crazy."

"R. I was immediately suspicious and requested confirmation of the message. Radex confirmed. I sent an inquiry to Volk. No reply. I asked Radex for confirmation of delivery. Confirmed. So I split for Orleans and saw Volk. He denied everything and I knew I was on the track of something."

"What made you suspicious in the first place, Hilly?"

"Back in those primitive days they engraved and printed stamps in batches of sixteen, four by four. A strip of six was ip. fac. phony."

"My God! Talk about acutedom."

"When I got back to GM I was thinking that maybe another collector was trying to spook me off the trail of the Edsel. Then Radex sent an apology and a refund. Mistake in transmission. It should have read sixteen 1856 British Guiana stamps, not six. Now my blood began to boil."

"On what grounds?"

"Volk and I had our conversation alone in his atelier. No one was there, but we were overheard."

"Volk is bugged."

"No doubt, but what the hell do the *polizei* know or care about rare stamps?"

"The price."

"Never mentioned."

"Um."

"We were overheard by something else and it was trying to cover up a bungle. A third attempt was made to lure me out of GM, but I won't go into details. It was a challenge I couldn't resist. I did what the cossack couldn't do—tracked down the Group, all dispersed by fake messages."

"Why?"

"Later. I found out about the Extro network, Dr. Guess, and the whole damned lunatic conspiracy."

"The Group knows?"

"More or less. I got the hard data from Poulos."

"Where is he? Also dispersed?"

"No, trying to track down the renegade. Yes, the Greek told me about that and I agree with his assumption. It's a dangerous mishmash. Crucial. He or she has got to be destroyed before the Group is destroyed. No one of us alone is a match for him, and that's why I think he had the Group scattered—to pick us off one by one."

"Any idea who it might be?"

"Not a clue. We've got an average proportion of rotten members. Take your pick."

"Just one thing. Are you saying the Extro can make mistakes?"

"I thought you were above blind computer worship, Guig. Yes, they can make mistakes and so can the Extro's collaborator, Dr. Guess. Even between them they can make mistakes, and that's how we're going to find Guess and his three freaks. What d'you think, Guig? Are they equipped with a putz and a twibby? Both?"

"I don't know, Hilly, and I don't want to find out. It gives me the chills."

"When we locate Guess we'll find out. Now, we have a three-pronged attack. Guess and the capsule are hiding out somewhere here on Earth."

"They might be in orbit."

"Not a chance."

"Expound."

"He lofted the capsule out of U-Con after it killed your girl. Houdini and Valentine took off. You were in shock. The capsule went up and nobody noticed."

"Into orbit?"

"How? He needed a rocket vehicle for that and he had none. The capsule must have gone up as far as repulsion would take it and then drifted."

"Why not fall down?" Natoma asked.

"It had gas jets to maintain attitude in space. Evidently they were enough to keep it up and take it to wherever Guess wanted it. So he's on Earth somewhere. Now the three prongs. Mrs. Curzon, you will inquire about your famous and distinguished brother everywhere. You love him and you're worried about his disappearance."

"I am, Mr. Hillel."

"I believe you and so will everyone else. You will make a pest of yourself. Force people to avoid you as the plague. Send constant messages to Guig reporting progress."

"But if there is none?"

"Then use your imagination. We can send fake messages, too. Everything you do will reach your brother by the network. It may draw him out to reassure you."

"I understand. I hope so."

"Guig, yours is more technical. How much gas was available in the capsule? How far would it take it? You'd—"

"It had full tanks of compressed helium."

"Hmm. Anyway, you'd better diagram that. Check UFO sightings and reports; a space capsule is an unusual sight here on Earth. Dr. Guess will need power to maintain the capsule pressure and refrigeration. If it's under cover, the solar vanes can't charge the batteries. Check every energy source within your plot for a new demand or drain. And here's a tricky one. What if the cryonauts develop no further than infancy? Mature in body; infantile in mind."

"My God! I never thought of that."

"No one else did."

Natoma said, "Boris told us he was reborn with all skills after CNA-Drone."

"DNA-Clone, darling."

"Thank you, Glig."

"Not the same thing, Mrs. Curzon," Hilly said. "Guess will have to train and educate them, first of all in speech. Check every supplier of educational modes for retarded children who are autistic. Address of every order received in the past month. It's a drag, I know."

I shrugged that off. "And the third prong?"

"Mine. The hardest of all. Why were three separate attempts made to get me out of GM?"

"But the renegade and the Extro have been dispersing the entire Group."

"True. They're afraid of us. But they could have got me out of GM by leading me to the Edsel. Why didn't they? Perhaps the car doesn't exist. A possibility. Perhaps they made a mistake in their estimation of my character. A possibility. But I'm looking for a third possibility."

"Which is?"

"I have no idea. I don't even know if it exists."

"What do you think, Hillel? Is Guess a monster?"

"N. N. N. The Extro and the renegade are the monsters. Unfortunately we must counterattack through Guess, who's merely a bad boy."

"Bad boy!"

"I repeat, bad boy. He's dealing with breathtaking discoveries and he's drunk as a kid in love for the first time. I don't fault him for that. It's so unusual it would intoxicate anyone."

"Then what can we do?"

"Sober him down. Basically he's a good boy; a frightful nuisance now but no source of lasting danger. Keep your sights on the real evils, the Extro and the renegade."

"Are they an intimate commingling, too?"

"*Quien sabe?* Now we must break this up, alas, and go to work, each of us independently. No more of the mama-papa shoot, Guig. I'm sorry, but you've had your honeymoon. Remember, you must Telex and Radex to each other constantly, but no message sent or received should be believed. Ignore them."

"But what if—"

"There is no what if. You told Boris this would be a bootleg chase. So it is. Lie to each other. Fabricate. Be outrageous. That will throw the network into fits wondering whether you're using a code it can't break. And always remember it will be fabricating phony messages too, so believe nothing and go on with the chase. The three of us operate alone. Understood?"

"Y, sir."

"Gung. Give me a half-hour start. Delighted to have made your acquaintance, Mrs. Curzon. Don't forget to collect your chickens, Guig."

"Don't forget Sequoya is my brother," Natoma called.

The Jew turned and smiled. "More important, he's of the Group, Mrs. Curzon, and we're always extra kind to our meshugenehs. Ask your husband what we went through with barking Kafka." Then he was gone. Acute and fast.

"Kafka?" Natoma asked. "Barking?"

"He thought he was a colony of seals. Will this concrete be too hard on your back?"

"Yes, but not on yours."

So we gave Hilly his half hour and I did remember to collect the chickens.

SIX-FOOT LEMUR DISCOVERED IN MADAGASCAR. LIVING FOSSIL NOTIFY YOUR BROTHER. URGENT.

SEQUOYA REPORTED ON THETIS.

TELFORD SAYS YOUR BROTHER WORKING ON CURE FOR ASTHMA IN GRASSHOPPERS. CAN CONFIRM? MAY MEAN NOBEL PRIZE IF HE CAN LOCATE ASTHMATIC GRASSHOPPERS.

N CONFIRM. HAVE HEARD HE HAS JOINED INCA CULT IN MEXICO.

EDISON SAYS YOUR BROTHER AND CAPSULE IN ORBIT SAYS GUESS FEELS LIKE A BRASS MONKEY N BELIEVE EDISON.

SEQUOYA NOT IN MEXICO. WHAT ARE YOU DOING IN P&G?

MUST BE MISTAKE IN TRANSMISSION. N P&G AM IN TINKER TOY. YOUR BROTHER CLOSE BUT ANCHOR ICE MAKING SEARCH DIF-FICULT

URGENT. COME AT ONCE TO GARBO. HAVE BROKEN MY HIP.

SO SORRY. N LIKED YOUR HIP. ON MY WAY TO SEE GUESS IN SAN MIGUEL ALLERGY.

RESPECTFULLY REQUEST DIVORCE.

BRINGING COUNTERSUIT FOR THE CRIME OF PHLEBOTOMY COM-MITTED WITH YOUR BROTHER. HOW DID YOU BREAK YOUR HIP IN GARBO?

N GARBO. AM IN DIETRICH. HIP UNDAMAGED.

YOUR BROTHER TELLS ME CAPSULE SAFELY HIDDEN BUT N SAYS WHERE. HAS HE TOLD YOU?

IN LOVE WITH EVIL ECZEMA. RESPECTFULLY REQUEST DIVORCE OR YOUR SUICIDE. MY BROTHER TELLS ME NOTHING.

URGENT INFORM SEQUOYA ANOTHER LIVING FOSSIL SIGHTED IN CANASKA. A DINAHSHORE. IT IS GERMAPHRODITE.

URGENT P SEND CREDIT. HAVE BEEN BILLED BY TRACER AS-
SOCIATES FOR EXTRA   MILES COVERAGE RESULT OF YOUR MES-
SAGES.

IMPOSS.   MILES IS TO THE SUN AND BACK. IS THAT WHERE
YOUR BROTHER IS NOW?

CORRECTION. N MILES KILOMETERS.

REPEAT: STILL TO SUN IS YOUR BROTHER IN ORBIT WITH CAP-
SULE?

CORRECTION: USED BINARY INSTEAD OF DECIMAL. FIGURE
SHOULD READ   MILES. Y. SEQUOYA AND CAPSULE IN ORBIT

The Jew was right as usual. We had the Extro network
throwing fits; distorted transmissions, phony messages,
dumb corrections. Meanwhile I was pursuing the course he'd
plotted for me. The capsule was up to its ass in gas, enough
to take it as far as Houston, Memphis, Duluth, Toronto. No
point in mapping that. There had been a dozen UFO sightings in Nevahado, Utoming, Iowaska and Indinois. Also Ha-
waii. That was a bust, too.

I did just about as well on the energy drain. After half
a dozen consultations with the enclave I discovered that
they no longer tried to trace the thefts. It was cheaper to
add it all up and charge everybody a surtax to cover it.

Ah, but the Autistic Instruction Modes! That was the hot
lead. A barrage of orders for crash courses had come in to
the branch offices from something calling itself the Neo
School. The orders were forwarded to the main office in
Tchicago which, alone, knew where to deliver them. There
was a strong chance that this was Hiawatha and his three

baby machisbians. I would have to go to Tchicago and do some snooping.

But in the course of all this it dawned on me that while I was tracking the Chief I was being hounded myself. It started small and built. Salesmen from private composts paid calls. Wedding cakes in horrid glowing neon were delivered COD; also beds, clothes, carpets, spirits, acids, and belts for hernia. I began to receive bills from physicians for absent acupuncture, and confirmations for bookings to Venus, Mars, and the Jupiter and Saturn satellites, all luxury class.

Then it got worse. You add human worship of computers to an electronic revolt and you have a rough scene. There's nothing the damned machines can't do when the humans bob their heads and take infallibility for granted. At least the Druids worshiped trees, which are sensible and trustable. You can't corrupt a tree.

Six criminal indictments were filed against me by the Provacateur General's machine. Followed by announcements of my death by suicide over Solar Press Interplanetary wires. Then my passport and credit cards were revoked as counterfeits after routine computer review. I was now a man without a country.

My seven banks and brokerage houses informed me curtly that their accounting printouts indicated I was heavily overdrawn. No further courtesies could be extended. I was now bankrupt. Then my former home—now the Chief's—burned to the ground. I'd taken the precaution of moving every treasure from the tepee to the house for safekeeping. All destroyed or stolen. I spent the night sifting through the cold ashes looking for a fragment of memory. The looters had been before me and left nothing but their excrement and an odd weapon which must have been dropped unnoticed in the excitement. It was a short dagger with a broad, pointed blade. The handle was two parallel bars joined by a crosspiece. I slid it into my boot. It might help me locate the looters and recover some of the stolen things.

I would have given up that night if I hadn't had a vivid image of how Hillel and Natoma would ream me out. That gave me Dutch courage. So next morning I cash-fared onto a linear bound for Tchicago. It was hijacked to Cannibal, Mo. I was transferred along with the other passengers and many bewildered apologies to a linear bound for Tchicago, and this time we were jacked to Duluth. Transfer and confusion again ("These are all computer routed and piloted!") but this time the Guig-jinx was smart. So they wanted to keep me away from Tchicago? R. I transferred to the Buffalo shuttle and they let me get there.

So here I was at the far end of the Erie reservation and this time I had a break. The gate was guarded by a Cherokee tour of duty and one of them was a totemic relation who recognized me. He grinned, knocked his fists together four times, put me in a chopper, and lofted me to the Guess marble wickiup.

I must have looked awful. Mama stared at me, burst into tears, and swept me into her billows. Then she stripped me, bathed me, put me to bed, and fed me a broth that lined my ribs. I never had a mother like this. I loved her. An hour later stately papa came in accompanied by a goblin—all head and not nearly enough body to go with it. Slavic eyes and high cheekbones. A character out of "The Hall of the Mountain King."

"Like bwenas tarthes, man," the goblin said in mellifluous Spang. "How esta you?"

"I'm more comfortable in XX," I said. "Do you speak it?"

"But of course. I am Larsen, Professor of Linguistics at the college. You're not ill, I hope, Mr. Curzon."

"Just tired, spent, exhausted."

"The Sachem asks first about you, his new son. I will tell him." He told papa in Cherokee. Papa shook his head and clicked his tongue. "Now he asks about his other son and daughter."

"Both are alive and well, to the best of my knowledge."

"That is ambiguous, Mr. Curzon."

"I'm aware of it, Professor Larsen, but the facts are so complicated it would take the rest of the day to explain. Just say alive and well and happy."

After a palaver the goblin said, "The Sachem asks why they are not with you."

"Tell him I'm on my way to join them."

"And this is a courtesy call?"

"Yes and no."

"Ambiguity again, Mr. Curzon."

"It's part of the complication. I must borrow some cash."

"But you are reputed to be a millionaire many times over, Mr. Curzon."

"And so I am. Again more complications."

"I must hear them. I have never been so tantalized. Excuse me." He turned and quonked with papa. Then back to me: "The Sachem says certainly. Of course. How much will you need?"

"One hundred thousand."

Larsen was startled; not so papa. He nodded calmly and I loved him. I never had a father like that. He left the room and returned with ten neat packets of gold-colored notes, meaning they were thousands. He stacked them on the bedside table, sat down on the bed, and peered into my face. He put a hand on my brow and murmured.

"The Sachem says that despite your fatigue, marriage to his daughter seems to agree with you."

"Please tell him that she has become more beautiful than ever."

"I had better not, Mr. Curzon. On the reservation it is regarded as unmanly to admire one's squaw."

"Thank you, Professor Larsen. Tell him that Natoma is a hardworking squaw."

"That should please him, I think."

The door burst open and the hardworking squaw charged into the room, looking like an agitated goddess . . . that is, if the gods ever were chic. She threw herself on top of me. "What is it, Glig? What is wrong? Why are you in bed? Am I hurting you? Why are you here? Where should you be? Did you know I was coming? How? Why don't you say something?"

When she gave me a chance I said something, and managed to ask her what she was doing here.

"I had to come," Natoma said. "I had to reload with sanity. I've seen my brother and I'm furious."

I was dying for her news but there was no more time for talk; dinner was waiting. Papa, the professor, the kid brothers, and myself at the table while mama and Natoma waited on us. My incomparable wife had the charm to revert to tradition on the reservation. She wore deerskin, kept her head lowered, and actually blushed when the naughty boys made coarse marriage jokes which Larsen refused to translate.

When I signed to her to come out with me for an evening walk she nodded but gave me a wait signal. She had to help mama with the dishes. When at last we left the wickiup she walked three humble paces behind me until we were out of sight. Then she threw herself at me and nearly knocked me down.

"I love you. Oh, how I love you! I would love you if you were hateful. You've rescued me from all this."

"You would have rescued yourself, Nat."

"How could I? I never knew there was another world. No, you liberated me and now I'm entire."

"And so am I. It works both ways."

She took me to her childhood hideout, a giant cedar of Lebanon in which we could climb up, sit close, and hold hands without caustic comment from the Erie conservatives.

"Who goes first, you or me?" she said.

"You."

"Mr. Hillel was right. My brother came looking for me."

"Where did he find you?"

"In Boxton."

"I never knew you were there."

"The machines were keeping us apart."

"Yes. And? Did he try to reassure you?"

"No. He frightened me. He's not just a bad boy; he's cold, cold, cold. Heartless."

"Ah."

"He's not my brother anymore."

"Not now, but he will be again."

"He told me that it was cry havoc for the human race, which had been asking for it for a thousand years. Death and destruction. No mercy."

"*Dio*! We know he and the network mean it."

"He told me to go home where I'd be safe. The network can't get through to the reservation. There are other places, too. Sahara and Brazil and—and—I forget because I wasn't listening."

"Why not?"

"I lost my temper. I told him—Why are you grinning?"

"Because I know that temper."

"I told him he was a traitor to me, to his family, to his people, to this entire beautiful world you've shown me."

"Hoo boy. You were hot."

"I was. I told him I wasn't a squaw anymore; that you had turned me into a thinking, independent person, and that I would do everything I could to stop him and punish him, even if it meant getting the Erie tribes and nations to hunt him down. If they could beat the Mafia International they would have no trouble with him and that damned computer on his back."

"Pretty strong stuff, Nat. Would the tribes and nations help?"

"They will. We've done without electronics for generations, outside of the fence and a few simple basics, so they can't be cowed by a computer. And most of them are dying for a fight anyway."

"Even against the son of the Great Sachem?"

"They won't kill him. They'll just roast him over a slow fire, Iroquois-style, until he comes to his senses. That'll sober him down."

"Did you mention the real enemy, the renegade?"

"No."

"And what did he say to all this?"

"Nothing. He just turned and left me like you leave a piece of furniture."

"Going where?"

"I don't know."

"Back to the capsule?"

"I don't know. He left and I came home."

"Of course. And you'll stay here."

"N."

"Why N?"

"I want to be with you."

"Natoma!"

"Edward!"

We had it out so hard that I nearly fell out of the tree. I listed all the disasters wrought by the computer network. Nothing. Not even a tear for the Sèvres destruction. She only looked grimmer and more determined. She had taken the ball from flippant old me and was set to run or pass, so I surrendered. My goddamn Cherokee wife had the Indian sign on me.

And she outsmarted the anti-Tchicago network. We took the Buffalo shuttle to Pittsburgh. Pittsburgh to Charleston. Then it would be Charleston to Springfield and hovercraft to Tchicago. But someone must have slipped up on Natoma's passage vouchers. The Charleston travel desk paged her just before takeoff. Her Spang wasn't nearly as good as her XX, so I left her on the shuttle and went to the main desk myself to find out what the tsimmes was.

I reasoned with the smart-asses and they argued back— computer check (infallible) indicated the tickets were faulty. I planked down a gold-colored thousand and asked for a new voucher. Quick, please. They quick, but the automatics took over and the shuttle lofted while I was waiting. A hundred feet up it burst into an explosion that shattered it, smashed the walls of the port building, and knocked me into oblivion.

11

No one knew what his real name was and nobody asked. It was a lethal offense to ask that kind of question in the Underbelly. He was called Capo Rip. No one knew his origins. There were a dozen stories but he was such a liar that none could be believed: orphanage (there hadn't been an orphanage in a hundred years), street gangs, adopted by the Mafia International, synthesized in a laboratory, product of the artificial insemination of a gorilla. He was cold-blooded, indifferent to women, men, companionship, friendship. Icy and hard. He was a percentage player with such a keen memory for numbers and probabilities that he was barred from all gambling tables; he was a losing proposition for the house.

But percentage prevented him from killing. Not that he gave a damn about murder, but he didn't like the odds against. He never took a chance when the odds were against. "Bod once wrote that all life was six-to-five against" Rip said. "I don't try anything unless it's six-to-five for." Yes, Capo Rip could read, and he didn't play even-money bets. He always looked for the edge.

That made him the ideal cannon and the idol of the Bellyworld. He was strictly business; robbery, burglary, extortion, blackmail, bribery. He won tremendous respect. Best of all, the Belly learned that he was dependable; he never slashed, he paid all contract cuts promptly, and never welshed on an obligation. Bad percentage. He knew that loyalty could only be bought.

He lived quietly in small hotels, drop-ins, lodges, gambling houses—provided he kept away from the tables. He was never armed but had shown himself to be a cold crusher when cornered into a gut-fight. He always preferred the coward's copout from one-on-one trouble—no percentage in that—but some goons on a machismo trip wouldn't let it alone. Then he crunched. The Belly believed he could be light-heavy champion in all-out if he wanted to.

Capo Rip won so much respect that a small coterie gathered around him, uninvited. They were unknown bods without records and therefore of no account, but they seemed to be serviceable. One was a woman, also uninvited and unwanted but she remained loyal and laughed off outside propositions. No odds in them for her. Mercenary.

Rip's capers were ingenious. A few examples: The Exchange Brokerage House protected itself with a quicksand moat. The drawbridge was raised after hours and no one could pogo onto the pointed roof. Capo Rip froze a path across the quicksand with dry ice and skipped quietly over the skulls of long-gone failures for the heist. He bribed a secretary at the Foreclosure Trust to type on her terminal keyboard in Morse clicks giving him crucial security information. He ripped the vaults.

A governor's fifty-year-old wife began to turn youthful; hair glossy, skin transparent and lovely. Rip checked the governor's staff. A ravishing young secretary. He checked the rejuvenation salons. The wife had no accounts. "Arsenious poisoning," he said, and the governor paid, and paid and paid. Posing as a pianolo tuner he came to the home of a celebrated but cautious collector, casing for a rare Russian gem, a seven-inch goddess carved out of the largest emerald in history by Fabergé three centuries ago. Nowhere in sight. He returned with a compass and located her in a steel casket plastered up in a wall. He sold seven replicas molded out of synthetics to demented collectors and then had the chutzpah to return the original gem to its original owner. The Belly loved that.

Between the heavies he worked the petty buncos: medical frauds, radium pitchers, glass caskets, the honeymoon and obituary racks, the cataracts swindle, building lots in Atlantis; *Atlantis*, for God's sake! Begging cassettes, fading-tape contracts. Oh, he was versatile and busy, busy, busy. His energy was unbelievable. The Underbelly estimated that his vigorish must come close to a million a month.

His capers were quiet. Capo Rip did not care for publicity, and that was one of the constraints he required of his coterie, which they respected. For unknowns they were remarkable; as silent as knives, never speaking. The Belly could not persuade them to talk, drink, gas, trip, gamble, communicate. They were dead-face deadly, so no one cared to get acquainted through a gut-rap.

The Underbelly could not believe it when Capo Rip and his Merry Men disappeared. He had started on a job and then there was none. They thought he'd been busted (improbable) but when discreet questions were asked of his professional fixer, who was in possession of a generous retainer, he reported that Capo had not been in touch with him. Capo Rip had gone up like a skyrocket, burst in a blaze of glory, and then vanished.

He was belted down in a berth that rocked. The belts were locked, he found out soon enough, but there was a dark stranger hatefully smiling at him constantly, always calling him "Great Capo." The woman was there, too, feeding him meals with a runcible spoon. Rip still didn't know her name and didn't want to, now more than ever. He took some pleasure from spitting the food into her face.

Whatever the place was, it swarmed with nurses and doctors in agitated conversation, using words like "platysma myoides," "abdominal aponeurosis," "rectus femori," and "ligamentum cruciatum cruris." Bewildering. The only one who made sense was a young surgeon who was a lycanthropist. He kept turning into a fanged wolfman and devouring the shrieking nurses alive, usually starting with the gluteus maximus. The dark man and the woman paid no attention to them.

"This is a hospital?" Capo Rip growled.

"No, Great Capo. You're watching a kiddie show, *Young Doctor Prevert.* I'm sorry. We can't block the broadcasts." And he took the captive to the head and guarded him with a burner.

"You bastard. I hate you."

"But of course, Great Capo. Lunch now."

Back to the rocking berth and the woman came to feed him.

"You bastard's bitch. You sold me out."

"Yes, Capo, but you don't know why, yet."

"Where am I? What am I doing here?"

"On a schooner in the middle of Lake Mitchigan," the dark stranger said. "What are you doing? Preparing to pay a price."

"How much?"

"First for what. No?"

"To hell with that. Name the price, you damned bastardly barber. I'll pay it, and I promise you you'll never barber anyone in the Belly again."

"I believe you, Great Capo." He started to leave and then

turned. "The price is telling me where I can find a man named Edward Curzon."

"Who?"

"Edward Curzon."

"Never heard of him."

"Oh, come now, Great Capo. With your connections and experience you must have come across him. And with your ingenuity and expertise you can find him for me. I'll contract for the hit and make it worth your while."

"I never hit. Bad percentage."

"I'm aware of that, which is why you're here under gentle persuasion. You must find and hit Curzon, Great Capo."

"Why me? I can put you onto twenty killers."

"To be sure, but none with your integrity. An essential part of the contract must be that it can never be traced to me. I can trust no jimp except you. Find and hit Edward Curzon, Great Capo."

"How did you snatch me on the Chalice job?"

"I set it up. I also have ingenuity. Now be reconciled. You must find and hit Edward Curzon."

"Suppose I agree. I can always sell you out, the way that bitch sold me."

"No. Your word is your bond. That's why you're here. Think about Curzon, Great Capo. When you're ready to agree, we'll talk. Surely you must have run across the name during your brilliant career. The name or something like it. Search your mind, Great Capo. Think hard."

Curzon? Or something like it? Curzon, Curzon, or something like it? The Capo thought hard. How many did he know in the Belly? There was Cur the Lion. Not worth hitting. A cheap jimpster who only worked a cold house. Larry the Lace Curtain. A society goniff who reported the comings and goings of the heeled for a rotten two percent. A shroff named Chan Kersey, who sold his chop to the counterfeit crowd. Curmin the Vermin, who ran a decoy swindle outside the legit gambling houses. Yellow Kid Kurze, who operated a big store in an abandoned bank building. Now *he* sounded likely, but the Kid was gentle and harmless.

The woman came in, balancing a plate of food and that goddamn runcible spoon. There was a hard gale and she had to balance herself against the lurch of the goddamn schooner, clutching at whatever was handy. Nevertheless she was thrown and the plate went up out of her hand. She was quick on her feet and poised when it came down, still right-side-up. She caught it, smiled at Capo Rip, and even winked.

"Krijeeze!" I yelled. "The Sèvres!"

She stared at me. I stared at her. "Wait a M," I said. "You're not my Nat. You can't be. I saw her die this morning. Who are *you?*"

She threw herself on me and began to cry and shriek like the wolfman was fanging her. Words finally came out of the screams, "Hilly! Hilly! Quick! He's found Edward Curzon."

The Jew rushed down into the cabin, clutching at anything. He stepped on the plate and crunched it. "Hi, Guig," he said. "My foot is full of beans."

"What the hell is going on? Half hour ago I saw Natoma die in Charleston. Now here she is with me on this thing that rocks and—"

"Schooner," Hilly said. "All sail; no machines. We're on Lake Mitchigan."

"And here you are and God knows who else and what else. Natoma, I love you as always forever, but give me a little breath space. I have to ask questions. Hilly, there's no Lake Mitchigan. It's gone the way of Erie."

"Not quite yet. There's a hundred-mile puddle left, and here we are in the middle where we can't be monitored."

"How the hell did you get me here so fast, Hilly?"

"Yes, it was fast," the Jew conceded. "It only took three months."

"Three—"

"You see, Mrs. Curzon? I warned you it would be total amnesia."

"Do you mean to tell me—that I—get off me, Nat. I've got to get up."

They unlock and I up, not feeling v. flippent. "You'd better tell me the whole story," I said.

"It couldn't be simpler, Guig. The linear explosion and what you thought was your wife's death knocked you into a massive epileptic seizure."

"I came out of it?"

"Not into sanity; into epileptic delirium. Complete loss of memory. Complete loss of moral control. Complete loss of humanity."

"Dio! And then?"

"You became Capo Rip."

"Who?"

"The most vicious jimpster in the Underbelly. There's no point in trying to restore your memory of that. I wouldn't if I could. Best forgotten forever."

"In other words, I turned into another vicious Sequoya."

"Don't say that, Glig."

"I do say it. He tried to kill me. He nearly killed you. What saved you?"

"You took too long, so I got off the linear to join you just before lift. The explosion knocked me unconscious. By the time they found me in the wreckage you were gone."

"And then?"

"I recruited four feisty braves from the reservation and we found you in the Belly. Then I found Hilly in GM and told him everything I knew. He set this up."

I gave Natoma a hard look. "I'm sorry. I'm going to hit our brother."

"Please, Glig, no. Don't be Capo Rip anymore."

"I have to hit our brother."

"The Group won't stand for one of us killing another," Hilly said.

"No? If Guess'd blown me up, plenty of them would have cheered."

"And if you kill Guess?"

"More cheers. And what do you intend to do with the mystery renegade? Send him to a shrink? Protective custody? Therapeutic recycling?"

"But Guig, you gave Sequoya perpetual life."

"Yes, by killing him once. Now I'm going to take back the gift by killing him again. I'm an Indian giver." I aimed a finger at Natoma. "And I don't care if it destroys my marriage."

Natoma turned to the Hebe in despair. "Hilly. Help."

"I can't, love. He's generated the purpose I talked about on the Heath, and now he's too much for us to control. Don't you see it? Gottenu! I never thought he would turn so savage. He actually scares me."

"What did you shoot me with to bring me out of this?" I asked.

"You're behind the times. We don't inject anymore; we use estrogens."

"What was it?"

"Let's get something straight," Hillel said in level tones. "You're feeling your new muscle now, but don't try to clout on me. It's none of your business what I used to bring you out of the delirium. The whole event has got to be forgotten. I can't control you, but by God you can't control me. Either we confer as equals or get the hell out of here. You can swim to shore."

He was right. I gave him an apology bow. "Gung. Have you located the Chief?"

"Y. With your help."

"Mine? Imposs. I never got near him. Where is he?"

"About a quarter of a mile below us."

"What! In the lake?"

"Under the lake."

"Expound."

"The network tried to keep you out of Tchicago, and me out of GM. What connection could there be between the two? That gave me the third possibility I was hoping for. GM used to be a city named Detroit. There are hundreds and hundreds of miles of exhausted salt mines under Detroit, leading all the way to Tchicago. I was prowling one end and you were threatening to get to the other. Dr. Guess and his creatures must be somewhere in the middle. Possibly just underneath us."

"How could he get the capsule into the mine shafts?"

"They're not shafts; they have the dimensions of boulevards."

"Why the demand for salt?"

"They used an extraction process. Sodium for energy."

"Ah! And the Chief is probably tapping the original power lines for his damned capsule."

"Possibly."

"As equal to equal, Ililly, first things first. Y?"

"Y."

"We have got to pinpoint Guess. I want a look at him and his freaks."

"Agreed."

"The hit comes later. Shut up, Nat. Any job needs careful casing."

"Now you sound llke Capo Rip."

"Whether I remember him or not, a part of him must still be with me."

"I can see that."

"Do we work together or from opposite ends?"

"I would say opposites."

"Gung. I'll need help. Who would you suggest? Someone from the Group?"

"N. One of your wife's braves."

"Are they available?"

"They're aboard. The trouble is, they speak none of our languages."

"I'll come and interpret," Natoma offered. Damn brave.

"No," the Jew said firmly. "You're dead and you'll stay that way on this schooner."

"It's all K," I said. "She taught me to talk Sign while I was teaching her XX. I'll be able to communicate. Who's the best tracker?"

"Long Lance," Natoma said, "but he's not as good a hatchet as Arrow Edge."

"I told you there would be no killing yet. This is just an exploratory. Now shut up, Nat, and do what Hilly says. Stay dead. We'll discuss our brother when I get back, and there's plenty to discuss. Who was so angry she wanted him roasted over a slow fire?"

"But I—"

"Not now. Does the network think I'm dead, too, Hilly?"

"Presumably. You disappeared after the blowup."

"What about this Capo bod?"

"I've often wondered, Guig, whether your brilliance-potential lies in the conscious or the unconscious. Now I know. When your subterranean took control it couldn't have picked a better cover. Of course the network is aware of Capo Rip. It's aware of everything. But it would be impossible for the Extro to link that cold-blooded jimpster with gentle, kindly Curzon."

"Not gentle anymore."

"Perhaps. We shall see."

Suddenly I went weak and had to sit down. My face probably turned green because Hilly smiled and asked, "Seasick?"

"Worse. The worst. I just thought of a possible result of the explosion that slammed me into the delirium."

"Ah. The big L. I'm afraid you'll have to sweat it out, Guig. Remember, it isn't inevitable."

"I don't understand what you're saying," Natoma broke in. "What is big L? Why is Guig so upset?"

"He'll explain to you another time, Mrs. Curzon. Just now he needs distraction and I happen to have a fascinating bijou handy." He opened a locker and took out the oddball dagger I'd found in the ruins of the house. "Any particular reason for carrying this in your boot when you were Capo Rip?"

"I don't know anything about him now. Why?"

"I know your original motive. Mrs. Curzon told me. Do you know its value?"

"No."

"In the thousands. It's an extremely rare antique, many centuries old."

"What is it?"

"A katar. An ancient Hindu dagger."

"Hindu!"

"Yes. Once again you've been invaluable. You've identified the mystery renegade. He dropped the dagger when he was destroying your house."

"The Rajah? No."

"The Rajah. He's the only Hindu member of the Group."

"It's out of the question. There must be another explanation. A jimp lost it."

"A jimp carrying a dagger you only find in museums? The Rajah dropped it."

"It was stolen from a museum."

"Try the grip. The only Spangland hand this katar could fit would be a child's. The Hindu aristocracy have always been v. small-boned. The Rajah is the renegade."

"That beautiful, exquisite prince? Why? Why? Why?"

"It will give me great pleasure to ask him in person . . . if I survive to hear the answer. Now shouldn't we start the Rajah-chase?"

"R. Nat, bring me Long Lance. I want us both war painted when we start tracking. That'll throw them a curve."

"Gottenu! You don't intend to stalk Guess on foot through hundreds of miles of caverns?"

"What would you suggest?"

"The same thing I'll use. Hovercraft."

"They're machines. They can report."

"To the Extro? Not from a quarter mile under rock."

"Then to Guess."

"How? He needs the Extro as his switchboard, just as the Extro needs him. Apart, they're nothing."

"R as usual, Hilly. Hovercraft it is, with supplies. Did you find any cash on me when you snapped the snatch?"

"Not much. Twenty thousand or so. We'll never know where you stashed Capo's ill-gotten gains."

"I know," Natoma said.

"How much, Nat?"

"Enough to ransom Sequoya."

"Y. I can see we're going to have one hell of a discussion. However. Twenty will do nicely. Gung. Get Long Lance, Nat. So it's me from Tchi and you from GM, Hilly. We'll meet somewhere in the middle, and for Gottenu's sake, don't shoot. Remember, the only good Indian is a live Indian."

The Hebe smiled. "Now you sound like the old Guig again. I like him better than Capo Rip."

"I don't. Gentle and kindly? S. Let's move it."

"Extro. Alert."

"Alert."

"Where is Hillel?"

"Where are you?"

"You know damned well. The capsule blabbed all the way to GM."

"But it cut off. How?"

"We're a thousand feet under solid rock where you can't reach me. Where is Hillel?"

"In GM."

"W?"

"N Known."

"The network must deflect him. He's dangerous."

"N poss when my switchboard is cut off."

"You function in nanoseconds. Issue instructions now, while I'm available."

"Issued. He is to be destroyed like Curzon."

"N, N, N! I did not want Curzon destroyed, only deflected. The same holds for Hillel. Do not ever dare exceed orders again."

"N? What can you do? I am invulnerable."

"And arrogant. When I have time I'll find the chink in

*your armor. Alert the network that I'm holding you all ac-
countable."*

"*It is alerted. It is listening to us. You must know."*

"*And your new aide?"*

"*I have told you. He cannot hear me.*

"*I can only hear him."*

"*Through me?"*

"*You are the switchboard."*

"*His identity?"*

"*Still unknown."*

"*Gung. Out."*

"*Not yet. Q: What is adabag?"*

"*Ah."*

"*Q. What is gaebac?"*

"*So."*

"*Q. What is cefcad?"*

"*Where did you get that?"*

"*From you, Dr. Guess."*

"*H?"*

"*The words run through your mind constantly.*

*What is adabag, gaebac, and cefcad? This may be urgent
for us."*

"*Let the network answer."*

"*It has already reported N knowledge in any lingua. You
must have heard."*

"*Y. Out."*

"*Stop. When you cut off from me we are all deaf and
mute. This cannot continue."*

"*It will not as soon as I've finished my work. It will
explode. Out."*

Long Lance and I were brilliant. The lurid war paint made
us inconspicuous in Tchicago. We didn't buy a hovercraft;

Long Lance stole one, a turtle two-seater. The first thing we did was smash and gut the communications panel. We were now handling a mute bird. We located the downshaft to the salt mine under the wreckage of the Lyric Opera House and a square block of rubbish piled higher than the original bldg where I once saw a performance of *La Boheme* by Darryl F. Puccini.

We stocked staples and had to burn our way down through a quarter of a mile of trash to get to the mine proper. They'd been using the shaft as a dump for a century. It was almost like an archaeological dig; cans, plastics, glass, bones, skulls, rotted cloth, antique kitchen utensils, a cast-iron radiator, a gearbox, and even a hunk of a brass saxophone. B flat. I grabbed at and missed a rare Nixon nickel.

Long Lance goggled at the remains and I liked him for that. I liked him anyway. He was long, lean, assured, and coiled like a steel spring. Outside of Algonquin and Sign he spoke exactly three words: Si, No, and Capo. That was plenty. He must have made one hell of an accomplice for the late, great Capo Rip.

It was hot as blazes down in the mine and I was glad we were naked. I had a gyrocompass and we headed toward GM, Long Lance doing the handling. I'd taken it for granted that we'd need lights and stocked up on lamp-lands. Not so. The rock salt remnants in the boulevards were luminescent—radioactive probably—and emitted a green glow that gave us all the light we needed. Probably more roentgens than we needed, too. I wondered whether there was an estrogen which could treat radiation exposure. The big L was still on my mind.

It was a scene out of the Inferno; this great, glowing boulevard with a vaulted ceiling dripping green light, jagged corridors leading off left and right, and we had to explore every one until the hover couldn't squeeze through. I figured that if the turtle couldn't make it, the capsule couldn't. That saved a little time. We ate and slept once. We ate and slept twice. We ate and slept thrice. Long Lance gave me a look and I returned it, but we went on through the silence and the glow.

I thought about the Rajah, still not believing the Hebe and the evidence of the katar. How could I? The Rajah had always overwhelmed me with his magnificence. The Rajah had been and still was the supreme ruler and supreme deity of a small mountain state named Mahabharata, now shortened to Bharat. It had a few lush valleys for farming, but the Rajah's gross national product came from rich mineral resources. Every time technology or luxury invented a need for a new metal, there it was in Bharat. Example: When platinum was first unearthed in the Ural Mountains, it was later discovered that the women of Bharat had been wearing beads of rough platinum nuggets for generations.

The Rajah, when I first met him in the Grossbad Spa, was singularly exquisite; sooty black—unlike M'bantu, who is shiny—handsome aquiline features, great dark eyes, delicate bones. His voice was slightly singsong and lilted with humor. He was always beautifully dressed and beautifully mannered. He was not and still isn't democratic. Caste. Alas, Ned Curzon inspired instant aversion in him.

I was told that when he first visited Western Europe, back in the days of Napoleon, his conduct was appalling. As a supreme prince and god he could do no wrong in Bharat. On the Continent it was something else. For example, whenever the necessity arose he would relieve himself in public. No floor or potted plant was safe. He soon learned to behave himself and I sometimes wonder what hero had the temerity to teach him. Possibly Napoleon. More likely, his sister, Pauline Buonaparte, who entertained the Rajah as one of her lovers.

And this man of supreme power and wealth, with everything that anyone could possibly want, to turn renegade and attack the Group? Why? In his eyes we were beneath him. Everybody was. Caste. Did he want to become prince and god of the entire world? Nonsense! You only find that motivation in cheap fiction. I never believe anything that doesn't make sense to me, and this didn't make sense.

On the fourth day Long Lance stopped the hovercraft and made emphatic Sign to me. I emphatic. He listened hard for a few minutes. Then he got out, pulled a dirk from his belt, and worked it into the rocky floor. He knelt down, fastened his teeth on the handle, and listened through his mouth. Then he came back to me, took the compass, and examined it closely. He showed it to me.

By God, the needle had swung two degrees from the north toward the west and hung there no matter how we jiggled it. Long Lance grunted, retrieved his dirk, climbed back aboard, and began crawling the turtle. The first broad corridor on our left, he turned, went up a hundred yards, stopped, repeated the dirk bit, and came back to me. He made a globe gesture and said, "Si, Capo."

Like a damned fool I opened my mouth to ask questions which he certainly couldn't have understood. He said, "No, Capo," and signed me to listen. I listen. I listen. I listen. Nothing. I look at Long Lance. He nodded. He was hearing what I couldn't hear. What a tracker! I listen. I listen. I listen. And then I heard it. Music.

12

We pulled the hover back to the main boulevard and turned toward Tchi until we located a side corridor big enough to accommodate the turtle. We backed in deep enough for cover, got out, and went north again on foot. Long Lance had the dirk in his belt. I shoved a meat burner into mine, just in case. No sense taking chances. He was barefoot, feet like iron; I'd sprayed my soles with a half inch plastic. He was naked, painted, and the green luminescence gave him the appearance of hideous tooled leather. If I looked anything like him we must have made a charming couple.

Suddenly Long Lance gripped my shoulder, stopped me, and turned me around. He pointed to a smallish side corridor we had just passed, and made See-Sign. When I asked him what, he made Animal-Sign. What kind of animal? The answer was complicated but I finally twigged. He was telling me he'd seen a lion. Preposterous, but I had to show him respect. We went back to the corridor and looked in. No lion. We went in. A dark maze. No lion. Not even a snarl. Long Lance was unhappy and confused and wanted to make a thorough inspection. We had more urgent business on hand. I urged him out and we proceeded.

When we reached Capsule Street he took the lead, naturally, signing me to imitate everything he did. I imitate. It was a crash course in the art of sneak attack. As we progressed I became aware of a white glow up ahead, then a low drone, and then the music again—a sort of hum of voices. It went like this:

Not my idea of any tunes ever written by Peter Ilich Korruptsky (b. 1940, d. 2003, greatly regretted). As we went smooch-foot toward the glow, the Rue de la Capsule enlarged, and when we crept up to the source of the light and the drone, I gawked. It was an enormous chamber, lined with the old sodium extraction apparatus, and in the center was the capsule, patched into giant old energy cables and droning away. The Chief had picked the perfect stash. Then we spotted his three humming babies.

They were enormous; nearly seven feet high. They were dead white albino. They were built like men but there was something uncanny about their joint articulations; they moved like insects. Then I saw they were blind. They emitted their tunes as a sonar sound-echo. Naturally I had to look closely at their genitals. Hillel had guessed wrong. Not putz and twibby both; they were white rosebuds, very large, the size of my fist, and the buds kept opening into petals and closing into bud again spasmodically.

Suddenly I had a flash of memory. Once in Africa with M'bantu, the Zulu was showing me the ecosights. He kicked over a rough clay cone and I saw thousands of terrified termites scrambling for cover. They were white, they were blind, and McB told me that they communicated by uttering sounds which the human ear couldn't hear. Sequoya's babies were seven-foot termites, but they could be heard.

I made Sign to Long Lance that I was going in alone. He didn't like the idea, but you can't argue in Sign, you only make statements. So I went while he stayed. The three things sensed me almost immediately and came at me. I pulled the burner out of my belt, but they intended no harm; they were simply overcome with curiosity and delight. While I looked for Sequoya they explored my body with their hands and jabbered in music:

And then all together, hopefully in approval.

I answered with Scott Joplin, Gershwin, Korruptsky, Hokubonzai; all the great standards I could remember and hum. They loved the vintage ragtime which I think they thought were funny stories, and kept asking for more. I oblige and they kept falling on each other and me, convulsed with laughter. Very nice termites, you know. Almost lovable once you got over xenophobia, and a damned good house for a stand-up comic. But still no Sequoya. I went and looked into the droning capsule with my three fans crowding around me. *Niemand zu hause.* I yelled, "Guess! Chief! Sequoya!" No answer. The Shout scared the three things and they backed away. I reassured them with a few bars of "Melancholy Baby" and they came back to be petted. Really adorable. But human?

A low hiss came from Long Lance and when I looked he beckoned urgently. I disengaged myself from my fans and ran to him; no time for autographs. He made Listen Sign. I listen and listen. Then I heard it; the murmur of an approaching hovercraft. "It's Hilly from the other end," I thought, took Long Lance by the shoulder, and we both ran down to the Avenida Las Salt Mine. The Algonquin didn't like it but I gave him no time for statements. However, he did pull out his dirk. That was statement enough.

Just as well. It wasn't Hilly, it was the Chief in a hover stacked with supplies. Long Lance melted against a wall and disappeared; probably reluctant to mess around with the son and heir of the most powerful Sachem in Erie. Not so the son and heir of the great Capo Rip. I stepped out in full view, blocking the hover, one hand on the burner, which was idiotic, but I was in a fury. Guess stopped and stared in amazement, not expecting visitors and not recognizing me.

"H," I said.

"W? W?"

"You look prosperous, brother."

"It isn't Guig."

"Y."

"It can't be."

"It is. Decorated. Not for valor."

"Guig! But—"

"Y. You missed, you son of a bitch."

"But—"

"You almost got Natoma instead."

"N."

"Y."

"But I—"

"I know. I know. Tried to get her off. I got off instead because her Spang is n. so good. She sends her love. So does the Sachem and mama."

"And you?"

"Only trying to figure out how to kill you."

"Guig!"

"Y. It's going to be a hit."

"Why want to kill me?"

"Why kill me?"

"You were on the attack. It was Extro-defense."

"And Fee? Was she on the attack?"

He was silent, shaking his head.

"You know she was mad for you. She would have done anything for you."

"That damned Extro," he muttered.

"Now where have I heard that before? It wasn't me; it was the other guy what done it."

"You don't understand, Guig."

"Make me understand."

"You've changed. Tough and hard."

"I said make me understand."

"I've changed too. I've lost my pride. So much has happened to me. It's a challenge, I know, and I think I'm failing to meet it. So many variables and unknowns."

"Yes and yes. You've been in the habit of linear thinking in a straight line. Now you have to think in bunches."

"That's most perceptive, Guig."

"You may have lost your pride, but you haven't lost your arrogance. The son of the great Sachem."

"I'd rather call it ambition. And why not? When I was a kid my idols were Galileo, Newton, Einstein, all the great discoverers. And now *I've* discovered something. Can you blame me for fighting for it, tooth and nail? Have you seen my cryonauts?"

"I've seen you and the Extro network. Is that your discovery?"

"It's part of the bunch, as you put it. You must have seen my cryos. I know you, brother."

"Cut the blood schmaltz. Y, I've seen them."

"And?"

"You want me to be frank?"

"Y."

"They're beautiful. They're fascinating. They capture instant affection. They inspire instant horror."

"You have no idea of their potential. They think and communicate on the alpha wavelength. That's why they can't talk. They're brilliant. In a few months they've reached the university level. They're incredibly gentle—not an ounce of hostility. And they have a remarkable quality I've never heard of before—I don't think the concept has ever existed—they have electronic valence. You know how people respond to weather. They respond to the upper levels of the electromagnetic spectrum, above the visual level. Run a current through a wire and they're elated or depressed, depending on watts and amperes. Guig, they're wonderful. Why horror?"

"Because they belong on another planet."

"We are all on another planet; everyone, everywhere."

"Well said. You're astromorphic."

"Then?"

"Sequoya Edward, we're the Group. We owe loyalty and love to each other. Y?"

"Y."

"Sequoya Edward, we're of humanity. We owe loyalty and love to every man. Y?"

"Edward Sequoya, what about your kills?"

"Ah. You hit hard. I'm ashamed, now."

"How many?"

"I've lost count."

"This is loyalty and love?"

"To the Group, yes. I wanted everyone to become us, no matter what the price."

"And I have loyalty and love for my three cryos. I want everyone to become them."

"By killing off humanity? I'm biomorphic."

"It's that damned Extro," he growled. "It's the killer."

"Why can't you dump it?"

"Guig, you know about multiple personality?"

"Y."

"I'm suffering from multimultiple personality. I've got the entire electronic network in my head. That's why I'm hiding down here. It's another remarkable phenomenon which must be investigated, but not until I've finished with my cryos. I have time."

"So the Extro is running you."

"Y. N."

"You're running it."

"Y. N."

"Make up your mind."

"Which mind? I have thousands."

"Brother, I love you."

"I love you, brother."

"And I'm going to kill you."

"Cain and Abel?"

"Goe and catche a falling starre."

"Get with child a mandrake roote," he picked it up.

"Tell me, where all past yeares are," I went on.

"Or who cleft the Divel's foot."

"If thou beest borne to strange sights."

"You've skipped, Guig."

"I know. Go ahead anyway. I want to get to the point."

"Things invisible to see."

"Ride ten thousand daies and nights."

"Till age snow white haires on thee."

"Thou, when thou retorn'st, wilt tell mee."

"All strange wonders that befell thee. . . ."

That was enough for my argument, so I made it.

"The point, Chief. Strange wonders have befallen thee, brother. I envy you. I want to be part of it. I'm sure the entire Group will. But you start a massacre. W? Are you still fighting the ancient Indian wars?"

"No. No. No. That's gone with the past years. Is there a war? Yes. Yes. Yes. Now listen carefully, Guig. Ten thousand years ago we lived within our environment. We took only what we needed. We returned what we couldn't use. We were all one organism. We did not destroy the balance. Now what? We've destroyed, destroyed, destroyed. Where is the fossil fuel? All going. The fish and animals? All going. The woods and jungles? Going. The soil? Going? Everything? Going, going, gone.

"You're quoting verse, are you? Do you know this? '*You have brought down the firmament and yet no heaven is more near. You shape huge deeds without event, and half-made men believe and fear.*' By God, Guig, we are all half-made men, a failed species, believing and fearing and destroying, and I'll replace us. You said I was astromorphic. D'you think I want the plague of man to pollute the stars? We poison the cosmos at her roots."

"When you say replace you mean kill."

"No, we'll merely crowd the failed breed out with the new. The killing is the Extro. It's monstrous."

"And you can't dump it?"

"How? It's moved in on me forever."

"You don't want to anyway."

"No, I don't. It's too valuable a tool to throw away. The trouble is, I can't control it yet."

"Y. It's like a Battle of Giants, but you're outnumbered, brother, two-to-one."

"How do you mean?"

"There's another giant joined up with the Extro, and you're being used by them, you damned dizzard switchboard. You'll never control them."

"Maybe you'd better kill me, brother," he said wearily.

Now what answer could an angry man make to that? Thank God, at the moment a hover whispered up from the GM end, stopped, and the Hebe eased out. (Hilly doesn't hop.) He came up to us and said, "So we've got you surrounded. Dr. Guess, I presume. I'm Hillel, the Jew, and were there ever any British Guiana one-cents or was it all a paper chase? V clumsy. My dear Guess, you must learn to consult the Group when you want to swing a swindle. You can't depend on a computer."

Either Hilly's unexpected appearance or his aplomb left the redskin speechless.

"Supplies, I see," Hilly chatted. "Suppose you take them to wherever it is and Guig and I will help you off-load. I must have a look at your cryonauts."

The Chief got back into his hover, still wordless, and turned up Capsulestrasse. Hillel and I followed. Long Lance came out of the stonework and hissed. I shook my head and he melted again. Hilly nodded in approval. Nothing escapes him. He surveyed the extraction chamber with one sweep, and X-rayed the cryonauts with another. "They only speak music," I murmured. Hilly nodded and gave them "Hatikvah" while he helped the Chief unload. They loved it. The Chief was silent, probably trying to cope with the unexpected by thinking in bunches. I was silent, too, because I was in a damnable dilemma.

At one point Hilly whispered to me, "Look at this, Guig," and opened a small box. It contained a dozen steel sewing needles.

"So he's going to make clothes for them," I said.

"Not my point. Watch."

He put the box on the flagged floor. It swung around by itself and aimed at the power cables. Hilly turned it back, let go, and it swung around again.

"That answers the question," he said.

"What question?"

"The question you haven't asked yourself yet."

He saw I wasn't interested, dropped it, and turned to the Chief. "May we speak words without upsetting your most remarkable creatures?" he asked pleasantly.

"It depends on the music of your voice," Sequoya answered. "Apparently yours pleases them."

"Yes. A racial legacy. So does yours, evidently. So we can talk."

"About what?"

"An appeal. You and your cryonauts are about to make history. You will be remembered forever. Don't hide down here. Come out into the open and let us help and protect you. You know you can depend on us."

"No. This mission belongs to me."

"To be sure. And no one will be permitted to cut into any piece of your credit. It's all yours."

"No. I don't need help."

"All right, another appeal. Your astonishing symbiosis with the Extro and the electronic network. That must be researched. It's a giant forward step in evolution. Won't you let us help you?"

"No."

"Dr. Guess, you're making history and yet you seem to be aborting yourself. Why? According to Guig's reports you're no longer what you were. Why? Aren't you in control?"

"N."

"Are you governed by the Extro?"

"N."

"Do you govern it?"

"N."

"It's like a bad marriage. Does it know you're hiding down yere?"

"Y, but it can't reach me down here."

"Doesn't your hover tattle when you're up there?"

"A machine's memory is only as long as the sophistication of its electronics. The hover has awareness of the moment, no more."

"Existentialist. But the Extro remembers."

"Y."

"Is it alive?"

"Tell me what life is and I can answer."

"I can answer, Dr. Guess. It's alive through you. Tell me why you're hiding from your partner down here."

"Because I'm confused, damn you!" he shouted. The cryos recoiled. "Too much has happened to me and I'm trying to sort it out. I'm having difficulties with my cryos; they keep spooking and I don't know why. There's too much I don't know. For God's sake, leave me alone!"

"I understand and wilco, but in return you must leave us alone."

"I told Guig. I have nothing to do with the killings."

"Then you must stop giving life to the killers."

"How?"

"Leave this planet. Go beyond transmission."

"Never. I'll take cover but I'm damned if I'll run."

"Ah. You're headstrong. It's the recent elevation. Intoxicating. Guig was like that after Krakatoa, imperious and sulky. It will pass. It must. When it does, come to the Group. Ready, Guig?"

He turned and I followed him out. Sequoya watched us go, looking angry and bewildered and yet stubborn. The cryos chased after us, humming for more ragtime, but they stopped short at the entrance to the chamber. "That's the question you didn't ask," Hillel said. "The energy field holds them here. You're one rotten inductor, Guig."

"I'm one rotten everything."

"That's a silly self-down. Don't you know that the Group envies you?"

"For what?"

"Something too many of us have lost."

"What?"

"Passion. When you lose that you lose your humanity. Where's Long Lance?"

I hissed and Long Lance appeared.

"I want him to stay, watch, and report," Hilly said.

I made Sign. "Stay. Watch. Report."

He made Sign. "Report where?"

"Big canoe."

He nodded and melted. We got into Hilly's hover and took off.

"Two things," I said. "No, three. I must have it out with Nat. I want a conference with the Group. You know where they're scattered. Collect them."

"And the third?"

"There can't be a hit. This brilliant son of a bitch has got to be saved."

Hilly smiled. "Then there's nothing to have out with Mrs. Curzon." He began to hum "Hatikvah."

13

I scraped up all I could on short notice," Hillel said. "We're meeting in Retchvic. We can't be eavesdropped in Iceland."

"D'you think the Extro network tailed you to them?"

"Barely an outside chance. I used cash only; no ID. Your cash, by the way."

"Mine?"

"Capo Rip's. Mrs. Curzon handed it over to me."

"How much?"

"About a million and a half. I have the balance waiting for you."

"Who'd you get from the Group?"

"M'bantu, Tosca, Domino, Ampersand, Queenie, Herb Wells, and No-Name."

"Oh, God! Not that nothing."

"Then you, of course, myself, and our host, Erik the Red."

Y. Erik owns most of Greenland and Iceland. He has geyser power and probably owns half the hot springs in this heat-hungry world.

"No Poulos?"

"The Greek's not coming."

"More important business?"

"No."

"You couldn't get in touch with him?"

"No."

"That's not like you, Hilly."

"No one will ever get in touch with him again."

"What!"

"He's dead."

"What? No. Not Poulos...."

"A Malay kris through the heart."

I was speechless. At last I stammered, "I—No. Not the Syndicate. No. It couldn't happen. He's too brilliant—careful—aware...."

"Not enough for the Rajah."

"Where did it—"

"Calcutta. Last week."

"Give me a moment, Hilly...."

"All the time you need."

When I came below from the deck I washed my mouth and face. I was in control again. "You said a Malay kris. How do you know?"

"Left in his heart."

"But Malay?"

"A hired assassin. These kinks bind up their putz until they're in agony and then carry out the holy mission. The local *polizei* say it was planned like a commando raid, with support, flankers, and backups. God knows how many first-class jimps the Rajah has on his payroll. The Greek must have been closing in on him, and he didn't stand a chance."

"If the Rajah can hit the Greek—"

"We're all as good as dead. How do you feel now? I know because it took me the same way in Calcutta. Have you got the strength to give me your news?"

"I can try," I said heavily.

"Good man. Go ahead. Gescheft is gescheft. Business is business, and it's our only salvation."

"You are R, as usual. There was nothing to have out with Nat. She's all for stopping our brother and saving him. She just didn't want to go the hit route. I'll bring her along to Retchvic." It was painful, talking.

"Good. And?"

"Long Lance came back to the big canoe day before yesterday. Nothing to report. Sequoya is still down there educating his babies."

"Even better. We can go on using transport safely while he's separated from the Extro. The trouble is, we don't know when he'll come up again, so we'll have to move fast. Where are the braves?" Hilly was v. brisk. It helped.

"Nat sent them back to Erie."

"Gung. Let's move it to Iceland."

"What about this big canoe?"

"Gottenu! Who cares? We'll leave it. Maybe it'll start another Sargasso Sea in Lake Mitch. We're for Retchvic."

Erik's pleasance in Iceland was a giant, steaming greenhouse festooned with exotic tropical plants. The guests from the Group were all there when we arrived and all in character; but as I've said, we're all characters and always in character. A few touches: A drab little woman you wouldn't look at twice was Tosca, the compelling actress who has been sweeping the media for generations with her electrifying performances. The flamboyant diva in eye-catching costume was Queenie in drag. We have never been able to persuade him to undergo a transsex transformation. He says he prefers remaining a faggot. Erik isn't red and isn't even a Scandy. He looks like a jolly Karl Marx.

There were greetings, of course, and the gallant M'bantu

put Natoma on his arm and escorted her around, introducing her. He was particularly proud of the tremendous progress she'd made with her XX. I began to wonder whether I should shift my apprehensions from the Greek to the Zulu. Certainly both of them outclassed me, but when you get right down to it every member of the Group outclassed me with the exception of the nothing No-Name who now seemed on the verge of falling into a pitcher plant.

"This is Guig's meeting," Hilly said casually, "but I'd better brief you first. You'll all recall that when I contacted you I handed you a slip of paper asking you to come to Erik's immediately on an urgent matter. It warned you not to speak and to use cash transport without ID so that you couldn't be traced. I didn't use ear-beads or cassettes for a most interesting reason. The whole planet is enmeshed in the damndest electronic bugging network conceivable, the result of Guig's recruitment of our newest and most splendid Group member. He'll be our pride, but presently he's created a crisis which you know about, more or less. Here's the complete scene." Hilly gave it to them, fast and acute. Then he turned the meeting over to me. I got to my feet and here is the conference, names withheld on the grounds of Group privilege.

"First, I must reenforce what the Jew has told you. The renegade is a savage, dangerous enemy. The murder of Poulos demonstrates that, and no one knows who will be next if we don't stop him."

"You don't call him the Rajah?"

"No. I'm not so sure as Hilly because the Rajah doesn't make sense to me as a vendettist. Why? There's no reason I can think of. I hold that it might be anyone, including myself. Trust no one. Be on your guard."

"D'you think it might be Guess?"

"Not likely. He's merely the human switchboard that makes all this possible. The problem: How do you kill the switchboard? Shut up, Nat. You don't know where I'm headed."

"Poison is out. Just an hors d'oeuvre."

"So is gas."

"It's got to be an external killing."

"A stab through the heart, like Poulos."

"Or a burn."

"Blow him up, like the attempt on Guig."

"Simple beheading."

"Ugh!"

"Yes, we know. You nearly accompanied Danton in the tumbril."

"Whatever happened to Dr. Guillotine, by the way?"

"Died in bed, not regretted."

"If you want a neat, tasteful death, shoot Guess into space."

"How would that kill him?"

"Radiation exposure. Vacuum malnutrition. Or he might explode from internal air pressure."

"Be realistic. How can you shoot a naked man into space? Tie him to the nose of a rocket vehicle?"

"Then put him in a capsule and shoot him into the sun. That would ionize the package into a fizz."

"And how would we put him together again?"

"What?"

"That's the point. We can't lose him."

"Then why the talk about killing him?"

"To bring us face to face with the problem. How do we kill the switchboard without killing Guess? That's where I was headed, Nat."

"I apologize, Guig."

"It *is* a puzzle."

"Almost a paradox. How do you kill a man without killing him?"

"What about a time-shoot back six months so I can abort this damned crisis before it started?"

"It won't work."

"Why not, Herb?"

"You'll be a ghost."

"There ain't no such thing."

"I've tried it. I can't shoot a man into his own lifetime. The cosmos won't tolerate two identicals. One of them has to be a phantasma."

"Which?"

"The second."

"So possession is nine points of space-time, and we're back where we started. How do we abort the contact-catalyst without harming Guess?"

"You're not on target, Guig."

"N? W?"

"It isn't a question of killing the switchboard. Kill the computer."

"S! P! C! So obvious that it never occurred to me."

"You're too close to it. That's why you needed us."

"I'll deal some demurrers. The Guess-Extro symbiosis is unique. It should be explored."

"Too dangerous to delay. The situation is critical. Gottenu! I can feel the hot breath of the Rajah breathing down my neck."

"If the symbiosis is destroyed, a similar one may never occur again."

"The sacrifice must be made if we're to survive."

"If the Extro is killed have we any guarantee that it will stop the renegade?"

"It will. Not altogether, but to a great extent."

"How do you figure that?"

"He didn't start his war until *after* the Guess-Extro connection was established. When that's destroyed he'll be crippled; still deadly but manageable."

"The Group has always hated killing."

"N hatred for killing the renegade. He's a mad dog."

"Y. I only wish I knew why; it might make the problem easier to solve. Now let's tackle the next question: How do I get at the Extro?"

"You're taking this on yourself?"

"I must. I'm driven. How do I kill the Extro?"

"Fire. Explosion. Metal-burn Power cut. Etcetera."

"Without its knowledge that an attack is being mounted?"

"Are you sure that it will know?"

"That goddamn Squatter with its ragtag network knows everything we do, every move we make."

"Only provided Guess is in contact to make the circuitry possible."

"Have we any guarantee he'll remain buried in the salt mines?"

"N. We might try kidnapping Guess."

"How, without the knowledge of the Extro? The moment we haul Guess up to the surface that spying network will be activated, and you know goddamn well that a Moleman can't be drugged unconscious."

"You're driving too hard, Guig. Let's cool it."

"I can't. When I think of Fee-5 and Poulos, the Shortie killings, the—No, I'll cool it. Back to business. Calmly. The Extro knows everything we do and maybe everything we think. What can I use to outflank it?"

"Hic-Haec-Hoc," No-Name said.

My jaw dropped. This? From Mr. Nothing? Outclassed even by him.

"He can't think. He can't speak. He's a blank."

"But he obeys signs. Thank you, No-Name. Thank you all. If Sam Pepys can be located and can tell me where to locate Hic, I'll bring him and we'll try."

But I tried the time-shot first, anyway, and H. G. Wells was right; I was a ghost, invisible and inaudible. Worse, I was like a two-dimensional phone projection. I oozed. I oozed through bods and buildings and I felt damned sorry for ghosts. Herb and I had pinpointed my spot very carefully and I was shot to JPL and oozed my way to the astrochem lab just as the crowd of afflicted stockholders was hacking and coughing its way out right through me. Uncanny.

When I oozed in, Edison was barking with laughter. "That damn fool girl brought you fuming nitric acid. Fuming. And the fumes have turned this room into one big nitric-acid bath. Everything's being eaten away."

"Did you see her do it? Did you see the label? Why didn't you stop her?" The Chief sounded furious.

"No. No, and no. I've deduced it. Not an Emergent, just a Resultant."

"Dear God! Dear God! I've ruined the whole pitch to the U-Con crowd."

Suddenly me did the take and let out a yell. I didn't like his looks but I suppose nobody likes their own looks.

"What's the matter, Guig?" the Group called. "Are you hurt?"

"No, you damn fools, and that's why I'm hollering. I'm Grand Guignol triumphant. Don't you understand? Why didn't he know it was fuming nitric acid? Why didn't he choke on the fumes? Why isn't he eaten away now? Why wasn't he forced to run out with Fee and the rest? Think about it while I revel."

After a long moment, the Syndicate said, "I never believed in your campaign, Guig. I apologize. It was a million to one against, so I hope you'll pardon me."

"You're pardoned. You're all pardoned. We've got another Molecular Man. We've got a brand new beautiful Moleman. Still there, Uncas?"

"I can't understand a word you're saying."

"Take a deep breath of nitric. Belt down a stiff shot. Do anything you like to celebrate. Welcome to the Group."

And as we all left the astrochem and joined the hacking stockholders outside, he disappeared, but this time the pseudo-me followed him as he slipped out through a side iris and loped down a ramp, the ghost following and hollering. What I said was shouted and screamed: *"Chief, it's me, Guig. Listen! Hear me! Danger ahead. Hear?"*

He didn't hear me, see me, or feel me; just went about his pokerface excape. It was one of the most frustrating and exasperating experiences of my life, and I was relieved when Herbie Wells' mantis snatched me back. Herb saw my expression and shrugged helplessly.

"I told you it was a lemon," he said.

So Natoma and I waited on standby for the outjet to Saturn VI, otherwise known as the moon, Titan. Standby because it was strictly a bribe transaction. We submitted to the search for flammable materials without complaint. Titan has a methane atmosphere, poisonous and explosive when spiked with fluorine. Methane is also known as marsh gas, produced by the decomposition of organic matter.

People who don't travel think all satellites are alike; rocky, sandy, volcanic. Titan is a mass of frozen organic material, and cosmologists are still arguing about that. Was the sun hotter? Was Titan an inner planet (it's bigger than Terra's moon) snatched by Jupiter and delivered to Saturn without charge? Was it seeded by cosmonauts from deep space ages ago who abandoned our solar system in disgust?

Natoma came along, not because I needed her for Hic-Haec-Hoc but because you don't shoot Saturn in a week, it's more like a month and there's a limit. The standby wasn't too boring. We were entertained by the broadcast of Ice-O-Rama, a penguin sitcom. Zitzcom has just discovered that his daughter, Ritzcom, has accepted an invitation from Witzcom to spend the night with him on an iceberg. There are hilarious complications. The antarctic night lasts three months, and Zitzcom doesn't know that it was Ritzcom's twin sister, Titzcom, who accepted the invitation in a snit because her beau, Fitzcom, didn't invite her to the penguin slide-in. Oh, bbls of laughs.

I'd warned Nat that Titan was a mining moon (they quarry the organic layer and ship it out in frozen blocks) but she didn't really understand until we'd boarded the freighter and located our private cabin for two. That was the bribe. No passengers; no crew; just deck officers and no doubt a couple of them had been willing to doss anywhere for a substantial cut. The freighter stank. The compost it shipped in-jet left a permanent aroma of the grave.

I'd been smart enough to be prepared; a huge wicker hamper with enough deli for months, clean linen and blankets. A freighter to Saturn is no luxury jet, and although there's a captain there's no such thing as a captain's table, a steward, formal meals. It's all catch-as-catch-can, with the staff helping itself to the frozen food and drink stocks whenever so inclined. You merely endure and survive at the minimum, which is another reason why Titan will always remain a mining moon.

We stayed in our tiny cabin a lot, talking, talking, talking. So much to catch up on. Natoma grieved with me over Poulos and tried to cheer me up. She wanted to know all about CNA-Drone. I told her all I could about DNA-Cloning, which wasn't much, but then the technique isn't much, still in its infancy. Then she insisted on knowing why I had deep depressions, and what big L was. I had to tell her all about Lepcer.

"You must never, never, *never* run another physical risk," she said severely.

"Not even for your sake?"

"Most of all *never* for my sake. There will be no big L this time. I know it because I have second sight, all the Guess women do, but if you ever run a risk again I'll have you roasted over a slow fire. You'll wish you had the big L then."

"Yes'm," I said meekly. "That linear explosion wasn't my fault, you know."

She pronounced a Cherokee word that would probably have shocked our brother.

Nat had been boning up, practicing reading XX. "Titan is the largest of Saturn's satellites," she reported. "It is seven hundred and fifty-nine thousands miles distant from Saturn. Its sidereal period is—I don't know what that is."

"How long it takes to go around."

"Is fifteen dot nine four five days. The inclination of its orbit to the ring plane—I looked those words up—is twenty apostrophe. Its—"

"No, darling. That's the astronomer's symbol for minutes. They measure space in degrees, minutes, and seconds. A degree is a little zero. A minute is an apostrophe, and a second is a quotation mark."

"Thank you. Its diameter is three thousand five hundred and fifty miles, and it was discovered by—by—I don't know how to pronounce this name. It's not in the dictionary."

"Let me see. Oh. Not many people do. Huyghens. Higenz. He was a very great Dutch scientist a long time ago. Thank you, love. Now I know all about Titan."

She wanted to ask questions but I promised to take her to what used to be Holland and show her all the sights that still remained, including Hi-genz' birthplace, if it still existed. Saturn was quite a sight itself as it came looming up. Nat had already charmed her way onto the flight deck and would spend hours staring at the cold, belted, spotted disk and the widening rings inclined ten little zero.

Alas, only the two inner rings remain. Despite violent protests by ecologists and cosmologists, the Better Building Conglomerate had been permitted to harvest the third outer ring for some kind of better building aggregate. There was a housing crisis and BBC paid enormous taxes. One infuriated astronomer had been euthanized for burning the chairman of the board.

If you think the inspection was tough when we embarked you should have seen what we went through when we arrived. As we came down the long tunnel to Mine City we were searched over and over again for combustibles, quasicombustibles, ferrous metals, anything that could produce a spark or a flame. Titan lived on a perpetual brink of disaster. One spark outside and the methane atmosphere could turn the moon into a nova.

The city was freaky. This is how it was born: The prospectors quarried out the frozen marsh compost to a depth of fifty feet. When it extended for a square mile, the crater was roofed over with plastic by ORGASM (The Organic Systems and Manure Company, Ltd). Narrow streets were blocked out in a rectilinear pattern, houses were built, and there was your mining town on your explosive mining moon. It was dark; the sun was no more than a brilliant arc light, but it did receive a lovely thermal glow from Mama Saturn. It was damp to eliminate any chances of electrostatic sparks. It stank of halogens and methane and the compost choppers.

No hotel, of course, but a residence for visiting clients with clout. I bluffed our way in. "I am Edward Curzon of I. G. Farben, and I cannot understand why you did not receive my message from Ceres. Kindly contact Directeur Poulos Poulos to verify." I also tipped in a lordly manner and did what it had taken me years to learn; behaved quietly as though I took it for granted that my orders would be obeyed. They obey.

I found Hic easily enough on the fourth day. I had a nerve-fire finder and all I had to do was move out beyond the quarrymen in each quarter—checking production techniques, you understand—and take a con. On Day Four the finder pointed and I followed it, hopping and galloping, for about ten miles until I came to a compost hut, rather like the sod houses the primitive pioneers used to build for themselves in nineteenth-century America. It was glittering with crystals of ammonia, as was all Titan. There were spectacular meteorite cracks and craters in the ice cover, and volcanic magma boiled up ("boiled" in the relative sense; Titan's mean temperature is minus one hundred and thirty little zero Celsius) forming pools of liquid methane. Saturn was rising dramatically behind the hovel, and Hic-Haec-Hoc was crouched inside like a predator about to spring on his prey.

Now, I know the popular impression. Say 'Neanderthal"
to anyone and an instant image of a caveman carrying a
club and dragging a lady by the hair pops into their mind.
Well, the Neanderthalers couldn't do much carrying or dragging; their thumbs were badly opposed. They were incapable
of speech because of the inadequate musculature of mouth
and throat. Anthropologists are still arguing about whether
it was speech and the thumb that produced Homo sapiens.
Certainly, Homo neanderthalensis had the equivalent cranial
capacity; it just never developed. If you can read XX, look
up Homo neanderthalensis and you'll have some idea of
what Hic looked like; a punch-drunk, prizefighting loser.
But strong. And like most animals, he lived a life of constant
terror.

I'd removed my helmet but I don't know whether he
recognized or remembered me. As No-Name said, he can't
think; but he understood my grunts and signs. I'd been farsighted enough to fill a pocket with sweets and every time
he opened his mouth I popped one in, which delighted him.
That's how the Russians used to reward their trained bears.

It was one hell of a session. I could give you the signs
in diagram but you wouldn't understand them. I could give
you the grunts in phonetic symbols but they would be
meaningless to you. But Hic understood. It's true that he
can't think, but only in the sense of memory and rational
sequence. He can absorb and understand one idea at a time.
How long it remains with him depends on how soon it's
dispossessed by survival terror. The sweets helped.

After I'd signed, grunted, bullied, and sweeted him into
obedience it was hell getting Hic into the extra thermal I'd
packed out, but he couldn't come in out of the methane
naked. Questions would be asked. I got him sacked at last
and back we schlepped to Mine City, Colossus of Compost,

Mother of Methane, Daughter of Destruction, with the two-ringed Saturn behind us. Damn Sequoya, he was right about Mankind-F. How can you fight a bod you agree with?

After a careful inspection Natoma said, "He must be shaved from top to bottom. We'll take him back as your feebleminded brother." She looked at me perplexedly. "Guig, how the devil did he ever get out here?"

"Stowaway, probably. A Moleman can endure months of that cold, and he ate anything that was handy."

Between signs and sweets we managed to bathe and shave Hic-Haec-Hoc. Natoma decorated him with graffiti which made him look like an average. Hic liked Nat and was comfortable with her. I think maybe he never had a mother. On the other hand he also liked his bath. I'm sure he never had one before.

He slept on the floor of our cabin during the freighter in-jet. Only one trouble; he didn't like any of our hamper food and the compost stench made him hungry. I couldn't get any for him—all sealed in the freight hull—and he started eating the most lunatic things; our linen, fire extinguishers, luggage, books, playing cards. We had to keep a constant watch (he ate my watch, by the way) or he might have chewed a hole in the freighter hull.

He'd become accustomed to Titan's methane atmostphere and didn't like the air in the jet. Natoma took care of that by spraying insecticide up his nose. Altogether, a problem child, and he was so brute-strong that you had to be cautious with him. But Natoma handled him beautifully. I think her experiences with the Erie warriors probably gave her the expertise.

As we started our approach to Earth, Natoma gave a thank-you luncheon party for the deck officers. She used the last of our provisions and even heated some of them up, a tremendous luxury. How did she do it on a jet where there were no ignition tools? She made a bow-drill and sawed away until she got an ember going. Shredded plastic for tinder. Chunks of plastic for fuel. And then a fire in an aluminum basin. No fool she. The officers were enchanted, and so appreciative that two of them proposed and all of them made plans to smuggle us out of the spaceport with no passport problems for my idiot "brother" who'd lost his on Titan. (And no warning to the Extro network which, of course, they knew nothing about.) We would be home free.

And when we put down we discovered that we'd acquired a hitchhiker.

14

At my age you learn to accept the unknowable with grace. You may ask, then, why the difficulty in accepting the Rajah, and the ease of accepting the spacehiker? Patent. The Rajah was the answer to a fact, an explanation which I could not yet accept because an integral part was missing. The hitchhiker made its appearance from an unknowable spacewhere. Neither explanations nor motivations were involved. It was a fact which could neither be denied nor fitted into the cosmic construct. That fact had to be accepted as *Ding an sich*, a thing in itself.

Impossible to name its original hatitat. Uranus, Neptune, or Pluto, which had not yet been visited, much less explored for indigenous fauna and flora? The asteroid belt? Perhaps a refugee from the halo of millions of comets shuttling in from space, around the sun and out again? It might even be a reject from some contrauniverse, spat into our system through a minuscule White Hole.

Metabolism? N Known. My hunch later—fed on the electromagnetic spectrum, which meant that out in space it was floating in a sea of food. Locomotion? N known. Possibly rides the stellar winds in space, which would account for its hitching a ride on the freighter; it couldn't buck the solar wind without help. Reproduction? N known, period. Reason for being? No living thing can answer that. Description?

Well, when we disembarked from the freighter there it was, clinging to the hull, to the incredulity of the officers and the jetport mechs. It reminded me of a myxomycete, a "slime mold" I'd studied at Trinity College; if it was anything analogous to that order the reproduction question was answered; by spore formation. It was a giant flat slab of cytoplasm, about the size of a 3 × 5 scatter rug, translucent, and you could see thousands of nuclei inside, all connected with a demented lacework of I don't know what. And the nuclei twinkled at you as though the thing were sharing a joke.

Naturally I insisted on taking it along with us, to Natoma's horror—it filled her with revulsion—but Hic-Haec-Hoc fell in love with Twinkles and slung it over his shoulders like a cape. Twinkles extruded its edges to get comfortable and blinked at Hic, and damned if Hic didn't blink back. I was glad that Hic had at last found a friend. Twink wasn't immobile. It would take off from Hic, flapping its edges like a buzzard, and go exploring. Then it would return and they had long conversations.

We'd put down just outside Mexas City, which had ordered the compost, and we took a transit into the city to catch a linear north. The transit crashed and Nat leaped to shield me. My pride was hurt. She snapped, "Big L," and that settled that. We flagged a free hire-pogo ambling back from the port and instead of landing in Mexas City it pancaked with a smash. My wife again. At the linear port a fuel reserve blew up and we had to scatter. I'd twigged by this time.

"He's up," I said to Natoma.

She nodded silently. She knew who and what I meant, and it hurt her.

"The Extro network is in action again," I said.

"But how does it know where we are?"

"The freighter probably snitched. Now the network is gunning for us."

"We're being attacked?"

"Y. All out."

"What do we do?"

"Stay away from machines and electronics. Go north on foot."

"A thousand miles?"

"Maybe we can dig up some silent transport on the way."

"But won't Mexas City report where we're going?"

"N. Only that we're leaving. They won't know where we're going and we're not going to let them know. This is going to be a tough ordeal for us. From here on we don't talk, not a word. Hic will lead us; the Extro can't pick up anything from him, and I'll instruct him with signs." I got out a slip of paper (a banknote, actually) and wrote: *And any time we pass a piece of electronics we smash it.*

She nodded again and we moved it out of Mexas City, me silently and patiently instructing Hic-Haec-Hoc. He finally got the idea, took the lead, and we became a lost army of three. I didn't count Twink.

It was v. interesting. I could tell when we were approaching a town of any size when its broadcasts appeared, flickering before us like a mirage. We hoofed it to Queretaro where our Fearful Leader was sent in and picked up three horses. I'd given him cash along with my instructions but he probably didn't know what it was for, and most assuredly stole the nags. We rode bareback until San Luis Potosi where Hic stole a small wagon. Nat plaited makeshift cords for a makeshift harness. In Durango the Fearful Leader didn't do so well. I'd grunted and signed *"knives"* to him. Apparently he didn't get the message. He brought us two hammers and a shingling hatchet, but at least that made the destruction easier.

The army was spreading a trail of electronic demolition like Sherman's March to the Sea, but the network couldn't know it was us; machines are always breaking down for the sake of deserving Repair Syndicates. We camped nights with a sagebrush fire and roasted everything Hic and I could forage. It was tough. We had no cooking or eating utensils. We got water by crushing cactuses, century plants, and prickly pears between flat stones, but we had nothing to store it in.

Then we got a break. We passed an abandoned dump. I explored the rusting, moldering rubbish and, hallelujah! produced cooking and eating tools from forgotten automobile parts; two deep old fenders, eight hubcaps (for plates), and a gasoline tank which I had to hammer loose from the remains of a chassis. That was for water storage. I hammered one of the fenders flattish for a frypan, and raised the sides of the other for a stewpot. We were in business.

Now we really foraged. Natoma taught me how to catch rabbits, Indian-style. When she spotted a big jack sitting up and surveying the terrain, she'd give me the sign and I'd sort of meander past, not getting within spooking distance. The jack would keep his eyes on me suspiciously while I wandered about aimlessly. Meanwhile Nat was creeping up on him from behind. A quick grab and she had him. Not always, but often enough.

We had a windfall once. We'd just crossed a dry arroyo when I noticed black clouds laced with lightning many miles to our left. I stopped the party, pointed to the distant storm, then to the arroyo, and lastly to the gas tank. We waited.

We waited. We waited. Then there was a distant rumble followed by a growing roar, and a foaming flash flood torrented down the arroyo. I washed the gas tank repeatedly and finally filled it. The water was full of sediment but it was potable. Then came the windfall; a thrashing, kicking sheep was born down to us by the tumbling water. I grabbed a leg. Natoma grabbed the other. We hauled it out. I now draw the curtain on the godawful business of butchering and skinning a sheep with a shingling hatchet.

Curiously enough, Twink didn't seem to need any food, and that's when I first began to suspect that it was feeding on something outlandish like high-tension wires. It had intelligence. After a week of watching Hic and me foraging it got a piece of the idea. It would blink at Fearful Leader—I wish I knew what language they were speaking—and take off. It would return with all sorts of junk clutched to its plasm; rocks, sage, dead branches, bleached bones, a bottle turned purple by the sun. . . . But one glorious evening it brought back a thirty-pound peccary. More hatchetwork.

Ozymandias crashed in on us the night we'd caught a twenty-pound armadillo and were wondering how to cook it. I don't exaggerate his advent. It was heralded by approaching bangs, crunches, breakage, flounderings; it sounded like a blind brontosaurus blundering through a jungle. Then he appeared in the firelight, threw his arms wide, knocking over a cactus, and nearly tripped into the fire.

Merlin nicknamed him Ozymandias, from the last sentence of Shelley's poem: *Round the decay of that colossal wreck, boundless and bare the lone and level sands stretch far away.* Oz was colossal. He stood two meters high and weighed 150 kilos. (That's 6"8" × 330 lbs.) He was a wreck. He's eaten and drunk his way around the entire system hundreds of times, leaving lone and level sands where once fine food flourished. He was also a wrecker. Oz can't go anywhere or do anything without breaking something, including himself. Hardly an asset for our expedition, but I was grateful to him for rallying 'round.

He's strickly a metropnik—you never find him outside a Center City—and his idea of action clothes for the wilderness was hilarious: heavy mountaineering boots, tasseled wool stockings, leather shorts, canvas safari coat, and a Tyrolean hat, including the shaving brush. But the dear maladroit had an impressive hunting knife hung from his hip, and that would come in handy. He had a rucksack slung over one shoulder, and from the bulges I could tell it was filled with wine bottles. From the spreading stain and steady red drip I could also tell that at least one of them had been wrecked already.

Ozymandias opened his mouth for a hearty roar of greeting but I signed him off. He shut his mouth, winced, and felt his tongue. Bit it, no doubt. From then on our conversation was conducted written on banknotes, like a couple of deaf Beethovens. I won't reproduce our shorthand, and anyway Oz broke my stylus. What it got down to was this: The Group knew I was fetching Hic-Haec-Hoc, and Pepys told them Hic was on Titan. Oz did something v. brilliant, he thought. He sent a reply-paid telex to the Titan authorities requesting the return date and destination of Edward Curzon and wife. *But*—clever, clever—Oz used an alias. The information was sent, and that's how the network knew. Oz picked up our trail of smashed electronics—he's not altogether a nudnik—and followed. He surmised that others might do the same.

He greeted us all the same way; hugged, kissed, and tossed us into the air. Oz is a tosser. You have to be prepared to land on your feet; he misses his catch as often as not. He fell in love with Natoma at first sight; he's always falling in love at first sight. He was taken aback by Twink but tossed it anyway. No kissing. When I asked his advice about the armadillo he was assured and brief. *Roast it in the shell*, he wrote. Then he inspected the rucksack, pulled out a broken bottle, and wept, pointing to the label. Vosne-Romanée Conti, the finest and rarest of burgundies. However, he cheered up the next moment, shrugged, laughed, tossed the broken bottle in the air, and threw it away, cutting himself in the process.

We had a transport difficulty with Ozymandias. He couldn't ride a horse; he'd break its back. Natoma got out of the wagon to ride the horse I'd been on (the other two were hitched to the wagon) and Oz got in. He overturned it, scattering our gear. We put it all together and Oz tried again. This time I made him crawl over the tail and sit. It worked. We were now a lost army of four, on the march.

We proceeded to Obregon where Hillel picked us up. He was in a hover, took one look at our scene, and didn't stop. Acute and fast. He'd no doubt smashed the instrumentation and I couldn't understand his exaggerated caution. He went straight on over the horizon as though he'd seen nothing. We heard an explosion and a half hour later Hilly came running back to us. Then I understood. His left arm was gone. I was aghast.

The Jew nodded and smiled.
The Rajah?
Y.
How?
Too complicated for writing. It was brilliant.
But you escaped.
At a price. Poulos was the warning.

Regeneration?
Perhaps. You're the next candidate. Be careful.
W me?
He's killing in descending order.

Hilly spoke a greeting to the horror-struck Natoma with his eyes, popped a handful of candy into Hic's mouth, patted Ozymandias on the cheek, and examined Twink with fascination. Twink had never come across a three-limbed Terran before and had to explore the Hebe. Hilly twitched through the examination as though he were receiving electric shocks. Then he took off and was gone for a few hours while we rested and I tried to stop Natoma from crying. Oz produced a flute d'amour from his rucksack and played sweet, mellow sounds.

Hilly rode back on a vintage bicycle which he'd promoted somehow, and the army continued on to Chihuahua where M'bantu joined the party. Five deaf Beethovens. M'b left us and returned, riding a donkey, his long legs scraping the ground. Twink was bewildered by M'bantu's color and had to examine, naturally. The Zulu understood and immediately stripped. He twitched and jerked through the inspection and finally went over in a dead faint. We pulled Twink off his head and hovered over the Zulu, doing things, until he recovered consciousness. When he'd regained some strength I wrote, *Suffocated?*

N. Brain drain. Lost brain energy.
Sucked out by it?
Y.
Electro nerve charge?
Y. Don't let it come near you naked.
W. naked?
Clothes insulate a little.

By now our silent army was foraging a path nearly a

half mile wide and destroying any possible tattletale machine. M'bantu was an old hand at living off the land and brought in a delightful change of diet; wild yams, wild onions, wild parsley, lily bulbs, parsnip, and strange roots. Hilly, smart as ever, had the sense to bring in a few pounds of rock salt. I must esplain that although a Moleman can consume anything, we do prefer good food. Ozymandias proved himself to be a master chef and improvisor.

Erik the Red joined us outside Hermosillo, and that will give you some idea of the continuous zigzag course we were pursuing. We had to cross the Rio de la Concepcion to get to Nogales. The river was in flood. We were grateful for the chance to have a wash, but we had to leave all our heavy gear behind. We hoped to live off the land as before. We were dreamers.

The farther north we got the more pop. ex. we encountered plus all the mecho-electronic amenities which civilized people demand and take for granted today. We started to travel by night, holing up in obscure places by day, always in the same deadly silence. No more smashing anything. Too much to destroy. We turned into Artful Dodgers.

Between Chula Vista Del Mar and San Diego Erik left us one rest period and returned an hour later and gestured us to follow him. We follow. He led us to a railroad track and an abandoned hand-flatcar. We got on and began pumping our way north, taking turns. It was exhausting work and I was grateful when we ran out of track south of San Diego.

We camped and M'bantu left us. He returned, yanking a camel, two zebras, and a buffalo after him, persuading them to cooperate in animal language. No doubt stolen from the San Diego Zoo. We were now mounted again. North to San Clemente (now a national shrine) where Oz left us and returned slightly damaged with emphatic gestures to follow him. We obey. He led us to a wharf and an empty lifeboat. We rowed north up the coast. Exhausting work and murder on the hands and ass. Thank heaven the leaky relic foundered off Laguna (another tribute to the Wrecker) and we had to swim ahore, me hauling Hic-Haec-Hoc in a cross-chest carry. He could breathe water but the idiot had never learned to swim.

We stripped to let our clothes dry in the sun and lay down to rest, with the exception of Twink, who took off to explore the sea. The last I saw of Twink before I fell asleep was a soaring up out of the water with a furious dolphin flopping away in its plasm. When I opened my eyes again there was a majestic diva in a scarlet caftan standing over us. Queenie.

"Well," he said. "Trespassing on my private cruising ground. I didn't know you were so well hung, G—" At this point he was cut off by Hilly's hand over his mouth. With a finger Hilly wrote in the sand, *N talk.*

W? Queenie wrote.

Extro.

&?

On way to kill it.

Knows you're here?

Hopefully, N.

That's why you can't talk?

Y. Or go near electronics.

Can help?

Y. Stay here and be conspicuous.

Always am.

Be more so now.

Decoy?

Y.

Hillel tramped out the sand-writing and Queenie sashayed off to be hit on the head by a live skate dropped by Twink. "You—You thing!" Queenie cried. He didn't know how right he was. The beach was littered with Twink's catches.

I felt it was my turn to promote some silent transport. I got into my tutta and took off inland. When I returned two hours later they were all up, dried out, dressed, and having a ball chattering with each other on the sand. I made *suivez-moi* gestures and they followed me to a dilapidated airport where a huge sign in seven languages read: SEE THE SIGHTS SLOW AND COMFY IN A IZVOZCHIK GLIGER. N GUARANTEE. N LIABILITY. N REFUNDS.

We got into the sailplane, the pilot followed, counted head, nodded, and sat down at the controls. A decrepit World War II jet hooked onto us with a hundred-yard cable, took off, and dragged the gliger after it. At two thousand feet it unhooked and went home and we were free to see the sights slow and comfy. I nodded to M'bantu, who yanked the pilot out of his seat and dragged him aft while I replaced the pilot at the controls.

This was old hat for me. Fact, not boasting. I'd won a dozen gliger rallyes when I was a kid of seventy. I rode the thermal updrafts and the southwest wind north while the pilot raged and the Zulu soothed him with a fist. Although the sailplane was mute none of us spoke. It had become a habit.

Damn if I didn't land in the same TV dump where I'd taken two girls home ages ago. It was a messy putdown but no one was hurt except the gliger. We left the pilot burning for satisfaction and took off, but I did see the Red toss a packet of bills onto his chest before he left the plane. We slud out of the dump and through streets to the tepee where the three wolves were still on guard. M'bantu spoke to them and they let us enter. I expected to find Sequoya there. N. Was he up or down?

Now I accelerated. I left in silence, went and bought a multiburner, a cc of Codeine-Curarine, a jolter, and a utilities map, still in silence. I returned to the tepee, jolted myself with a massive shot, and memorized the map. I had half an hour before the Codeine-Curarine would hit me. When I had the map by heart I gave my perplexed companions a smile of confidence, which I did not feel, motioned to Hic to follow me, and left.

I was able to get Hic to the sewer manhole before the drug hit me. He was still carrying Twink on him but I didn't object. I wasn't going to break up a beautiful friendship. We went down into the sewer and started crawling toward Union Carbide when the Codiene-Curarine bombed me.

What it does is splinter the psyche. I was fifteen, twenty, fifty people with their memories and hang-ups; dreaming, angry, thrusting, frightened. I was a population. If the Extro network was aware of me it would have as much trouble sorting out who I was and what I was up to as it would have with Hic-Haec-Hoc. Codeine-Curarine is deadly fatal, but not for a Moleman. However, a lot of Shorties shoot it for that one last kick.

The one percent of the realsie me led us through the sewer, counting yardage until we came to the approx. spot. Out the burner and cut hatch through top. Not bad. Plastic conduit N far off. Ear to. Rushing wind. Exhaust from Extro complex air-con. Burn. In. Crawl. *La mia mamma mi vuol bene. Einen zum Ritter schlagen. Oh, Daddy, I want to die. L'enlevement des Sabines. Shtoh nah stolyeh? Hold on thar, stranger. Una historia insipida. Your son will never walk again. How do you feel about that? Merde. Agooga, agooga, agooga. Like sing out dulce Spangland.*

Knock/oh jazz/head/oh jazz/against grille/this is the consequence/look/of ill-advised asperity/computer complex below/arte magistra/empy W?/Vrroom/grille must go/give me liberty/too strong for me/or give me/out burner/burn/or give me W?/pull grille back/slide out and drop ten feet to floor followed by gorill who probably/sholem aleichem/ wants to mug me/look around look around nothing in complex W? H?

Look at gorill. Look familiar. Punch-drunk fighter. One percent me now becoming ten percent. Very nice edge, Capo Rip always said. Who? Rings a bell. I'm dying, Egypt. N, can't kill a brother. A what? But going to kill one now. N. The Extro. Kill the Extro. Si. Oui. Ja. Kill the Extro. Hic, kill the Extro. Why we're here. Hic, with your bare hands; rip, tear, break, smash. Hic, kill the Extro. That's it over there, center. And Sequoya came out from beyond the Extro. Suddenly I was all me.

"Hi, Guig," he said pleasantly. The three cryos came out and joined him, emitting their radar music. They were wearing maladroit homemade coveralls.

"Hi, Geronimo," I said, trying to match his genialdom. "You knew I was coming?"

"Hell, no! We picked something up from the conduit through cable crosstalk but it sounded like a hundred bods. You?"

"Y. Then you *can* read our minds?"

"Y. How'd you turn yourself into a mob?"

"Codeine-Curarine."

"Brilliant! Listen, Guig, I've been plagued by lunacy from the Extro ever since I came up. You?"

"N."

"Who's that with you?"

"Oldest member of the Group. Hic-Haec-Hoc."

"Ah, yes. The Neanderthaler. What's that cape-thing on his back?"

"A creature we brought back from space."

"No! You don't mean to tell me—"

"I do. Highly advanced exobiology for you to research, if you can persuade Tycho to let you keep it."

At this moment the broadcasts began their regular carousel of commercials, and the complex filled with men, women, girls, children, doctors, lawyers, cartoon characters, all selling something. It was bedlam and it drove Twink mad with curiosity. It took off to examine the host, but since they were only three-dimensional illusions Twink kept flapping through them.

"I've been waiting for you for ages, Guig."

"Didn't you know where I was?"

"Not after Mexas City." He hesitated. "How is she?"

"Fine. Still angry with our naughty brother."

"She has a temper."

"Why wait for me here, Chief?"

"I had a lot of work, weeks of it, debugging a program for the production of hermos here on Earth. And I knew you'd show up, sooner or later."

"D'you know why?"

"To make a deal with me and the Extro."

"Including the Rajah?"

"Who?"

"Ah! Then you don't know his identity yet. The renegade killer who's joined forces with the Extro to use you. He's murdered Poulos. He nearly got Hillel. I'm probably next." I turned to Hic and made forceful signs and grunts. He got the idea again, at last, and headed for the Extro. The Injun was perplexed.

"What's all this, Guig?"

"Not a deal, a hit. We're going to take the monkey off your back. We're going to kill the Extro."

He let out a yell that scattered the frightened cryos and made a dive at Hic, who was attacking the panels and fascia of the damned machine with his powerful hands. I made a dive at Guess, tackled him knee-high, and pulled him down.

There was no need for Sequoya to defend the computer; it had heard everything I said and was defending itself. Lights were shattering, with the fragments aimed downward; the air-cond blew up, more shrapnel; electronic locks on doors and software files burst and barraged us, circuits shorted and high-tension cables came sizzling down. Then the satellite computers were sacrificed. They began to blow up, and it seemed that the Extro would sacrifice every human in the complex, too.

An animal howl from Hic cut through the darkness and dementia. Guess and I froze and stared. One panel had been ripped from the Extro and we saw a lion within, glaring at us. The commercial carousel cast a confusing kaleidoscopic light on it. After a moment I saw that the lion was standing on its hind legs. After another I saw that it was a man wearing a lion mask. And then I realized it wasn't a mask. It was a deformed face.

"Oh God! The big L."

"What, Guig? What? What?"

The Chief and I climbed to our feet. "Lepcer . . . The final leonine stage. . . . It. . . . He. . . ."

He shambled out of a dim clearing in the Extro that looked like a small camp walled with electronic units. He was crook-gaited and spastic, yet with ominous power; the strength that comes with loss of control and the agonizing hypersensitivity of terminal Lepcer, the honing of the senses that precedes final anesthesia. And he stank. He filled the center with his big L. Hic-Haec-Hoc whined and disappeared.

"So many years since the spa, my dear Curzon," the Rajah said, poised and courteous as ever. His voice was hoarse and broken, but still singsong. My mind squealed and darted, trying to escape what had to be faced.

"And this, of course, is the latest addition to the beautiful Group. I was beautiful myself once. Can you believe it, Dr. Guess? Yes, I know you. I have been watching you from the shadows for some time. I have been watching the entire Group. Give Dr. Guess my name, Curzon. My name and rank."

It took all my courage to speak. "His Serene Highness, Prince Mahadeva Kauravas Bhina Arjuna, Maharajah of Bharat. The Group calls him the Rajah."

"Delighted, Dr. Guess. I do not offer to shake hands or smite palms. Royal princes do not so greet commoners. It might be permitted to kiss my hand, but the touch of my skin is loathsome, even to myself. My dear Curzon, you did not tell him that I am also the avatar, the transfiguration of Siva on Earth."

"I didn't know, sir. Apologies." My heart was watery but I was not to be outdone in poise. "So the renegade is really you, your Serene Highness. I could not believe it when Hillel told me."

"Renegade, Curzon? Only a Jew unbeliever would say that. God, Curzon." Abruptly he bawled, "God, Curzon. The divine Siva. *We are Siva!*"

I was convinced at last. Lepcer was the missing factor. The big L had turned an exquisite into a malignant enemy; stalking, lurking, destroying, literally a lion. This was the animal Long Lance had seen in the salt caverns. This was what had spooked the cryos and was deranging the Extro.

"I congratulate you on your choice of a hiding place, Rajah," I said. "Your command post at the center of action? No one would ever dream of looking for you here. How did you make room for yourself in that damned clutter?"

"Discarded a few units, Curzon. It was less than a prefrontal lobotomy for the Extro, although it protested. Why is your pulse chattering, Dr. Guess? Are you fearful of Siva? Deny nothing. I hear it. I see it. A god senses all; everything is known, and this is why Siva's destruction and creation are received with humility and love. Yes, humility and love for my destruction and regeneration of the void."

"God in heaven!" I burst out. I was shaking. "Where is the regeneration for Fee, Poulos, Hillel's arm, my home. Our—"

"Alas, not the little girl. I regret I did not destroy her. That was before my advent. The Greek, yes; a beautiful death. The Jew escaped me, but not a second time. No one escapes Siva twice."

"Alas, not the little girl?" Sequoya repeated in a choked voice. "You regret you did not—! Alas?"

"Humility and love, Dr. Guess. It is the true worship of Siva." Suddenly he raged in the Chief's face. *"Humility and love! I am the all, the one, the destruction and regeneration, and the linga is my sacred symbol. See! See with humility and love."*

He displayed his enormous, rotting symbol. We backed away in revulsion.

Abruptly the rage was replaced by sweet reason. "You will love me even as I destroy you, for I am the maker of miracles by virtue of the penance and meditation of fifty years."

"You've suffered from Lepcer for half a century, Rajah? I—" But I was stammering so badly that I had to stop.

The lion head nodded graciously. The lion face almost smiled. "It is permitted to address me by that name, my dear Curzon. Siva is only one of our thousand names. Above all, we prefer Nataraja, the Cosmic Dancer. So we are most often idealized in sacred images."

He uttered a croaking, sawing song, *"Ga-ma pa-da-ma pa-ga-ma ga-ri-sani-sa-ni ga-ri-sa. . . ."* This is a slow 4/8 and 3/2 rhythm. Then faster, *"Di na a na di na a na di na a na ka a ga a ka ga dhina na dhina na dhina-gana. . . ."*

And he danced to it; solemn ritual stances, quick jerking movements, then pauses for poses; around us, around the Extro center, through the broadcast bedlam, through the debris and the crackling sparks of the shorted cables. He danced his cosmic dance with the convulsive frenzy of a spasmic rubber doll with arms, legs, hands and feet that seemed to crook the wrong way and flung their own debris. Each time he jerked his head left and right, tatters of hair scattered. Nails dropped off his fingers and toes. Each gasp for breath sprayed blood.

"This is the horror that's been using me?" Sequoya squeezed out.

"With the Extro," I mumbled. "They've been going steady."

"I'll take the goddamn machine. You take the damned god."

"Wilco. Give the word."

We were both in a fever. The Rajah swept up to us. *"Dhina na dhina na dhinagana. . . . "* The lion face glaring at us as hypnotic as the dance. The rubbery arms swung wide with tremendous power and knocked us apart.

"Now!" the Chief exploded, stumbled to the Extro, and

began tearing at it. The burner was slung around my neck and I swung it forward to make the hit. It had to be a brain or heart shot. Siva was posturing before me in a sacred pose, arms high, hands cocked down, but there was a katar in one hand, sidebars protecting the sides of the wrist, fist clenched around the crosspice, and the broad blade punched down at my heart. All that hypnotic singing and cosmic dancing for this one moment.

I was absolutely confounded, but the burner saved me. I'd swung it before my chest and the katar plunged through it and muscle-deep into me. The burner shattered, blew widdershins, and I went over backward with the Rajah all over me; one blunted hand crunching my neck, the katar thrusting at me like a goring bull. I thrashed desperately, trying to escape a severed throat or a split heart. I couldn't yell to Guess for help and I was blacking out when I was released as unexpectedly as I'd been attacked.

There was the Rajah, squirming and hissing in Hic's hands. Hic loyal? Helpful? Coming to my rescue? Imposs. It must have been the instinctive hatred and loathing that makes so many animals turn on their sick and rend them. Hic transferred his powerful grip to the lion head, held it firm, and whirled the body in the air in a tremendous circle around the neck. There was one *crack*. The Rajah's neck was broken.

I gimped to my feet again, staring. Hic had hit the wrong target, and yet it was the right one. Only I saw that there were two bodies. The other was Sequoya, with Twink wrapped around his head. Much later I reasoned that its electrotropism must have been attracted by the powerful combination of Uncas and the Extro; particularly after the frustration of the shadow broadcasts.

A strong voice spoke. "That's enough, Curzon. He's dead. Get that thing off."

"Dead? No. I wanted—" Then I looked around in bewilderment One of the cryos repeated, "Get that thing off."

"But—but you can't talk."

"We can now. We're the Extro. Get the thing off Guess. Quick, Curzon. Move!"

I pulled Twink off the Chief.

"And no more demolition. Don't let your friend start again."

"Give me a good reason."

"We're in control now. It's shifted to us. You know us. Will we permit it to go on making war?"

It had to be a quick decision and it was a tough one. I pulled Hic back from the Extro (he'd probably forgotten his mission anyway) and let him keep company with Twink again. The cryos knelt around the Chief and examined him with hands and ears.

"Dead, all right."

"Everything's stopped."

"No, the heart is still spasming."

"That's like the case with electrocution."

"We'll have to regulate it again. That's the least we can try."

I wondered whether they were speaking from their own knowledge or the Extro's; probably the latter, which was all right provided the hateful thing was properly humbled. They began an extraordinary cycle of operations. The Chief was pummeled, bent, flexed, stretched, loted, dangled, prone-pressured, and mouth-to-mouthed; again and again, always in the identical tempo, 78 to the minute. My own pulse was running much faster. At last they stopped and put ears to the Chief's chest.

"Nominal," they said. "We've got him back from the edge." They looked around with their blind eyes.

"I'm here," I said. "He's going to live?"

"For a long time. Do you trust us, Curzon?"

"I have to, don't I?"

"No. You can kill us easily. If that's the way you want it, get it over with now."

"After that, I trust you."

"Ta. We won't let you down. We'll make the Extro behave. Why lose it?"

"Why indeed."

"We're going to repay your trust. Give us all available data on Lepcer. Maybe the Extro can suggest a line of research leading to a remedy. Don't count on it?"

"Thank you."

"Try to get some viable tissue from the remains of that girl to us. It may not be too late for cloning. Don't count on it."

"Would you lovable freaks care for a few bars of 'Hail to the Chief'?"

They burst out laughing. "Take Guess, Curzon. He's all yours. Keep in touch."

I knelt alongside Guess. "Cherokee," I said, "it's me, your brother. Everything's going to be gung."

"Ha-ja-ja," he burbled.

"You're rid of the Extro. The cryos have taken it over and I believe they can be trusted to do right."

"Ha-ja-ja."

I looked at the cryos, who were busy restoring the damage Hic and the Chief had begun. "Hey, bods, he sounds like a baby."

"Oh, he is, Curzon. When the Extro pulled out it left nothing behind. He'll have to grow up all over again. Not to worry. He has plenty of time."

15

Hic had to help me carry Sequoya out. The Chief couldn't walk. He couldn't talk. He was helpless. And he peed and shat in his tutta; he'd have to be diapered. I was relieved to get out of the complex before the cryos asked me to get rid of the Rajah. I flagged a pogo, we hauled Tecumseh in and made the tepee in one jump. The Group was waiting there, worried and tense. When they saw us lug the infant in they were flabbergasted.

"It's all over now," I said wearily. "We can talk and think out loud. We can take transport. We can do any damn thing we please. No more war."

"But what happened to Guess?"

"He'll be his old self in about twenty years. Just now all he needs is cleaning up. Give me a stiff belt and I'll tell you the whole story."

I tell and they listen, taking turns looking over the six-foot baby. Natoma was so fascinated by the events and so relieved that our brother had come out of the crisis alive that she forgot to be upset by his regression. All of them were delighted by the end of the Rajah threat, particularly Hilly, and no wonder. I could see he wanted to thank Hic-Haec-Hoc, but he knew better. There was no doubt that the Neanderthaler had forgotten all about it by now.

I said, "I know you all want to leave and go about your

business, but please stay a little longer. I have one more mission and I may need your help afterward."

"What is it?" Ozymandias asked in an asthmatic voice as thick as his body.

I told them about the cryo offer.

"Too late," Hilly said. "I'm sorry. She's been in too long."

"I've got to try anyway. There's always hope."

"Not much."

"It's too dark, Guig. Dangerous. Wait until morning."

"The longer I delay, the less hope."

"Don't go, Edward. You'll never find her."

"I've got to try, Nat."

"Please listen to me. I—"

"Damn it, don't you think I know it's a ghoulish search?" I shouted. "I know it's a rotten job, but I've got to try and get a part of the body for DNA-Cloning. If you can't support me in my try because you're jealous or whatever, at least don't dissupport me, or whatever I mean."

"You've made yourself v. clear, Edward."

"R. Forgive my manners. I've had a hell of a day and the worst is yet to come."

"We'll go with you," M'bantu offered.

"Thank you, no. More than one would only make it easier for a patrol chopper to spot us. I'll go it alone. Sit tight, all. I'll probably need you for messenger service. Back in an hour."

I took a pogo to the edge of the burial ground and as I got out a chopper thrummed overhead playing its brilliant beam down and around. The light held on me for a moment and then moved on. I had no idea when the patrol would be back. It depended on how many private ops it had to police.

It was night. It was nightugly, not because of the fear

of death but from the revulsion of the living for rot and decay. You could smell the decomposition choking you as you approached; ammonia, nitrates, potash, phosphates, carrion putrefaction. Death couldn't be wasted these days; every end product of life went into compost.

El Arrivederci filled about five acres—the public composts occupied ten times that space—and used the concrete foundations of the old Waldorf West Hotel which had been torn down forty years ago to make room for an office complex never built. The two thousand evictees had blocked the entire undertaking with a squatters' rights lawsuit. The case had not yet come to trial and most of the parties concerned were rotting in composts themselves. Progress.

The foundations looked like a squared-off labyrinth; odd-sized boxes, squares, rectangles, even a few diamonds and pentagons, depending on what stress supports the original architects had designed. They were concrete walls, six feet high, three feet wide, and flat on top providing a walkway for workmen and funeral corteges. There weren't many of the latter. You go to a compost once and never again, and the word gets around. The corpses are layered in with other organic refuse and chemicals, and the piles are kept flat on top to collect rain. After a long wet spell bones thrust up out of the decay.

Bones are always a nuisance when it comes time to empty a pit and ship the matured compost out. There's a giant steel mesh mounted on pillars in the loading area. It's used to screen out the coarse rubbish, and the heaped bones and skulls make it look like a *danse macabre*. I'd seen all that the day I followed Free-5's body to the pit to make sure she was treated respectfully.

This was night. The night was dry ... the whole week had been dry ... and I was startled by the "fire-fang," as it's called, shuddering in some of the pits. It's generated by the intense heat of fermentation and the flames were parti-colored from the chemicals. I could see by the light of the fire-fang and didn't need the lampland torch I'd brought to find my way.

I threaded across the compost on the walkways to the small pit where I remembered Fee being placed. The miasma was strangling me. The pit was dark, no flames, so I switched on the torch. Just a flat surface of straw some three feet below. I steadied my nerve and dropped down. The straw was spongy. The heat was burning, and I knew I'd have to work fast or I'd be roasted unconscious. I clawed the straw aside, reached a layer of crushed limestone, shov-eled that back with my hands, and there was a bloated body, peeling, shredding, rotting. Not Fee. A man. I vomited.

He must have come in after Fee. You've got to move him. Move him, Guig. Be a mensch and move him. I braced myself and used a foot to roll him out of the way and he came apart at the joints, emitting a gangrenous gas. I retched bile. Underneath him was a layer of dried blood, and under that was another large adult in the final stages of decomposition. Only a few fragments of skin and patches of hair adhered to the loose skeleton. *If Fee's under that she must be gone if it's gone. Gone forever, Guig. Hopeless. Don't count on it, they said....* I dry retched again.

A voice cackled in Spang, "Bod doan dig it."

Another, "Nadie tell'm us leave nada?"

I flashed the lampland up. Three wild grotesques bright against the black sky. Grave robbers, flashing with corpse jewels.

"Got a union carda, bod?" the third called.

They dropped down into the pit. They were armed with heavy femurs and I would make an addition to the compost, alive or dead. I had no weapon and I backed away from their advance, reaching for whatever valuables I had on me to toss to them. I kept the light in their eyes to blind them but they merely squinted and hefted the thighbones. *We'll meet again v. soon, Fee.*

My digging must have introduced enough air into the compost to trigger combustion. A flicker of fire-fang welled up from the cavity and spread over the entire pit. The three goons went up a wall, burning. I went up the opposite wall, burning. While they were putting themselves out, I got myself out of *El Arrivederci*. Only then did I start slapping and beating.

I didn't have to do any talking when I rejoined the Group in the tepee. They knew. They didn't ask questions, even about the condition I was in; clothes nearly burned off, hair nearly burned off, blistering and stinking of compost. They got up quietly, took a last look at the Chief, who'd been cleaned up, and whispered their sympathy to Natoma. Then they left to return to their own life-styles. Why did they whisper? It wasn't funeral; just a delay in Sequoya's life. Y. I'm so vivo. There was a delay in mine coming, too.

"I'll have to help you bathe and change." Natoma smiled. "I have two babies on my hands."

"Thank you. This one is a v. tired baby."

"And then you'll sleep."

"I don't dare, love. If I go to sleep now it'll be for a week. We've got to get our brother home first."

"That's not wise, Edward. You're still driving too hard."

"I know you're right. I—You were right about Fee. I should have listened."

"You don't know how right," she said in a curious tone. I was too exhausted to make anything of it.

"But please let me wrap up the whole package tonight. Then we can be together again, alone. You don't know how I've missed you."

Natoma cried out. The three cryos had entered the tepee silently, carrying a heavy burden wrapped in plastic. No warning from the wolves; M'bantu had taken them with him. I stared. The cryos were still blind but now moved with assurance. The new computer connection, perhaps?

"This is the sister? Your wife?" They seemed to be aware of everything.

"Y."

"She must not fear. Tell her who we are."

"I've told her already."

"And will she trust us, too?"

"You saved my brother," Natoma said.

"As he saved us."

"Then I must—No. Then I *do* trust you."

"She's a good woman, Curzon, and brave. We know now how our appearance shocks people. You must go, all three of you. There will be a pyre behind this tent and you should not see it."

"That's the Rajah?"

"Yes. His rot is not for the compost; only for burning."

"But why here?"

"We will live here. We've taken over everything for Sequoya; his home as well. With his sister's permission?"

"You have it," Natoma said.

"Then go, please. We have much to do here, and even more to do directing the Extro. For that we need solitude."

"Solitude? Won't you work in the complex?"

"N need. We can control the Extro on our wavelength from anywhere. We've programmed it to respond to our electronic valence."

"My God! You'll be like God Himself."

"No. God is neither man nor woman."

"Then what is God?"

"God is Friend."

It was hell for Mr. and Ms. Edward Curzon getting brother into another pogo and worse getting him into a linear to Erie and off. The Shoshoni were on duty at the west gate and they lent a hand without asking any questions, for which I gave them good marks. They hovered us to the marble wickiup, carried Sequoya in, and put him down on a couch. He wet the couch. Mama looked him over and began to sob in Cherokee. The kids ran in, wide-eyed. Mama snapped an order at them. They ran out and in a few moments the Sachem entered. He looked.

"It's all yours," I said to Natoma. "You'll have to explain. Give them as much of the picture as they'll be able to understand. I don't think you should mention the Moleman bit. That's too much."

I left, went to the wall where Sequoya and I had sat together so long ago, and let the morning sun warm me. After a couple of hours Natoma came out, looked around, found me, and came and sat down alongside me. She was subdued and depressed. I didn't say anything.

At last she said, "I explained."

"I knew you could. What did you tell them?"

"That you and my brother were doing scientific research with a computer and he had an accident."

"Good enough. How did they take it?"

"Not very well."

"I don't blame them. Their splendid, brilliant son. I hope they live long enough to see him become what he was."

"My father says this would never have happened if he hadn't met you."

"I never knew it would turn out like this. How could I? Grant me that."

"My father says you have taken his son away from him."

I sighed.

"My father says now you must replace him."

"What!"

"You must be his son."

"How?"

"Here."

"On the reservation?"

"Yes. Here. In Erie. You must never leave."

"Dio!"

"And Sequoya will be your son. You must raise him and bring him back to what he was."

"But that will take years out of my life."

"Yes."

"That's a hell of a sacrifice."

"Yes, but what about mine?"

"Yours?"

"I'll have to become a squaw again."

"Not to me. Never."

"But to Erie, always."

"Dearest love, he's in good hands. We can go away; to Brazil, Ceres, the Corridor, Mexas, Africa. We have the whole solar before us and you haven't seen all of it yet. Yes?"

"No, Edward. I must stay and help, but you can go away."

"From you? Never."

"Then you'll stay and do what father says?"

"Yes, damn it. Goddamn it, yes, I'll stay, and you knew I would. All this pussyfooting around!" She looked at her naked toes. "I love you for a hundred reasons. Most now because you never let me down. You never will."

"Never."

"Now I'll tell you something I promised never to tell. It's your reward."

"I don't want any rewards for doing the right thing."

"I knew you'd never find Fee's body."

"And you were right."

"Because I knew it was gone."

A long moment, but I couldn't twig. "I don't understand."

"After she was killed and you were suffering so, Jacy took you out to comfort you."

"I remember."

"Borgia and I went to the compost. I wanted Fee buried in a private grave just for you. Borgia said no and talked about rebirth."

"What? DNA-Cloning?"

"Y. She said we were in time and she got Fee back. It cost an enormous bribe."

"And you never told me."

"Borgia said she had luck with Boris, but it was still so iffy that she didn't want to get your hopes up. She made me promise. Anyway, I couldn't understand what she was talking about. My XX wasn't v. good then."

My heart began to pound. "So? Now?"

"She said she'd write and report progress."

"And?"

"She hasn't yet."

"Then I can hope. Dear God! I—I can't tell you how grate—And I made that vicious crack about jealousy."

"I'll forgive you if you'll forgive me."

"No bargains. It's just us together, forever."

"Not quite," she said solemnly. "I'll grow old and die, of course, while you go on forever. That's what hurts most. It must have tortured poor Fee, who didn't even have—But I know you'll be with me to the end. Who else would you have to take care of you?"

"We don't have to think about that for a long time."

"You'll probably want to run away."

"Probably, but I won't."

"They'll all believe I'm your mother."

"Or a rich old lady I married for her money."

She giggled a little. "Why didn't you ever hook up with one of the eternal ladies?"

"I suppose because I prefer human beings. The Group isn't really human, you know."

"You are."

"We have a long time before us in Erie—we can take vacations, I hope, and see the solar—so you may change your mind about that."

She smiled. "I'll go tell my father. Meet you in the tree in an hour."

"Why not now?"

"I have to help mother bathe and diaper your son."

So here I am, here I am in Erie, son of the Mighty Sachem, prince of poppies, fink of firewater, and it's damned hard work. They've renamed me White Eagle. I study Cherokee, Ugly synthesis and customs at the college. I obey. I refer all major decisions to the Sachem. I exercise with the braves and submit to their derision. My wife walks three steps behind me with her head lowered. What she does after hours is nobody's business but mine.

I have this recorder on which I'm keeping my journal in XX. I sent word to Pepys, and the Group visits occasionally. M'bantu stayed six weeks and had a glorious time. He made friends with everybody and was formally adopted by the Mandan nation. Tosca came and studied tribal dances for her new production of *Salome*. Disraeli brought a financial report. Apparently the cryos had forced the Extro to shape up and I was back in business again. I was able to repay the Sachem's loan. Queenie came but the Pawnees on duty wouldn't let him in. He was livid.

I think I'm beginning to gain some clout in Erie. The other day a deputation from the tribes and nations arrived at the wickiup with an internecine problem and they kept addressing me as "Great Eagle." Next week I go on duty as Chief of the west gate for the first seasonal tourist invasion. Natoma promises to do a paint job on me that will fill them with awe. The Sachem has given us permission to take June off and we're for the moon.

Dio! My son is crying again. Escuse me.

AN OPEN LETTER TO OUR VALUED READERS

What do Raymond Chandler, Arthur C. Clarke, Isaac Asimov, Irving Wallace, Ben Bova, Stuart Kaminsky and over a dozen other authors have in common? They are all part of an exciting new line of **ibooks** distributed by Simon and Schuster.

 ibooks represent the best of the future and the best of the past...a voyage into the future of books that unites traditional printed books with the excitement of the web.

Please join us in developing the first new publishing imprint of the 21st century.

We're planning terrific offers for ibooks readers...virtual reading groups where you can chat online about ibooks authors...message boards where you can communicate with fellow readers...downloadable free chapters of ibooks for your reading pleasure...free readers services such as a directory of where to find electronic books on the web...special discounts on books and other items of interest to readers...

The evolution of the book is www.ibooksinc.com.